Baby, You're Worthy

Baby, You're Worthy

Shantaé

URBAN Renaissance

www.urbanbooks.net

Urban Books, LLC
300 Farmingdale Road, NY-Route 109
Farmingdale, NY 11735

ISBN 13: 978-1-945855-81-8
ISBN 10: 1-945855-81-9

First Trade Paperback Printing December 2018
Printed in the United States of America

10 9 8 7 6 5 4 3 2 1

Distributed by Kensington Publishing Corp.
Submit Orders to:
Customer Service
400 Hahn Road
Westminster, MD 21157-4627
Phone: 1-800-733-3000
Fax: 1-800-659-2436

Prologue

Moving as fast as her short legs would allow, Nikki breathed a sigh of relief as she neared her destination. Minutes earlier she'd said good-bye to her friends and their families, and now she was headed to her car, which sat at the end of the long driveway leading up to Alana and Jakobi's luxurious home. Marcus had offered to walk her to her car, but she left as soon as he went to grab his things. She knew it was childish of her to just leave like that, but if she wasn't able to shake the scene swiftly, she would be forced to be alone with him, and she didn't think she had what it took to pretend tonight. She'd discreetly watched him interact with his family throughout the day, but anytime he came in close proximity of her, she practically ran in the opposite direction. The power walk she was doing right now was a prime example. She wanted to throw a tantrum and stomp her feet like a bratty four-year-old when she heard his deep voice calling out behind her right as she reached for her door handle.

"Aye yo, Nikki, hold up. Let me holla at you real quick," he said again as he hit a slow jog in her direction.

"I was so close," she mumbled to herself.

"Why you just dip out on me like that?" He frowned, looking her up and down in confusion. The look on her face said that stopping to talk to him was the last thing she wanted to do right now, but he didn't give a damn.

"Marcus, don't do this to me tonight, please," she whined, not bothering to answer his question. In an attempt to mask her attraction to him she feigned aggravation anytime he approached her. It was all she could do to keep from throwing herself into his arms anytime he stood before her, looking like he was looking with his fine self. Everything about this man was perfect to her. Tall. Muscular physique. Bushy, untamed eyebrows paired with beautiful sleepy-looking eyes and kissable lips all wrapped up into one lovely dark chocolate package.

"Damn, is it like that? Why you always giving me such a hard time, Li'l Bit?" he asked, calling her by the nickname he'd given her when they first met. Nikki would never admit it to anyone, but she loved it.

"Marcus, I don't mean to give you a hard time. It's just that we do this every time we see one another, and nothing is going to change. At least, not on my end," she informed him. Marcus was persistent in his pursuit of her, and it was nerve-racking. Well, that was a lie she constantly told herself. She actually loved the attention she received from him, but going there with him as far as a relationship could never happen. In the beginning, she was always sweet and polite when she rebuffed his advances, but seeing as how that hadn't worked, she now played the annoyed role. It wasn't how she really felt, but she did what she had to do to protect herself.

He stood with his arms folded across his chest, smiling that smile that made her heart quiver. The intensity of his gaze made her uneasy. It was one of the reasons she couldn't be near him for an extended period of time. She could literally feel her entire body heating up. No other man affected her the way he did, and that was frightening.

"So you ain't gon' ever give ya boy a chance, huh?" He'd asked her out more times than he could remember and she always turned him down. Why he kept trying to get next to her was beyond him. She was the complete opposite of any female he'd ever shown interest in. Her ass was bougie and educated, and she spoke proper English, but she was also a beautiful woman. There was this innocence about her that drew him in from the first night he laid eyes on her. Of all the women he'd been linked to, there was something that this particular female possessed that made him want to know more about her and just be a part of her world.

"I'm sorry, Marcus, but the answer will always be no," she answered with her hands clasped in front of her, leaning back against the door of her cherry red Lexus SUV. "Besides, we have absolutely nothing in common, so what would be the point?" she added.

She was laid-back and quiet for the most part. Marcus, on the other hand, was a natural comedian who was full of life and was known to get a little rowdy. Nikki tended to keep her thoughts and opinions of others to herself, while Marcus had no problem telling you exactly what was on his mind, even if what was on his mind was rude as hell and likely to hurt your feelings. He was a certified thug, and she was a professional, educated, cultured woman. What would she look like bouncing around town with someone like him? How would her colleagues and family feel about her dating a man with no education beyond high school, who'd been deep in the streets for most of his life? It wouldn't be a good look for her, and that's why she rejected him at every turn. Add to that the hurting he could potentially put on her heart, and she was all the way cool on hooking up with Marcus Tate. Keeping her thoughts of him at bay was an entirely different struggle, however.

"Have you ever heard the saying 'opposites attract,' Li'l Bit?" he countered, moving closer into her personal space, initiating a stare down.

"Of course I have, but in our case, it doesn't apply," she answered softly as she watched him lick those pretty lips of his. His closeness was having an effect on her, causing her to feel things opposite of what she was telling him.

Marcus didn't miss how her eyes had become darker under his gaze. Her formerly closed-off posture was now relaxed, and her arms were now dangling at her sides as her eyes rested on his mouth for a few seconds before coming up to look into his unblinkingly. He really felt that if he leaned in to kiss her, she wouldn't object. Baby was open to him right now, giving off vibes that contradicted the words spilling from her mouth. She wanted him but was fighting it for some reason. Nodding his head in understanding, he decided on a different strategy.

"Fine," he conceded, backing away from her. Marcus noted the frustration on her face as he moved farther away. Although it had taken quite some time, it seemed that he'd finally started to penetrate the wall of protection that she'd built.

His retreat caused Nikki to finally blink and release the breath that she'd been holding the entire time. She'd stood there in anticipation, thinking he was about to kiss her. Why hadn't he? Did she want him to? In that moment, she was sure that she did, and the realization made her nervous. This exact situation was the reason she fought him so hard all the time. Her body and mind became traitorous in his company. She felt things with him, foreign things that she couldn't rightly identify, but she didn't like it. The feeling was amazing, but it was too much. A simple smile or innocent touch from him caused her heart to race, palms to sweat, and tongue to become tied. She turned to putty in his presence, so she knew that he had the power to really damage her if she gave in.

"How about we agree to just be friends then? I won't bother you about going out with me anymore, and you can still date them wack, corny-ass mu'fuckas you used to fucking with. We're around each other all the time, so it shouldn't be a big deal for us to be friendly like everyone else. It's cool for us to be friends, right?" he proposed.

Her heart dropped, but she tried to mask the dissatisfaction she felt when she realized what his proposal actually meant. Marcus suggesting that they just be friends meant that he was finally giving up on something romantic developing between the two of them. Happiness and relief were two emotions she expected to experience, but at that moment she was anything but. Instead of fessing up, she played it off the best way she could.

"Of course we can be friends, Marcus, and you can continue to date the classless, trashy women you're used to going out with," she said with an uncaring shrug.

"Touché," he said with a chuckle. He couldn't get mad at her clap back because that's exactly how he liked his women: downright disgusting and down for whatever. Well, at least that's how he liked them before he met her. Nikki was different, and that's what he liked most. "Since we gon' be cool and shit that means you can come to the grand opening of my tattoo studio next weekend. And to show you how serious I am about us being friends, you can even bring a date. You'll probably be bored as fuck with whatever square-ass nigga you decide to bring so I'll be sure to keep you entertained," he teased. Before she could protest, he snatched her phone from her hand and proceeded to enter his number before handing it back to her. "If you can make it, hit my line and let me know," he said before turning and walking away.

She laughed out loud when she looked down at her phone to see that he saved his number under **Future Husband**.

"You laughing now, but mark my words, Li'l Bit." He grinned confidently while simultaneously wiping the smile right off her pretty face. Nikki knew right then that being his friend was going to be hard.

Chapter 1

"Goddamn, bring y'all ass on," Marcus mumbled to himself. He glanced down at his watch again, unable to hide his irritation and impatience. He was posted at a car wash on Belt Line, waiting for the slow-ass workers to finish detailing his Tahoe. Any other day he would insist that they take their time to ensure his baby was pristine and shining like new money, but today he was in a hurry to meet Nikki at the Studio Movie Grill to see *Straight Outta Compton*. He didn't want to be late, although nine times out of ten he knew that she would be. Her ass couldn't be on time for shit, but by now he was used to it. He wasn't far from the theater, so as soon as they brought his whip around, he hopped in and quickly pulled out of the lot.

On the way over he thought about what a great friend Nichole Grant had become to him. What had started out as a game to get closer to her and give her a chance to get to know him had unexpectedly blossomed into a special friendship. Of course, he was still somewhat feeling her, but he had decided to accept things for what they were. Nikki wasn't interested in him that way, so if friendship was all she could offer him, he had no choice but to accept that. Not being able to see her or talk to her on the regular was not an option for him.

Their tickets were purchased in advance, so after scanning the receipt on his phone, the cashier printed out his paper tickets. He was surprised to find Nikki sitting in the lounge area and scrolling through her phone while awaiting his arrival. She looked good dressed down in destroyed white skinny jeans and a white lightweight hoodie with the word "Dope" across the front in black capital letters. She wore the all-black Timberland boots he'd gifted her for her last birthday to complete the look. Her short hair was shaved on one side with a cool design carved in, and her bangs swooped down over her eye on the opposite side. She was getting bolder with her hairstyles, and he loved it. Instead of a marketing research specialist for a major Dallas corporation, she looked like an around-the-way girl complete with shiny nude lip gloss and large hoop earrings. Marcus was dressed down in jeans and a hoodie as well, but he wore all black. His entire fit was Saint Laurent, and he had on the same black Timberlands that she was sporting. It was weird how they always ended up coordinating without really trying to.

"What's up, Li'l Bit," he said, catching her off guard. She looked up with that big dimpled smile he'd grown so fond of. Nikki was a petite cutie, hence the nickname he'd given her. Baby was about five feet two inches and maybe 115 pounds soaking wet. He practically towered over her at six foot three. Although they bore no facial resemblance, her slim, thick frame put him in the mind of the singer Teyana Taylor, from the nice full breasts and flat, toned stomach on down to the petite but curvy ass. Her little ass was definitely fucking around with that body.

"Hey, Marcus," she said, standing to hug him. They hadn't had the chance to hang out in a while because they had both been busy, so she was really happy to see him. It was a trip that someone she claimed to loathe in the beginning had become someone she couldn't imagine not being a part of her life.

"Let's get in here so we don't miss the previews," he said, ending the hug and rushing her along.

"You and these previews," she said, laughing as she adjusted the strap on her small cross-body Chanel bag. Going to the movies was one of Marcus's favorite things to do, and they always had to be extra early when they came so that he wouldn't miss any of the previews. He told her it was because he needed to stay up on anything interesting that was coming out.

"Hey, Marcus," a sultry voice called out behind them as they walked toward theater number seven. He glanced over to his left to see Jazz, a dancer from Sensations he'd fucked with a while back. She was with another chick who looked to be in the same profession. Both girls were beautiful but were dressed a bit too provocatively to be at the movies. He nodded his acknowledgment but kept it moving. Jazz didn't know if Nikki was his lady, but she had the nerve to speak and make her presence known. *Trifling ass,* he thought.

"Still out here being Smoove I see." Nikki shook her head at him. It never failed. Every time they were out together he ran into some random female he knew. The chicks were bold, too, some walking right up to him to touch or hug him as if she weren't even standing there. Although he didn't belong to her, they didn't know that, and they didn't seem to care either way. His taste in women was questionable as well, and she had no clue why he was so hell bent on going out with her when they first met. It was obvious that she wasn't his type.

"Don't start that shit, Li'l Bit," he warned.

"Whatever, Smoove," she teased.

He ignored her and walked ahead to locate their seats with her following close behind. He hated that when he was with her, he constantly bumped into hoes he used to deal with. He was sure that seeing that shit didn't help change her perception of him and his reputation as a player. Over the last few years he had slowed down tremendously, and besides hanging out with her the only chick he spent time with was Meka, and that only happened behind closed doors.

He and Tameka Porter went way back, but this Jazz chick was a random woman he hit off one night at the end of her shift, and that was well over a year ago. He remembered her acting a fool on stage that night. Baby had all the major players vying to take her home after she finished her set, but he ended up being the chosen one. He was always the chosen one with the ladies, except for when it came to the one he really wanted.

He'd already shown Nikki that he was about something, but she still didn't see him. He now owned four tattoo studios throughout Texas and he no longer sold dope, but that wasn't enough to win her over. Friends were all they would ever be, and he tried convincing himself that he was cool with that.

The feel of Nikki nudging him broke him out of his thoughts, and she gave him a look that told him she was only teasing with the "Smoove" comments. He simply smiled and turned back to focus on the screen.

Nikki knew that smile meant they were good and he hadn't taken offense to her joking with him. Marcus had about five different smiles, and each one was stored in her visual memory bank. Although she couldn't act on her feelings, Marcus Tate was an extremely handsome man who she enjoyed spending time with. Besides Alana and Kelsey, he was her only close friend. Their attraction had been established from day one, but friends were all they would ever be. All the women in his life were major turnoffs, and she couldn't see herself trying to compete with them. She assumed that her limited experience with men would probably be a deal breaker for him anyway. In her opinion, they just weren't meant to be.

"That movie was so freaking bomb. I'm so glad you convinced me to come, Marcus. And the music, oh my goodness, so amazing! The guys who played Eazy-E and Ice Cube were so good. They all did a wonderful job, but those two definitely stood out," she exclaimed as she looped her arm through his.

Marcus just stared at her, amused by her excited rambling. "Follow me to my truck wit'cho proper ass. 'So amazing,'" he imitated her before laughing. "I got something for you." He'd copped her the *Straight Outta Compton* CD as well as the vinyl for the record player he'd purchased for her just last month. He got tired of her saying she wished she had a classic vinyl turntable, so he found and purchased the perfect one online for her. "Say, you know the dude who played Ice Cube is his son in real life, right?"

"Really, Marcus?"

"Yup."

"Well, he did a great job playing his father. And to think I was sitting there praising the casting director for finding someone who looked so much like him. Now I know why," she replied, feeling silly for not realizing it before.

"Hell yeah, dude had Cube's walk down pat and everything. Here you go," he said, handing her the gift after closing the door of his truck. "I figured you would want those after seeing the movie."

"Thank you so much, buddy," she said, grinning while examining the CD and record. "My vinyl collection is getting pretty extensive because of you," she said, smiling up at him.

"You sure you don't have time to have a few drinks?" he asked, not ready for their time together to be over so soon. "We could hit Razzoo's for a couple of worm burners since it's right there," he suggested, nodding to the other side of the parking lot at one of her favorite restaurants.

"I wish I could, but I have to get home. I have a presentation to perfect for work, and I can't afford to half-step on this one," she told him.

"I understand, and I know you gon' kill shit with your presentation. Just call me sometime this week so we can compare schedules. That way we'll know the next time both of us are free so that we can plan something. I missed you, Li'l Bit," he admitted.

"Aww, I missed you too, Smoove," she said, laughing.

"Here you go with that bullshit," he laughed as they approached her car.

"Language, Marcus, language," she admonished him.

"Man, please. If you ain't used to my mouth by now, you never will be. You already know how I do," he said as he opened her car door for her. She was forever giving him grief about the language he used, but it was how he talked, so she would just have to deal with it.

"Fine, potty mouth. I don't know who is worse, you or Kelsey," she said, giving him a parting one-armed hug. "Thanks for the movie and the gift. Next outing is on me."

"You're welcome, and you know I'm not trying to hear that other shit you talking," he said, referring to her statement about paying the next time they got together. He wasn't having that, and she knew it.

"Whatever, Marcus. Have a good night."

"You too, and don't forget to text me and let me know you made it home," he reminded her before going to his truck. He chucked up deuces to her as she pulled away.

What he wouldn't have given for this to have been a real date so that he could've kissed her good-bye or gone back to her place with her. Maybe fuck her down real good and spend the rest night with her wrapped tight in his arms, but that wasn't for them, so he shook that thought off and headed home.

Chapter 2

"This shit here gon' be clean as fuck when it's finished," Marcus boasted of the jersey tattoo he was doing of their last name on his brother's back. They were at his tattoo studio, Smoove Ink, located in a high-traffic area in central Dallas.

"I'm already knowing, bro. Can't wait to see the finished product. The way you incorporated Moms, Pops, and the twins' names when you sketched it was dope as fuck," Jakobi said, singing his praises.

"Shit, you know I had to freak it all the way out for you," he replied, thinking about his family. He missed his parents and twin sisters terribly, but he was grateful to still have Kobi here with him. Without his brother, he didn't know where he would be. Thoughts of his lost loved ones still saddened him after all this time, so he decided to change the subject. "We all set for next weekend? Alana told you I dropped off some meat the other day, right?"

"Yeah, she told me. Said you came through there with about six cases of ribs. Definitely a good look because you saved me a trip. Alana ass been having me ripping and running all over town picking up shit." Jakobi feigned annoyance. He actually didn't mind doing it. There wasn't shit he wouldn't do for Nari Alana Tate. Didn't mean he couldn't talk a little shit while he carried out her request though.

"It's all good. When I was in West Dallas fucking with Nate and Big B the other day we ended up stopping by

Jerry's. I walked up out that bitch with every single case they had in stock, bruh. Shit, you know I'm gon' eat my fair share and then some, so I thought I would be kind enough to contribute to the cause," he said, laughing. "Big Rick gon' be on the grill, too! Shiiidd, it's about to be on and popping. That fool gon' have that meat falling right off the bone, and my ass gon' be right there to catch it," he said, making his brother laugh.

"Hell yeah, and we gon' kick it hard like always. You know my wife lives for this shit, so she went all out on the food and entertainment," he said.

Jakobi looked forward to the holidays nowadays because for the first time in a long time he remembered what it felt like to be a part of a family. Reuniting with Alana had been the best thing to ever happen to him, and he was still thanking God for making it possible. Her best friends, Kelsey and O'Shea, along with their people had welcomed him and his brother into their lives with open arms. His wife's father was cool, but it took a minute for him to form a bond with her mother. He didn't fuck with her too much in the beginning because of the way she treated his wife, but they actually had a better relationship these days, and as long as Alana was happy he was good. Plus, he wanted to set a good example for his children, so he put his feelings to the side and got to know Cheryl. Turned out she had changed her ways, so they got along just fine now.

The brothers lost their parents and twin sisters in the midst of some street beef Marcus was involved in years ago. Since then it had just been the two of them. They had other living family members, but they'd disowned Marcus for being the cause of their family being murdered, so Jakobi didn't fuck with them at all. If they had no love for his older brother, then he had no love for them, and nothing anyone said could change that. His brother had been there for him in every way possible since he was born, and for that, he was rocking with him until the wheels fell off.

"Dad, when you gon' let me get a tattoo?" Jakobi's fourteen-year-old son, Gavin, asked, looking up from his phone for the first time since they'd been there.

Sucking his teeth, Marcus spoke up before his brother could even respond. "Boy, stop! Yo' mama would beat yo' ass and ours, so you may as well give it up."

"You ain't never lied," Jakobi concurred. "I'm sorry, G, but yo' mama would kill me. I ain't no punk or nothing, but I ain't trying to see those hands. I've seen her in action, and I don't want them problems," he joked with his son, making him laugh. His wife was a wild little thing and wouldn't hesitate to get shit popping. When it came to her three children, she went even harder. "Maybe when you turn eighteen me, you, and your mom can sit down and talk about it."

"Okay, Pops, that's cool," he agreed and quickly went back to texting on his phone.

"What y'all got up when y'all leave here?" Marcus asked Jakobi.

"Headed to the house for dinner with the family. You should come through when you're done. Nikki gon' be there."

"Oh, yeah? Her dwarf ass ain't say shit when I talked to her earlier."

"Yeah, I think she's bringing some new nigga she supposedly talking to," Jakobi lied, attempting to piss his brother off. He knew he succeeded when the low buzz from the tattoo gun suddenly stopped. He smirked as he felt his brother burning a hole in the back of his head.

"Fuck you talking about, JB?" Marcus fumed. Nikki dating someone was news to him, and he was pissed at hearing it. Maybe that was why she failed to mention going to his brother's house for dinner tonight. He didn't know why he was so tight about the shit. It wasn't like they were fucking with each other like that. Still, he still felt a way.

"I'm fucking with you, fam," Jakobi said as he killed himself laughing.

"Nigga, you childish as fuck for that," Marcus snapped, embarrassed that he'd shown Kobi his hand like that.

"If anybody childish, it's you two niggas. Still living in the land of denial, walking around acting like y'all ain't in love. Y'all the only ones who don't see the shit," Jakobi said, shaking his head at his big brother. He wished his brother and Nikki would just hook up already and quit playing games. All this time had passed, and they still hadn't gotten together. Friends of theirs who had secretly made bets that they would hook up were starting to think it might never happen.

"Ain't nobody in denial. That's the homie, and that's all there is to it," he informed Kobi.

"Homie? Whatever, my nigga. That's yo' damn wife, and you know it," Kobi snickered.

Marcus didn't waste time on a reply. He simply shook his head at his brother's assumption that something more would eventually develop between him and Li'l Bit. He would give anything to have her as his wife, but she wasn't having it. If it hadn't happened by now, he doubted it ever would.

"Marcus, baby, oh Gawddd!" Meka screamed as he gripped her pretty, brown ass and pounded into her from behind. Arms stretched out ahead of her with her upper body completely flat, ass tooted up perfectly as he rammed into her like a crazed maniac, she relished every single thrust. A crazy combination of pleasure and pain shot through her every time he hit bottom, bringing her to another violent orgasm. "Yessss, just like that, shit!" she cried, her body convulsing as the most delightful sensation consumed her entire being. He was in rare form tonight, and she was reaping the benefits of his superb stroke game. Since showing up to her Cedar Hill home unannounced a few hours ago, they had been fucking like rabbits, going at it nonstop. She'd missed him something terrible and had to admit that she felt slighted that he stayed away for so long.

"Come catch it," he said, removing the condom from his long, meaty dick. Meka already knew what that meant, so she quickly turned around and took him into her mouth to greedily swallow his release. "Damn girl, that shit feels so good," he groaned as she continued to suck him dry. She then proceeded to push him back on the bed with one hand while reaching toward the nightstand with the other to grab a condom and place it on his still-erect dick. She then mounted him and proceeded to ride him like a woman possessed. The same energy he gave her when he was serving her the back shots was returned to him tenfold. He enjoyed the feeling of her squeezing, bouncing, and grinding on his dick as she quickly brought them both to spine-tingling orgasms.

"I don't know what has gotten into you tonight, but I love it," she said between shaky breaths as she placed soft kisses on his rock-hard chest. Lately, when he came through, he would get his nut off and then be right back out the door, but tonight he brought his A game.

"You trying to say a nigga ain't been handling his business in the bedroom or sum'n?" he asked, looking down at her. A selfish lover he was not. Well, he wasn't normally a selfish lover. Lately, he hadn't wanted to be bothered with her and only came by to smash and dash. Her comment made him feel bad for using her body today.

"That's not what I'm saying at all. It's just that it's been a minute since we went more than one round. You know you always put your thing down, Smoove," she said, rising to look at him. He always made sure she got hers, but she was used to him coming through and giving her that work until the wee hours of the morning. These days she was lucky to have a full hour of his time.

"My bad, man. It's just that I've been crazy busy lately. I'm thinking of expanding again and opening up another shop in Oklahoma City," he informed her.

"That's what's up. I'm really happy for you, Marcus."

"'Preciate that."

He had been really busy lately, but Nikki was the main reason things had changed between him and his longtime lover. At present, Meka was the only chick he was having sex with, and that was only because he couldn't be with the woman he really wanted. The nights he came from hanging out with Nikki were usually the nights he would make a beeline over here to get his rocks off. He knew that was fucked up, but he couldn't help it. It was either that or beat his shit as he fantasized about Nikki, and he felt like he was too player to be doing that shit. He went so hard tonight because as he fucked Meka, he'd imagined she was Nikki.

Before having dinner at Pappadeaux earlier that evening, he'd taken Nikki to a car show. She was becoming more open to doing things that he suggested they do when they hung out. He went to museums and plays with her, and in turn, she would accompany him to concerts, car shows, and tattoo-related events. Whatever they did together, they always ended up having a fantastic time.

Following their first encounter a few years ago, he felt she was too snooty for his liking, but once he got to know her, he found that she wasn't that bad. Around him, she was relaxed and not as uptight as he first assumed. Earlier that day Marcus watched and laughed at how fascinated she was by seeing all the candy-painted,

tricked-out vehicles at the show. She was constantly
handing him her phone so that he could capture pictures
of her and whatever car she thought was cool. Not to
mention all of the radio personalities in attendance. She
just had to have pictures with them as well. Marcus was
well known around town, so he ran in the same circles
as a lot of those people, so shit like that didn't move
him. Many of the dudes whose cars were on display were
associates of his as well. Nikki herself grew up around
the rich and famous people her father represented as
an entertainment attorney, summers spent in L.A. and
all. But she still seemed to get excited meeting the local
celebrities. He thought she was adorable.

To an outsider, it probably seemed like they were dating because of the way they behaved. And in some ways,
it did feel like they were in a relationship, but they didn't
have sex or the drama that being in a situation like that
sometimes brought about. There was one point during
the day when he ran into one of his potnas and stopped
to chop it up with him for a minute. When he caught back
up with Nikki, there was some nigga all up in her face,
kicking game, and it seemed she was entertaining the
shit. Seeing her interact with another man that way had
him tight, but he kept quiet. It wasn't his place to say shit,
right? Not long after that, they were stopped by a group
of scantily dressed women who recognized him from
around the way and wanted to take a picture with him.
He noticed Nikki roll her eyes and mug the hell out of the
boldest one in the group, who passed him her number for
everyone to see. He made sure that Nikki witnessed him
tossing the number in the garbage just to ease her mind.

Why they behaved this way knowing they were just
friends was beyond him. Her reaction did tell him that
her feelings might be changing, but he didn't know what
to do about it. He wanted to approach her and see where

her head was at, but he didn't want to push her away or give away that he still wanted more than friendship with her. On the cool, Marcus was unsure how long he could continue pretending. After he did this favor for her on the job for her brother, he planned to scale back how often they hung out. It was obvious that his plan to get close to her on some friendship shit had completely backfired. That night he fell asleep with Nikki heavy on his mind as Meka snuggled up next to him in bed.

What the fuck is up with these dreams? Marcus silently asked himself after he was jolted from his sleep just a few hours later. It was the same dream he'd had ever since he met her. He didn't have the dream every night, but he had it enough to piss him the fuck off. Everyone he loved was there, and she was the guest of honor. Shit always seemed so vivid. The happiness he felt was real, and his heart would beat out of control with anticipation, but the elation was always short-lived. Waking up to realize it was all in his head was crushing. If he really sat back and thought about it, he would realize that he only had the dream when he was asleep in bed with another woman.

Beads of sweat lined his forehead as he sat up and began looking around the room for his clothes. He glanced over at Meka as she lay sprawled out on the other side of the bed, naked. She was sexy as hell to him and always had been. Having a baby had left light stretch marks on her ass and stomach, but baby girl was thick as fuck with curves in all of the right places. He loved that she was authentic and wasn't shit on her body artificial. They'd been sleeping together off and on for years, and he appreciated that she never pressed him to take their involvement further. He wasn't into any woman claiming him as her own, and he didn't believe in playing games with a bitch's feelings by making her think for one minute that she could ever change that about him. There was only one female for him, and if he couldn't have her, he would continue to do what he was doing.

"You leaving?" she yawned as she sat up in bed with her back against the headboard while stretching her arms above her head.

"Yeah. I got some shit to handle," he lied. His plan was to go home or stop by Jakobi's. His brother and sister-in-law wouldn't mind him coming by to crash in one of their many guestrooms until morning. All he knew was that he needed to get the hell up out of Meka's place. He recognized right then how far gone he was for Nikki, because there used to have to be some serious shit going down for him to tear himself out of Meka's arms or her bed.

"A'ight, just hit me up when you got some time to come through again," she said before grabbing her phone and pretending to scroll through her Facebook feed.

She was really getting sick of him playing with her, and she honestly didn't know how much longer she could continue to engage in this game with him. He'd always told her that he fucked with her the long way because she didn't trip on him or nag like other females did when a nigga gave them the dick on the regular, but she found herself getting fed up. They had been fucking around with each other for years. He came into and went out of her life as he pleased, and each time he left, he took a piece of her with him. It might be a few days, a week, or sometimes months before she would see him again, and each time, she would greet him with open arms and legs. She understood that Marcus only did what he did because she had allowed him to do it for so long, but something had to give. The situation was affecting her mentally, and she didn't want to go back to that gloomy place.

"Come lock up," he told her once he was dressed.

"Right behind you," she sang cheerfully, which was the exact opposite of how she really felt. At the door, he kissed her good-bye while squeezing a handful of her ass before turning to leave. These days even his kisses were different, and the way he handled her body had changed as well. Not to get it fucked up, the shit was still good, exceptional even, but she could tell that his mind was elsewhere.

From the beginning, she'd known that she wasn't the only woman in his life. They didn't call the nigga Smoove for nothing. He loved all types of women, and they loved his handsome chocolate ass back. Up until a little over two years ago, she knew that she reigned supreme above all the others. These days she wasn't so sure. The possibility that there was another woman out there who had miraculously been able to capture Marcus's heart didn't sit too well with her. She sure hoped that wasn't the case, and that was for his sake and the sake of whatever bitch he was secretly agonizing over.

Chapter 3

"Hey, baby girl," said Nicholas Grant when Nikki finally joined the family outside for the festivities. It was Labor Day weekend, and their annual party was in full effect. Family from near and far had come together at their huge estate to celebrate. He was especially happy to see his youngest daughter, who everyone had deemed his favorite. He would never admit it to anyone, but she really was. They had a special bond that was established the day she was born. Coming into the world at twenty-nine weeks and weighing only two pounds, six ounces, she had been a fighter since day one. He remembered her being so tiny that she fit perfectly in the palm of his hand. From the day she was able to come home, after months of battling numerous complications in the neonatal intensive care unit, every member of their family spoiled little Nikki rotten. She was his heart, and everybody knew it.

"Hey, Daddy," Nikki replied in the sugary-sweet voice that was reserved just for her father. She hugged him tight and accepted the usual kiss to the temple from her favorite guy.

Her brother and sister both cut their eyes at the exchange before making eye contact with each other. The older siblings loved them both tremendously but couldn't help but be a little envious of the relationship their father and Nikki shared. Brandy was the oldest at thirty-five, Junior was the middle child at thirty-two, and Nichole, affectionately known as Nikki, was the youngest at thirty. She was the apple of their father's eye and was the one who looked most like him. Bran and Nicholas Jr. favored their mother more, from their fair skin right on down to their long, curly hair. Nikki had a decent grade of hair as well, but it wasn't that water-wave stuff that her older siblings had. She shared the same chestnut brown skin tone as her father and had big, beautiful doe eyes, long lashes, and the cutest, deepest dimples. She was also very sweet with an infectious smile and personality that people couldn't help but love.

Despite her good qualities and looks, Nikki was single and had no potential prospects on deck. Her friends were always telling her that her standards and expectations were too high, but she didn't agree. The idea she had of the perfect man for her was engraved in her mind and heart, and she was willing to hold out until they crossed paths. There was no such thing as settling for less when it came to the man of her dreams. Her career was very demanding and kept her busy, but she longed to add a husband and some children to the equation real soon.

"And how are my eldest babies doing?" asked their father.

"Just fine, Dad," answered Brandy, getting up to hug him. He embraced her tightly before kissing her cheek.

"Everything is everything, Pops," said Junior. "Buutttt how long are you going to call us babies?" he added with a light chuckle.

"You three are my world and will always be my babies no matter how old you get." *Especially you,* he thought about Junior. Nicholas Jr. still lived at home and had no clue what he wanted to do with his life or when he would strike out on his own again. He'd made plenty of attempts but somehow always ended up back on their doorstep with his single duffle bag. Junior dropped out of college after his second year, stating school just wasn't for him, and of course, his mother made excuses for him and welcomed him home with open arms. He had been back and forth ever since. They assumed that when whatever woman he was freeloading off of got tired of taking care of him, she would ship his butt right back to his folks.

Both of his girls had their stuff together, and he was extremely proud of that. Bran was gorgeous. She had been married to her high school sweetheart for three years, but they divorced last year. She was the mother to the Grants' only grandchild, Alexander. She followed in her father's footsteps and had gone to law school, but she specialized in corporate law while he was an entertainment attorney. Her career seemed to be on the rise, but in his opinion, his daughter had become bitter after her divorce, and he hoped that she would one day find love again. In order for that to happen, she had to be open to the possibility. Honestly, he felt that her ex-husband, Myron, was who she was meant to be with. He hoped that they would come to their senses and get back together soon.

Last but definitely not least was his darling Nikki. She was smart, spoiled, and a hopeless romantic. She was his princess, and now all she was lacking was her prince. He prayed that she found what she was looking for and that whatever guy she ended up with didn't mind catering to her pampered tail. Hearing the word no wasn't something she was accustomed to, so whomever she ended up with would have a real problem on his hands. A strong, no-nonsense man was what she needed, someone who would give her the world but also command respect and not hesitate to put her in her place when needed.

"So, Junior, what's the word on the job search?" he asked after glancing lovingly at all three of his children.

"It's going, Dad. Got a few interviews this week, so hopefully I'll find something soon," he answered. He hoped his response was sufficient, because he did not want to have this conversation with his father in front of all these people. It really didn't matter though, because everyone there was family and all well aware of his issues. Junior wanted to be settled and responsible just as his family did, but he was having a hard time finding his purpose in life. He couldn't see himself showing up to a nine-to-five job Monday through Friday doing something he didn't love. It was frustrating not knowing what he was meant to do with his life, and he was sure his family was equally frustrated with him.

His parents were under the impression that he lived off of the women in his life, but that couldn't be further from the truth. In his spare time, he messed around with his art and had actually been able to sell quite a few pieces over the last few years for a substantial amount of money. Nikki was the only one who was aware of what he did to get money in between jobs, and for now, that was the way he wanted it. His art wasn't something he wanted to pursue full time, at least not right now, so he didn't bother telling the rest of his family about it. When they saw how good he was, they would encourage him to make a career out of it, and that's not what he wanted. It wasn't that he didn't enjoy it. He just lacked the passion that he knew it would take to go all the way with it.

He could live on his own if he chose to, but for some reason, he liked staying with his parents. Being that he was the middle child, Junior sometimes felt left out growing up. Living in his parents' home somehow made him feel like he was getting time with them that he missed out on as a child. He actually owned a place that his family knew nothing about.

"I'm sure you will, son," his father replied.

His baby sister noticed him breathe a sigh of relief when his father didn't comment further. "Junior, I can talk to my friend Marcus to see if he has any openings at his tattoo shop. He recently mentioned he was looking for some help at the Dallas location. I believe it was something administrative, but I'm not exactly sure. I'm sure I can get you a meeting with him," Nikki offered.

"Good looking out, Nik," he replied. Working in a tattoo shop sounded like something he could manage, at least for a little while. "How your uppity butt end up becoming friends with someone who owns a tattoo studio though?" he asked with his lips turned up.

"Shut up, Junior," she laughed. "Marcus is Alana's brother-in-law."

"And you two are just friends?" he asked skeptically.

"Yes," answered Nikki. From the corner of her eye, she noted the look her sister was giving Junior.

"Really?" Bran butted in. She had been around her sister and her so-called friend on several occasions, and the way they looked at each other and the level of comfort between them was more than friendly in her opinion. Marcus cut for her sister, and if Nikki were honest with herself, she would have seen that she had feelings for him as well. The man hogged all of her attention and hardly let other guys close to her, and jealousy would flash in her sister's eyes anytime another woman lingered in his face for too long.

"Yes, just friends, Brandy. We've been friends for a long time now, but you already knew that," she said, rolling her eyes. Nikki felt that her sister should mind her own affairs and stop the speculation when it came to her and Marcus's friendship. She was getting sick of repeating the same thing over and over.

"Whatever you say, baby sis," Bran laughed sarcastically. She thought it was funny how defensive Nikki became when she suggested that she and Marcus were more than friends. Her reaction only confirmed how she felt, but Brandy would play crazy right along with her sister a little while longer.

Their mother walked up just in time and informed them that the food was ready. They all jumped up, eager to dig in.

Nikki smiled as she read the text from Marcus wishing her and her family a happy Labor Day. He always sent her the sweetest messages and never forgot about her on a holiday or a special occasion. If she told him about an important presentation or accomplishment at work, she could always count on good luck or congratulatory flowers and gifts. Marcus was the most giving and thoughtful man she had ever known. It wasn't so much the gift that she appreciated, but the thought was everything. Not even her ex-boyfriend Kendall was as considerate as him. Just the thought of her high school sweetheart still caused an ache to shoot through her chest. It wasn't as bad as it used to be, but it was ever present.

According to their life plan, she and Kendall would have been married for three years and welcoming their first child by now, but her man hadn't stuck to the script. After meeting at church as teenagers, they fell in love quickly, and after high school both attended college at Howard University, vowing to wait until marriage to have sex. However, not even a full semester into their sophomore year Nikki was crushed to learn that not only had Kendall not kept his promise to her, but he'd also impregnated the girl he secretly lost his virginity to. He claimed he was madly in love with the chick and begged Nikki to try to understand, swearing up and down that he hadn't meant to hurt her.

Regardless of his intentions, she was crushed, and initially, she blamed herself. She felt that if she had just slept with him, he wouldn't have felt the need to be with someone else. She quickly let that way of thinking go and came to realize that she and Kendall just weren't meant to be. Even if she had given up the goods to him, he probably still would have ended up creeping on her. She had ignored his wandering eye and suspect behavior throughout their relationship because she was blinded by her desire to be married and start a family. Honestly, the real reason she stayed with him for as long as she did was that she didn't think she would find another man willing to wait for marriage to have sex.

She'd dated off and on after Kendall, but telling guys she was a virgin and intended to stay that way until she wed wasn't an easy thing to do. There were guys who would immediately end things with her, and then there were the ones who tried to run game or seduce her with hopes of changing her stance on premarital sex. She refused to budge and felt that she deserved a man who was willing to wait for her. As big of a ladies' man as Marcus was, she just couldn't see him as one to give up his women or sex just to be with her, so yes, they would remain just friends.

He and his family were doing it just as big as the Grants were for the holiday. If she had some spare time after this was over, she planned to go over, if only for a little while, to hang with her friends. Honestly, she wanted to see Marcus, and the holiday get-together was the perfect excuse to do so. Sure, she wanted to kick it with her friends Kelsey and Alana but seeing Smoove would be an added bonus. She just hoped that he wasn't there with one of his lady friends. It had been a while since he'd brought another woman around, and she wondered if he was seeing anyone. Women naturally gravitated to him, and she hated that. She used to love when he would rush them away just to come over and shower her with attention, begging her to let him take her out. She always said no, but he never stopped coming for her. Secretly she used to hope that he never would. They were past that point now, and she could honestly say she enjoyed having him as a friend.

"Always have been a daydreamer," she heard her father say behind her. She was so deep in thought that she hadn't even heard him walk up.

"Hey, Daddy," she said, still smiling.

"What has you out here grinning so hard?" He smiled, taking a seat beside her.

"It's nothing. My friend just sent me a text wishing our family a happy holiday. I thought it was sweet," she replied.

"Is this the same friend you and Bran were discussing earlier this afternoon?" He noticed the way her eyes and facial expression changed when she spoke of this particular friend of hers, and he didn't buy that "he's just a friend" business any more than Brandy did.

"As a matter of fact, it is. And before you say anything, I'll tell you like I've tried telling Bran. We are just friends. I could never date a guy like Marcus," she said, trying to convince her father.

"Now you said all that, and I didn't even ask you anything," he laughed. Yeah, his baby had it bad.

"I know, Daddy, but I see the way you're looking at me," she laughed.

"Whatever. Let me ask you something. Why do you say you could never date a man like him? What's so bad about this guy that you can be friends with him, but you wouldn't want to date him?" he asked curiously.

"It's not that he's bad, he's just different. He's nothing like us. Marcus didn't go to college. Told me he barely finished high school. He's a little rough around the edges. And his mouth, goodness, he curses like a sailor," she said, laughing some more. Suddenly, her expression turned serious and she continued. "I don't want you to judge him, but he also used to be heavy in the streets and even sold drugs at one point. He's not into that anymore. He's turned his life around and makes his money the legit way. Marcus is a good person, but he's just not someone I would get involved with. He's not my type at all, and I'm not his. Besides, he's too much of a player, so things are better this way," she said with a little regret in her tone.

"I understand what you're saying, Nichole, but I want you to think about this. Before I met your mother, I was a wild one. You might not believe that, and I won't go into detail, but I was out there bad. Did some things that I'm not too proud of, but when I met your mother, she made me want to be a better person. I drastically changed up my lifestyle and the way I was moving so that I could be someone she would deem deserving of her love. All I'm trying to tell you is that you should never overlook any man because he's lived a different life from you. It's all about the feeling, baby girl. If he treats you well and makes you feel good, his past shouldn't matter. How you feel when you're in his presence will tell you if he's the one. All you'll be able to see is him, and you'll realize that there's no other place you'd rather be," her father told her, putting her up on game.

Before she could dwell on the butterflies she felt in her stomach or the heart palpitations she had every time she was near Marcus, her mother walked outside with an unexpected guest at her side. Christine Grant was the epitome of beauty, style, and grace. At fifty-four years of age, her mother had the look of a woman in her thirties. She and Brandy could pass for sisters instead of mother and daughter. Nikki hoped and prayed she looked as good as her mother when she reached that age.

"There you two are. I've been looking everywhere for you, Nichole. There's someone I would like for you to meet. Eric, honey, this is my youngest daughter, Nichole.

Nichole, this is Eric Palmer. His mother and I used to work together, but she left the university shortly after Eric was born," her mother said, making introductions. Christine was a sociology professor at a private university nearby.

When Nicholas realized what was going on, he frowned and cut his eyes at his wife. He didn't like the thought of her trying to fix their daughter up with random men, and she could tell by the look he shot her. Christine was purposely avoiding making eye contact with him. He was sure that this young man was a nice guy and all, but he wasn't cool with what she was trying to do. Although she played it off well, he could sense his daughter was uncomfortable, and his wife would hear about it from him later. He didn't want Nichole to think they weren't confident that she was capable of finding a man on her own.

"It's nice to meet you, Eric," Nikki said with a warm smile that extended to her bright, beautiful eyes. This was obviously a setup, and she was nervous but thankful that the guy her mother matched her with was good-looking. He could even be described as pretty.

"And, Eric sweetie, this is my husband, Nicholas. Honey, you remember Janine Palmer, don't you?"

"Of course I do. Welcome to our home, Eric." He extended his hand for the young man to shake.

"Thank you, sir, and it's great to meet you," Eric replied as he shook the hand of the father of this beautiful girl he'd been set up with.

"Likewise."

"Nicholas, do you mind assisting me in the kitchen?" Christine asked nervously. The woman knew her husband well, so she was prepared to get an earful from him about what she'd done. She wanted to get the lecture over with so that they could move on. It was actually her friend

Janine's idea to set their children up, and she reluctantly agreed. In her honest opinion, she didn't think Eric was a good fit for Nichole, but she felt that after they met and didn't click, that would be the end of it. When it was all said and done, she would have done the favor for her friend, and her daughter could continue doing her own thing. Her baby girl was amazing, and Christine had no doubt she would soon find the man she was meant to spend her life with.

"Sure," Nicholas replied then reluctantly followed his wife.

Now alone and blanketed by an uncomfortable silence, neither Nikki nor Eric knew where to begin or what to say to each other. She spoke up first. "Well, this is pretty awkward."

"Tell me about it," Eric replied with an uneasy laugh, scratching the back of his head. "Look, I'm sorry that we caught you off guard. When I agreed to accompany my mother here today, I had no idea that it was a setup. I have to admit that I'm very surprised, because you're nothing like I pictured you." He smirked.

"I hope that's a good thing," she said with one eyebrow raised.

"It's a great thing. You're beautiful." He smiled. He loved the dimples that graced both her cheeks. They were the deepest he'd ever seen. His compliment caused her to give him the same bright smile again. It was a beautiful smile, and the way her eyes lit up captivated him. There was an unfamiliar stirring in his gut when he looked at her, and that feeling made him a bit uneasy. It was his mother's intention for him to meet a good girl, fall in love, get married, and give her lots of grandbabies. He was enjoying his life just the way it was, so he didn't see any of that happening for him in the near future, or ever, if he was being honest. Despite his initial reaction to

Nichole Grant, he didn't plan to switch it up for her or any other woman for that matter. She was definitely a beauty though.

"Thank you, Eric," she said shyly.

"So, how about we start over and pretend that our busybody mothers didn't set us up and we just happened to meet each other here?" he suggested.

"That works," she said, becoming more interested by the second as he turned his back to her. She giggled at his attempt at role-playing. Turning around and behaving as if this were his first time ever seeing her, Eric's eyes traveled the length of her body then made their way back to her face, where he let his gaze linger for a while. His expression told her that he was pleased with what he saw. He then grabbed her hand and spoke.

"Excuse me, beautiful. My name is Eric Palmer. And you are?" he asked, giving her the cue to introduce herself again.

"Nichole Grant, and it's a pleasure meeting you, Eric," she said with her eyes appraising him the same way his had done her. He smiled, and immediately they both laughed. He had successfully moved the situation from awkward to chill, and she was glad for that. "Can I get you something to drink, Eric?" she asked as they moved toward the table to sit down. A group of her cousins were still out back playing a competitive game of volleyball, so she moved them out of the way to avoid getting smacked by a flying ball.

"Sure. What are you drinking?" he asked after noticing her empty glass on the table.

"Sangria. It's my mother's version, and it is absolutely delicious."

"Then I'll have the sangria." He smiled.

"Have a seat, and I'll be right back with that drink," she said, being a gracious host.

When she returned she had a drink for him and another for herself. After she took a seat next to him, the pair began talking. Nikki found Eric to be pretty cool. At thirty-one he was already very accomplished, and their backgrounds were similar, which was a bonus in her book. He was into commercial real estate and was with one of the most successful companies in Dallas. In addition to being very educated and someone she felt was on her level, this man was sexy as sin. The green eyes had her at hello, and his overall look screamed pretty boy. He was tall, at least six feet two inches, with a slender but athletic build. Judging by his clothes and the way they fit his body, it was obvious that he took pride in his appearance, which was a requirement of hers. Rocking labels wasn't necessary, but it was mandatory that her mate dressed the part. Marcus had a nice body as well and was always dressed to impress. She liked to shop with him more than she did her girls.

There was no spark with Eric, but he was definitely nice to look at. Who was she kidding? She had only felt that spark with one person, and she couldn't be with him no matter how she felt when she was around him. "So, I guess your mom is anxious for you to meet someone and settle down?" she asked to get her mind off of a man she shouldn't have been thinking about right now anyway.

"'Eric, baby, when are you going to get married and give me some grandbabies?'" he said, trying his best to imitate his mother, and Nikki laughed. "That's her favorite line to hit me with," he said while shaking his head.

"You are totally speaking my life right now. Don't get me wrong, I want those things, but I believe I'm capable of making that happen without any outside interference," she said, although she hadn't done such a good job on her own thus far. "I'm glad that I met you tonight though, so I hope that you're not too hard on your mother."

"I won't be. Because of her meddling, I had the opportunity to spend time with you." He smiled genuinely.

By the time his mother came out later that evening to inform him that she was ready to go, they had already exchanged contact information and agreed to meet up for lunch and hang out real soon. It didn't look like Nikki was going to have time to stop by Alana's after all, and that was probably for the best.

Chapter 4

Today Marcus was scheduled to meet with Nikki's brother, Nicholas, aka Junior. She'd asked him a few months back about the opening he mentioned to her, but he hadn't had time to sit down with him due to the holidays, and his tattoo schedule had been insane. Now that the New Year had come and gone, he felt it was time to get serious about filling the position. He was searching for a shop manager for his Dallas location so that he wouldn't have to be so hands-on. He was unsure if ol' boy was qualified, but on the strength of his and Li'l Bit's friendship, he agreed to a meeting anyway.

Marcus was even more interested in speaking with him after Nikki mentioned that her brother was an art major in college. Marcus didn't make it to college, but he had a love for art as well. While Junior was a painter, drawing had been Marcus's thing. In middle school, he was accepted into an arts magnet program at a school in Richardson. However, when he reached high school, he left the program because all he wanted to do was draw, and he didn't have the patience to learn the fundamentals and history behind it all. His parents were disappointed, but in the end, they let him do what he thought was best for him.

By the time he graduated he was selling dope and had put all his academic and artistic dreams behind him. Some days he regretted giving it up, but one thing he learned in therapy was to not dwell on what could have been. He used to beat himself up, saying that if he would have stayed focused on art, maybe he wouldn't have gotten mixed up with the wrong crowd, and maybe his folks and sisters would still be alive. He became fascinated by the fast life, money, and women, and it ended up costing him everything.

He got into tattooing as a teen and would occasionally do tats on his homeboys, but to him, it was just a hobby. He was talented but didn't take it seriously again until after he got out of the game. Every tattoo on Jakobi's body was done by him, and it was his brother's idea for him to open a tattoo studio. He took Kobi's advice and invested in some real estate then opened his first location in Dallas. Afterward, the success of his first shop, Smoove Ink, blew up. Now in addition to Dallas, they had locations in Austin, San Antonio, and Houston. Marcus traveled a lot to do tattoos in each city, and his wait list was usually six months or more at each shop. He was really that good, and he enjoyed what he did.

Discovering that there was actually life after the dope game was a very freeing experience. His baby brother expressed his relief that he was done with the life and told him on more than one occasion how proud he was of him. Jakobi would never know how much hearing that meant to him. For years Marcus just didn't give a fuck about life while Jakobi played the role of big brother. Lately, Marcus had begun reclaiming his rightful spot and was behaving like the eldest of the Tate boys, as it should have been from the beginning.

As he sat at the desk in his office going over some paperwork, the alarm chimed, alerting him that someone had entered the shop. Looking at the cameras, he zoomed in on the man. He could see the resemblance, so he assumed that this was the infamous slacker, Junior. None of his artists had made it in yet, but his shop assistant, Amina, was at the front desk and called back to let him know that his appointment had arrived.

"Marcus, I have Nicholas Grant up front to see you."

"Bring him on back, Mina," he said, putting his work to the side for the time being.

"Will do."

Less than a minute later she was escorting him in. Amina was a beautiful girl, and it seemed that Junior had taken notice. Marcus admired his attempt at remaining professional since this was lightweight an interview, but the lovely girl from Ghana had dude distracted.

Marcus met her a while back when she was bartending at a local strip club. She was a student and was all about her money. Customers tipped her well and showed her the utmost respect when she was behind the bar. Most of them anyway. He intervened one night when a customer was hassling her because she didn't respond to his advances and refused to let him fuck. Marcus ended up having to beat the man's ass for manhandling her. That altercation, along with her unwillingness to put the customer first, caused her to lose her job. When he opened his shop, she was the first person he thought of for a receptionist, and he hadn't regretted that decision one bit.

"What's up, Nicholas? It's good to finally meet you," he said, trying not to laugh at the way he was gawking at Amina.

"Marcus, it's good to meet you too. My sister has told me a lot about you," he said after he got himself together.

"Really?" he asked, surprised.

"Of course, and your shop is everything she said it was. Congratulations on your success, bruh," Junior said genuinely. No lie, this was the dopest tattoo shop he'd ever been in. The interior designer had done an excellent job with the décor. The front desk and waiting area looked like more of an upscale lounge with modern furniture and expensive artwork lining the walls. On the way to the back, he noticed that each artist had their own private tattooing room with their name engraved on the door and examples of some of the work they'd done. There was an entire wall with framed pictures featuring and dedicated to the rich and famous patrons who frequented this spot. Junior was thoroughly impressed. He was expecting some hood shit, but Smoove Ink was far from it.

"Thanks. I really appreciate that. Have a seat and tell me a little about yourself," Marcus said, motioning toward the chair on the other side of his desk before taking his seat again.

Marcus had learned from Nikki that Junior was currently out of work and was living at home with his parents, but the nigga sat in his office with Gucci on from head to toe with expensive bling adorning his wrist and ears. How was it that his broke ass could afford nice shit like that? Marcus figured he was either mooching off some bitch or mooching off his parents. Either way, it was time for his grown ass to fend for himself, and Marcus planned to assist him in getting his shit together.

Junior was far from broke, but Marcus had no clue. Nikki had left out the part about her brother making money selling his paintings, because it wasn't her business to tell. Junior was private about his artwork, and it was almost like he wanted to protect it from the world. He sold his work under a name that not even she knew.

Marcus immediately liked Junior, and he would look out for him because of Nikki. The man was nothing like he imagined and seemed to have it more together than he initially thought. After he finished telling Marcus what he already knew from the conversation he had with his sister, he talked about his work history and a brief stint in college. Junior was honest about where he was in his life and told Marcus his reasons for leaving many of his jobs. He wasn't being fulfilled and didn't want to settle just to please his family or anyone else. For some reason, Marcus understood where he was coming from.

After they talked, he gave Junior a full tour of the shop and formally introduced him to Amina as well as a few of his tattoo artists who had begun trickling in one by one. Marcus explained that his opening was for a shop manager, but he didn't feel that he had the necessary experience to fill the position at the present time. He planned to take him under his wing and train him. If at the end of six months he had proven himself, then the job would be his. Marcus also told him that he would have to take this seriously, because if he fucked up he wouldn't hesitate to fire his ass and he didn't give a damn who he was kin to.

Lastly, he mentioned the shop's policy on fraternizing. Romantic relationships between co-workers were prohibited, and Marcus had zero tolerance for the matter. In his opinion, it was bad for business, and not allowing it kept shop drama to a minimum. If he couldn't fuck clients and the fine-ass female tattoo artists, then no one could. Although Junior was excited and wanted to accept the job on sight, Marcus asked him to think it over and call him in exactly one week if he still wanted the position. This was his business, and he wanted Junior to take it as seriously as he did. He couldn't allow him to treat this as a game like he'd done with many of the other opportunities he'd been blessed with throughout his life.

"Expect a call from me next week," he told Marcus.

"A'ight, man. I look forward to hearing from you, and I'll call your sister and let her know how things went today. I know her li'l nosy ass will want a full report," he said, smiling.

"So, what's up with you two?" Junior asked curiously. He didn't miss the goofy-ass smile that appeared on Marcus's face just from mentioning his sister. He remembered what Nichole told him, but he wanted to hear it from Marcus. Dude seemed cool, but he loved his baby sister and was just as protective of her as the rest of the family was.

Reading between the lines, Marcus knew what he was really asking. "We're just friends, my nigga. I tried to holla at her when we first met, but you know her wannabe-socialite ass wasn't trying to fuck with a thug, so we ended up being good friends," he answered truthfully. "Does that answer your question?"

"Yeah, just friends." He smiled knowingly.

Marcus had no idea what that look meant, but it didn't matter. Their friendship was their business, and as long as they knew what was real, that was all that mattered.

"Wait, wait, wait," Nikki said for what seemed like the millionth time. It was her first time, and she was terrified thinking of the pain that was sure to come once he started.

Marcus was losing his patience. He tried to talk her into letting someone else do this, but she refused, stating she trusted only him to christen her body. "Fuck it, Li'l Bit. I'm about to ask my nigga Reedo to come do this shit. We been in here damn near forty-five minutes and I ain't even got going yet. This li'l ass dove and you're wilding like I'm about to perform open heart surgery on your midget ass," he groaned in frustration.

"No, Marcus! I only want you to do it," she whined.

"Well, let me do the mu'fucka then wit'cho crybaby ass," he said, not hiding his aggravation. He hated when she poked her lip out. In a way, he was glad she wasn't his woman, because she would be able to get just about anything she wanted up out of him when she did that shit.

"You're a mean fucker," she said, rolling her eyes at him.

"Since when you start cursing so much? Shit don't even sound right. 'Fucker!'" He mimicked her Valley girl tone as he prepared to begin again. "G'on and lay yo' proper ass down." He couldn't help but laugh a little.

"I've been hanging out with you too long, and I'm starting to pick up your bad habits, I guess." She tried not to, but she tensed up when she heard the noise from the tattoo gun. Marcus noticed and kept talking to distract her.

"Don't blame that shit on me, Li'l Bit. Fake classy ass. I knew you was an undercover ratchet," he said, making her laugh.

There was some discomfort, but it wasn't as painful as she imagined it would be. He joked around the whole time, so she was more focused on what he was saying than she was on the pain. She was scared her first tattoo was going to come out messed up, because she was shaking with laughter the entire time. Before she knew it, he was finished.

"All done," he said after he finished applying the ointment to her brand-new tattoo.

"Already?" she asked, surprised.

"Yup, take a look," he said, handing her the handheld mirror. He watched her stand up to check out her tattoo in the full-length mirror near the door, while he took the time to admire her petite body in the strapless black dress she was wearing. She needed to hurry up and put her jacket back on, because his body was reacting to the outline of her shape and the subtle curves that graced her frame. He loved the flaring out of her small hips, that li'l booty, and her apple-sized breasts that were sitting up nice and firm. It was hard, but he caught himself before she had a chance to peep him checking her out. Before discreetly adjusting himself up front, he addressed her. "What you think, li'l one?" She was already grinning, so he knew she liked it, and he was honored that she trusted him to do it for her.

"It's so pretty, Marcus. I love it." She beamed. She was still admiring her dove in the mirror when Amina rushed into the room. From the tears spilling down her face, it was evident that something serious was going on.

"Marcus, I have an emergency to tend to with my daughter at the daycare. They just called saying that her father, my ex, is there trying to check her out, and he's not supposed to do that because I have sole custody and an order of protection against him," she cried hysterically.

"Calm down and have a seat, Mina. You're too upset right now, and I don't want you driving up there in the condition you're in. Just give me a second to get someone in here to take you just in case that nigga is stupid enough to still be there when you show up," he said, fuming.

Nikki went over to comfort her while Marcus got on the phone and handled his business. She admired the way he took charge and looked out for his employees. No sooner than she had that thought, a big, burly, intimidating figure appeared in the doorway. For his own sake, Nikki hoped that Amina's baby daddy was long gone by the time they showed up. Hell, this man had her spooked, and she didn't have anything to do with what was going on. The look in his eyes had her literally shaking in her boots.

Even with his demeanor and the no-nonsense scowl he wore, Big B was a very attractive man and was always kind. Until you pissed him off, that was. He was a shade or two lighter than Marcus and stood at about six feet five inches. He looked to be at least 300 pounds of pure muscle and fineness.

After taking instructions from Marcus, Big B escorted the sniffling young lady from the shop to pick up her daughter. Nikki could tell Marcus was heated, and she didn't like to see him so amped up. She had to fight the urge to go over and wrap her arms around him to calm him.

"Looks like I'll have to cancel lunch, Li'l Bit. I'll be covering the desk for the rest of the day," he said regretfully.

"That's fine. You gotta do what you gotta do," she said, trying not to sound too disappointed. "How about I stick around and help you out? We can order food, and I'll even go pick it up for us."

"You sure you don't mind?" he asked, relieved at the thought of being able to spend more time with her.

"Not at all. Just think of it as payment for the beautiful tattoo you did for me and also for being an awesome boss." She smiled sweetly.

"Whatever." He blushed at her compliment. "You don't have to go pick up the food. Just tell me what you want, and I'll have someone pick it up and drop it off for us."

"Sounds like a plan."

They ended up ordering from Hardeman's BBQ, and as expected everything was delicious. She and Marcus took turns eating their lunch in his office while the other watched the desk and checked customers in. Once they were both done, she took over the desk while he cleaned up around the shop and checked on the artists. He basically did everything that Amina would have done if she were there.

She was a great shop assistant, and he hated that the young woman was dealing with so much. She was holding down this job and an internship, and she attended school part-time, all while being a single mother. The last thing she needed was a problem from a crazy-ass ex who didn't know when to move the fuck on.

She'd called a little while ago to tell him that she and her baby girl were safe, and she thanked him for sending Big B with her to the daycare. Dude had already left by the time they arrived, and he better be glad, because Big B wouldn't hesitate to fuck shit up. Marcus had to resist the urge to get the ex's information and go holla at the nigga himself. He was trying to do right, but fuck niggas like him made it hard to stay on the straight and narrow.

While Nikki took command of the desk, he went to his office to hop on the computer and make a few calls. If he couldn't go see about the nigga, the least he could do was make sure that while Amina was at work, she knew that her baby was safe. He didn't want her to be here worrying about whether her daughter was in danger.

"We have a delivery for Marcus Tate," a handsome Caucasian man said, snatching Nikki's attention. She was so busy flipping through the catalog of tattoos that she didn't hear the door chime letting her know that someone had walked in. Now that she had gotten her first one, she was thinking of all the other cool tats she could get. The ink had barely dried on her first one, and she was already an addict.

"One moment," she told the man before going to the back to get Marcus. "Hey, there's a guy up front saying he has a delivery for you."

"Damn, that was fast," he said, getting up from his desk. "Do you mind opening the door at the end of the hallway while I go sign for everything?" he asked, handing her a key.

She was curious about what he'd ordered but did as he asked. The room was empty but clean, with bright white, newly painted walls and brand-new carpet. Nikki wondered what Marcus planned to do with the space. Just as the thought entered her mind, men were coming in with what looked like equipment one would have in a nursery or daycare. One box contained a playpen. There was a rocking chair, a changing table, and tons of toys. Marcus spared no expense, and everything was high quality. He paid ahead to have the workers set things up. They hung the pictures of various cartoon characters and animals on the walls. Nikki's heart swelled when she realized what Marcus was doing for Amina.

"You're so fucking cool," she said as she nudged him.

"Language, Nikki, language," he said, smiling down at her. They were standing back, checking out how everything had come together. Right before their eyes, the room had been transformed into a mini nursery, complete with a crib. "You think she'll like it?"

"No, I think she'll love it. Knowing that her baby is safe will give her peace of mind," she answered.

"That's what I was hoping for. She's a good girl just out here trying to make something happen for herself, and she don't need to be worrying about this psycho-ass nigga trying to take her baby or do her harm. And if his bitch ass walk up in here with that bullshit, he gon' get carried out, and that's my mu'fuckin' word," he said seriously.

Nikki hated when he said stuff like that because it reminded her of the savage side of him, not the compassionate man who had gone out of his way to look out for one of his employees. Before she could respond, he was on the phone telling Big B to bring Amina up to the shop so he could get her approval on a few things and also see if there were any modifications that needed to be made.

Hours later, at nearly two in the morning, everyone had gone home, and he and Nikki were the only two left in the building. They were cleaning up and preparing the shop for business the next day.

"I've been meaning to ask you how things were going with Junior," she said as she sat at the desk, waiting for him to finish up. She hoped her brother was handling his business and wasn't slacking on the job. Cursing his behind out wasn't all she would do if he embarrassed her in any way.

"It's been going good so far. He's been on top of his shit, and he's a fast learner. I'm glad that I'm able to pass some of my workload off to him," he laughed. "Naw, seriously I think he likes working here."

"That's good to hear, because I would hate to jack his butt up for not taking this seriously."

"You wouldn't have to, because I made it clear when I hired him that I wouldn't hesitate to let him go if he wasn't serious about being here. I even got my man working with him on getting his paper right. It's the same dude I worked with to help me get my money situated after I gave up all that other shit," he said, referring to selling drugs. Marcus had fucked off a significant amount of cash over the years but was still sitting on a nice fortune. Jakobi hooked him up with his money man, and along with his businesses, his investments were bringing him big bread. Marcus was, in turn, passing the blessing on to Junior.

"That was nice of you. I think you'll be a good influence on him, Marcus." Despite her initial reservations, he had slowly but surely started to grow on her. She was starting to see him in a new light, but her fear of being hurt held her back from revealing her true feelings.

"I don't know about all that, but I'll do what I can," he said, flashing her that smile again. "You ready to head out, Li'l Bit?" he asked after a brief, uncomfortable stare down.

"Umm yeah," she stammered. "I should be heading home. It's late, and I still have a few things to wrap up before I go on vacation next week."

"I appreciate you hanging with me and helping out today. I owe you a full day's pay for all your hard work," he joked.

"It was no problem. I'm glad I could be of service, and I received a free tattoo out of the deal. I can't wait to get another one." She smiled, standing next to him as he locked up.

"I'm gon' tell you now that I will not be the one to do it if you act anything like you did today. All that damn whining and the shit ain't even hurt. 'Wait, wait,'" he imitated her in a teasing tone as they approached her car.

"Shut up, Marcus. I was scared," she said with her bottom lip poked out and her arms folded across her chest.

"Come on, ma, don't act like that. You gotta know by now that I would never do anything that was gon' hurt you," he said as he was lifting her up in a tight bear hug.

Her legs dangled as he continued walking through the parking lot. He loved the feel of her small body in his arms. It just felt like she belonged there. It would be a dream come true for him if he could be the one to love her and keep her safe in his arms just like this. He hadn't actually meant to say what he said to her, but his words were true, and although he was speaking about the tattoo, he hoped she believed he wouldn't hurt her in any other way either.

When he pulled back she was looking up at him, and what he saw was unexpected, stopping him dead in his tracks as he placed her on her feet. She was silently communicating to him with her eyes what her mouth wouldn't, but he refused to make the first move. If she wanted it, she would have to go for it. He'd spent far too much time doing the chasing where she was concerned. To say he was shocked by her next move was putting it mildly. Her lust-filled eyes remained glued to his as she slowly stood on the tip of her toes to kiss him.

After she placed soft pecks from one corner of his mouth to the other, baby went in for the kill and slipped her warm tongue into his mouth. Initially, he was shocked that Nikki was actually kissing him, but it felt so damn good. He never thought they would make it to this point, but he welcomed it, finally returning the kiss with just as much heated passion as she was giving.

Marcus's kiss took Nikki to another place, a place high above the clouds, and she wanted to remain there forever. His tongue felt like it was meant for her mouth only, and the way it moved around, taking complete control of hers, awakened all kinds of emotions within her. Surprised by her own boldness, she took over, sucking his tongue into her mouth to savor its sweet taste. She had never kissed or been kissed by anyone this way, and damn, she didn't want it to end. She wrapped her arms around his neck, taking it a step further. A little deeper. She was able to enjoy kissing him for nearly a full minute before she was suddenly snapped back to reality by the feel of his large hands palming and squeezing her ass. It was also at that moment she realized her panties were soaking wet. That had never happened to her before. With her hands over her mouth, she immediately began backing away from him, her eyes full of shame and regret.

"Shit," she cursed herself. "I'm so sorry. I shouldn't have done that, Marcus," she apologized, completely embarrassed.

"Don't be," he said, still shocked and turned on by how passionate she was and even more so by the way she sucked his tongue into her mouth during the kiss. He wanted her to do that shit again. She had his dick on straight brick. "Shit felt good as fuck," he added, being completely honest with her. However, the look on her face told him she wasn't pleased with his words.

"Goodness, Marcus, don't say that. I shouldn't have done that. We're friends, and that was inappropriate," she said, her hands covering her eyes. She couldn't take him saying things like that or looking at her the way he was right now. The kiss was fantastic, but right now more than anything she wished she could take it back. "I don't know what I was thinking," she whispered more to herself than him.

Marcus found himself getting pissed off because she was acting as if it were the end of the world. He hated that she felt kissing him had been such a mistake. As good as if felt, she still wouldn't give in, and that shit was blowing the fuck out of him. He knew when a woman wanted him, and she did, but she wouldn't allow herself to go there. Unable to mask his annoyance, he finally spoke. "It was just a kiss, Nichole. Chill the fuck out," he snapped. He was tired of trying to figure this girl out.

She looked up, surprised by his tone and that he had called her by her full first name. To him, she was always Nikki or Li'l Bit, but right now he was angry with her, so she was Nichole. "Marcus—"

"Don't worry about it, ma. Let's just act like the shit never happened. That's what you want right?" he said, giving her an out. The disappointment was evident in his tone.

"Please don't be upset. I—" she started but was cut off again.

"I ain't mad at'cha. Let's just go home. It's been a long-ass day."

"But—"

"Nichole," he said firmly.

"Fine, Marcus," she said before getting in the car. She wanted to protest further, but she could tell he wasn't having it. He was annoyed with her, and she didn't like that feeling.

"Text me when you make it home," he said before slamming her car door.

As she watched Marcus walk to his truck, the reality of what she'd done sank in, and she felt like crap. *What on earth possessed me to do something so impulsive and stupid? And why did it feel so damn good?* She hoped she didn't lose him as a friend behind this, but deep down she knew that things would never be the same between them.

He waited until she drove off before he pulled out of the parking lot. Through the rearview mirror, she watched as he turned and went in the other direction. She wondered where he was going this late at night, because his home was on the same side of town as hers, just a little farther out. She dialed his number, but he didn't answer. Attempting three more times but getting the same result had her piping hot by the time she got home. When she got there, she sent him a text letting him know that she had arrived like he'd asked, and he responded with a simple thumbs-up emoji. She immediately sent another text. Nikki knew she was tripping for being angry with him when it was her stupid kiss that started everything, but she couldn't help it. She was displaying typical girlfriend behavior and didn't even realize it.

My Dream: You can respond to my text, but you can't answer when I call?

Future Husband: Busy rt now. Glad u made it hm tho. Hv a good night.

My Dream: Marcus, we need to talk about what happened tonight.

Future Husband: Kinda tied up rt now.

My Dream: Fine. Call me tomorrow, please.

He didn't respond after her last text. Thoughts of him possibly being with another female caused jealousy that she had never known to consume her entire being. If she could just tell him what she was feeling, maybe he would be there with her instead.

The thing was, Marcus made her feel a way she had never felt before, and she was thinking of breaking her rule on premarital sex. Since she met him, she'd felt an attraction between them that was profound and alarming. Maybe she should tell him how she felt and just sleep with him. How would she feel afterward? Would she feel like she'd made a mistake? Why was waiting so important to her anyway? She asked herself these same questions all the time.

Sometimes she hated that she wasn't like the women Marcus was used to dating. She was thirty years old and had never been intimate with a man. Normally she didn't mind standing out from the crowd, but right now she wanted nothing more than to fit in with everyone else by giving in to temptation and satisfying the need that had been alive in her since meeting Marcus Tate. She could have gone years without sleeping with Kendall, but with Marcus, she was willing to throw caution to the wind. The differences between her and Marcus were starting to not matter as much to her.

Marcus was where he always went when he wanted to get Nikki off his mind. He had no choice but to come here. His raging erection had yet to go down since Nikki had slipped her arms around his neck and her tongue into his mouth. Relief was what he needed right now, even if the woman providing it was a substitute for the one he craved. Just like any other time, Meka welcomed him with a bright smile and a tight, soaking wet pussy.

Chapter 5

Marcus's mind had been racing all night, and he hardly slept at all. By six a.m., he finally said, "Fuck it," and hopped up to go work out in his brother's home gym.

After a quick shower, he came down to make breakfast for everyone. He had been hanging out at Jakobi's house a lot more than usual. The incident with Nikki had been swept under the rug, but he had secretly experienced his first heartbreak, and it wasn't an easy thing for him to get over. He had gone thirty-four years avoiding this very thing, and to think it happened with a chick he hadn't even smashed was troubling. Being around his family the last few weeks helped to keep his spirits up.

"Morning, Unc," Gavin said, joining him at the table.

"What's up, G," he replied, dapping him up.

"Good morning, brother-in-law," Alana greeted him as she entered the kitchen with his nephew Kash on her hip. His sister-in-law hadn't too long ago arrived home from working overnight at the hospital, and Jakobi was right behind her carrying his niece, Kiyarah.

"Hey, sis," he replied before kissing her cheek then moving past her to take his niece from his brother. The twins were just months away from turning two, and he knew not to go anywhere near Kash's rotten ass. That boy didn't fool with nobody but his mama. Baby girl, on the other hand, loved him to life, as did his oldest nephew, Gavin. Kiyarah was already squirming in her father's arms, reaching for Marcus.

"Hey, YaYa," he said, kissing her forehead. He leaned down to let her kiss his forehead too, as was routine for them. "I'll be glad when your brother stops being a tittie baby and shows his uncle some love too," he said, cutting his eyes at Alana while Gavin and Jakobi laughed.

"Don't talk about my baby, Marcus. I done told yo' ass about that. He just loves his mama," she said, kissing the boy all over his face before attempting to put him down. He immediately started to cry. Her baby boy was spoiled, and she knew it. Alana couldn't begin to describe how deeply she loved her children or the amount of peace they brought to her life. She was over the top with her love for them, and Kash's ass was the result of that.

"What I tell you? Damn tittie baby," he said, causing Alana to roll her eyes at him.

"I got him, baby. Go on up and get some rest. You been up with them since you got off work," Jakobi said before kissing his wife's cheek then picking up his crybaby son. Kiyarah had her mother's independent streak, so she was no problem, and of course, Gavin was a great kid, but that damn Kash was a real-life mama's boy.

Alana walked over to kiss her baby girl's cheeks and her oldest son on the top of his head. "I'll be up in a few hours, and we can run up to the mall to get those cleats you wanted," she told Gavin.

"Okay, Mom," he said with a mouthful of eggs.

"I planned on going up to the Galleria in a little bit, so he can just roll with me. You go on and get some rest, sis," said Marcus.

"Heck yeah, Mom. Can Uncle Marcus take me?" Gavin asked, jumping up from his seat at the table, a little too excited for her liking.

"Damn, son, it's like that? You don't want to go to the mall with your mama?" she said, pretending to be hurt.

"It's not like that. I just want you to get some rest," he said, trying to fix it up. He loved hanging with his uncle, and he knew he would get more than shoes if Marcus took him.

"It's all good, Gavin. I'll see you later, and thanks, Marcus," she said before stopping to whisper something to her husband that had him nodding his head and grinning from ear to ear. It seemed the couple was still in the honeymoon phase, and it was a beautiful thing to witness. Looking at them made Marcus wonder if there was someone out there who could give him the same thing.

At the mall, Marcus watched on as his nephew picked up more than shoes. In addition to the football cleats, Marcus got him tons of clothes and watched as Gavin got the phone numbers of at least three girls. The young girls these days were bold as fuck, too. Walking right up like it wasn't shit to put their game down on Gavin. His nephew reminded him so much of his brother it was crazy. It was no surprise that he was adored by the ladies, just as he and his brother had been.

Jakobi was a one-woman man now after reuniting with his first love after over ten years of being apart. After hooking back up with her, Jakobi learned he was the father of Alana's son, who she'd given up for adoption immediately after giving birth. It was a long and amazing story that was hard for a lot of people to believe, but it was true nonetheless. Gavin's adopted mother passed away a few years ago, and he had been with his birth parents since then.

Despite not being with his biological parents the first eleven years of his life, Gavin had adjusted well and had strong and loving relationships with his family. Last year, when Gavin approached his father about having his last name changed to Tate like the rest of the family, was the first time Marcus had ever seen his brother cry. Alana and his children were the only ones who could bring out Jakobi's emotional side, and Marcus was glad he had them.

As Marcus looked on, he smiled at the fact that his nephew was keeping his options open with the ladies, but he wanted to make sure that he knew to always treat them with the utmost respect. He didn't want Gavin to be anything like him when it came to the opposite sex. He wasn't a complete jerk to women, but he could admit that he wasn't always as considerate of their feelings as he should have been.

Despite being considered a player, Marcus never led women on and was always upfront with what he wanted and what he was about. Some women could fuck with it and others couldn't, but that wasn't his problem. With Nikki, however, he was a completely different man, and it wasn't something that was forced. Her being who she was brought all the good qualities out of him. For the right woman, a man would do what was expected of him without having to be told or coached. It was just sad that none of that mattered to her.

"Hey, G, you wanna grab something to eat at Grand Lux before we head home?"

"That works, Unc. I'm starving," he said, rubbing his stomach.

"Yo' ass always starving," Marcus laughed. His nephew was a football sensation, and all Marcus saw him do was eat and train. He took after his father in that way as well. As a teenager, Jakobi had had multiple offers to play at top colleges across the country, but he gave it all up and took a different path after the deaths of their parents and sisters.

After ordering lunch, the two kicked back and talked. He enjoyed catching up on what was going on in his nephew's life. Marcus loved his role as an uncle and looked forward to the day he could add "father" to his list of titles. Their food arrived, but before they could dig in, Gavin noticed his mother's good friend sitting a few tables away.

"Hey, there's Auntie Nikki," he said excitedly. He loved him some Nikki because she was so sweet and always gave him the best gifts.

"Where?" Marcus asked. He'd only seen her once since the incident at the shop, and he couldn't lie, he missed her a lot.

"Over there with some dude," Gavin said, pointing in her direction.

"Don't point, G. That's rude," he said as his mood instantly soured.

"My bad." Gavin shrugged.

The smile on Marcus's face was gone. He simply threw his head up as a greeting after making eye contact with her.

"Can I go over to say hello?"

"Naw, Gavin, she's on a date, and it wouldn't be cool to interrupt. Finish your food so I can get you back home. You know yo' mama and daddy probably put an APB out on us for being gone this long."

Gavin laughed because he wasn't exaggerating. His parents were very protective of him, and if he was out of their sight for an extended period of time, they worried.

Just then, Marcus received a text from Alana. "What I tell you? That's yo' mama asking when I'm bringing you home," said Marcus, shaking his head.

"Hey, you two," Nikki said as she walked up with her arms extended toward Gavin.

He got up and wrapped his arms around her waist. "Hey, Auntie."

"What's up," said Marcus coolly.

"Nothing much. How have you been?" she asked, looking at Marcus with a million questions in her eyes.

"Been good. You?"

He wasn't his usual self and seemed a little irritated. As she suspected, things had become weird between them after she kissed him that night. She was still kicking herself for that slip-up. Now he was avoiding her like she had Ebola, and she hadn't seen him in nearly a month. "I've been well, but the reason I came over was to ask you about that exhibition we planned to go to at the Dallas Museum of Art next week. I tried calling you about it, but I didn't get a response," she said, intentionally calling him out.

"Yeah, I've been a little busy. I gotta cancel though. I have to go to my Austin shop to check on some things."

He had actually forgotten all about the plans they made. He felt like a chump for not keeping it all the way real with her. The Austin trip wasn't a complete lie because they did have an issue with one of their artists bringing his street drama to the shop, but it wasn't so serious that he needed to go there to address it. His Austin manager, Dylan, was thorough, so he was confident that everything would be worked out. Although he hated to see the disappointed look on her face, she was on a date with a whole other nigga, so he didn't care how she felt right now. He couldn't allow this woman to continue playing with his emotions.

"Really? I was looking forward to going, but I understand that you have to handle your business," she said sadly. Nikki knew there was more to it but decided not to push further.

"Maybe you can ask your friend." He nodded in the direction of dude waiting for her to return to the table.

There it is, she thought. "Maybe I will," she said, deciding to be petty like him.

"You should." He shrugged nonchalantly.

"I guess I'll see you later. Gavin, tell your mother I'll call her later this evening," she said, trying to mask her hurt.

"Yes, ma'am." The boy saw the strange look she gave Marcus before she walked away. "Unc, what was that all about?"

"Nothing, G, just eat so we can go." He had officially lost his appetite and was glad when Gavin was finally done because he wanted to get as far away from Nichole Grant as possible.

It was clear that she didn't want to be anything more than friends, and he wasn't sure he could give her that. He used to really think she was just playing hard to get, but today she'd made it plain for him. Marcus still wanted her, so this friendship with hopes of winning her over shit was a wrap. He wasn't about to keep chasing after something that would never be his. Something unattainable and out of his league.

He felt it was probably the challenge that had him chasing in the first place. No female had run from him like she did, so he theorized that maybe he just wanted to get her to say that he did it. That's the only way he could explain his actions over the last few years. Being the man he was and doing the things he was doing to get next to her went against every player code he'd lived by all his life. He didn't even care for bougie, spoiled chicks, and she was definitely that.

Marcus felt like a sorry excuse for a thug right now, because Nikki had him behaving like a depressed, soft, fake-ass gangster. He shook his head as he made eye contact with her one final time before he and his nephew exited the restaurant.

"So, was that an ex-boyfriend you were talking to at lunch?" Eric pried. Although they talked on the phone and texted one another often, this was only their third date since meeting on Labor Day months back. He noticed the way her face lit up upon seeing the man there, but when she returned to the table the light in her pretty eyes was dimmed, and her mood completely changed. Eric didn't like that shit at all. They were now standing in line at the Starbucks located inside the Galleria.

"No, he's just a good friend of mine. We had plans to attend this exhibit next Saturday at the DMA, but he just informed me that he won't be able to go after all," she said despondently.

"Well, if it will erase that pitiful look from your face, I'll accompany you to the exhibit."

Her eyes lit up immediately. He liked that.

"Would you really, Eric?" she asked, surprised.

"Of course," he said, loving how easy it was to make her smile.

"Thank you. I would love for you to join me," she said before they placed their coffee orders. She was still disappointed that Marcus blew her off, but she was thinking that Eric going was probably better. It was time for her to start focusing on finding a husband anyway. She was done wasting time going on dates with her "friend" instead of going out with men she could actually have a future with.

Chapter 6

The Fourth of July rolled around, and family and friends were all gathered at O'Shea and Kelsey's summer home for a backyard barbeque. They had a place tucked away in the country, and the crew frequented the bed-and-breakfast-like estate a lot during the summer months. The couple liked to have their children out of the city when school was out, so when they weren't traveling for family vacations, that was where they spent time.

Today Marcus had the perfect distraction by his side for the holiday shindig. He hadn't spent any time with Meka in a while, so of course she was very happy to hear from him and jumped at the invitation to accompany him today. He was working the grill for the time being, with his date sitting close by, enjoying the festivities.

"You good on your drink or do you need me to get you something?" she asked sweetly. She was excited being there with him because outings with family or anything close to it wasn't their thing. Their time was spent strictly in the bedroom. There was no need to front. She was aware that she was a jump off. She knew her place but was hoping to change her position in Marcus's life. Over the years, she'd met like two of his friends, but this was the first time she had been in his brother's presence. She felt like him bringing her here today meant that the course of their relationship was changing.

"Nah, I'm good," Marcus told her as he held up his beer.

Meka was looking good as hell in a cute sundress that had her voluptuous ass on display. The way that thang jiggled and moved up and down when she walked had him hypnotized. He couldn't wait to get her back to her place tonight. It had been a minute since they hooked up, and he was looking forward to fucking her down until daybreak. After ceasing all communication with Nikki, he was feeling a lot better and more like the old Marcus. Slowly but surely he was getting back to being the player he was known to be.

"If you're bored, you can go inside to see what the ladies are up to in the kitchen," he suggested. He knew she wouldn't go. He only said it to be nice.

"No, I'm good out here with you," she said, shaking her head emphatically.

Today she seemed to stick to his side, and he hated that she felt out of place. He and Meka were of a different breed. They were both hood as fuck but still cool people. Although Alana and her friends were all down-to-earth and a little ghetto themselves, they were also dream-chasing, professional women with careers. He could see them being a bit intimidating to a chick like Meka. She was a party girl who didn't have to or even want to work because she was still living off the money that was left to her by her deceased baby daddy. Marcus used to not mind the fact that she didn't work and liked to kick it all the time, but lately he'd been wondering how long she planned to live her life that way. Her little girl was hardly ever with her, and she never spoke about her plans for the future. He felt as though he had no room to judge her, because a few years ago he was on that same shit with no future plans on the horizon and living life only for the day. He hoped that she would wake up soon and decide to do things differently, if not for herself then for her daughter, but he didn't plan on forcing his thoughts or opinions on her.

As the ladies gathered in the kitchen preparing sides and making pitchers of mixed drinks, Nikki's mind was miles away. Actually, it was mere yards away in the backyard. Marcus had been ignoring her calls for a while, and today he showed up with some woman she'd never met before. Although she had tried convincing herself that it was probably for the best, she was pissed about him blowing off their friendship. Honestly, that was only partially the cause of her jacked-up mood. She was trying to make herself believe that her attitude today had nothing to do with the beautiful around-the-way girl he was there with. The wall-to-wall, floor-to-ceiling windows gave her the perfect view of the couple. Watching their lovey-dovey exchange, she was sure her eyes would get stuck in the back of her head if she had rolled them any harder. Irritated was an understatement, and she wondered where the hell Eric was. Maybe if he were there, she would have her mind occupied with something other than Marcus and the beautiful brown-skinned girl.

"Nikki, what the hell?" she heard Kelsey gasp.

"What?" she snapped unintentionally.

"Your hand is what, smart ass!" her friend snapped back as she removed the knife from her hand.

Tearing her eyes away from the window, Nikki looked down at her hand and almost passed out. Unlike a majority of the women in the kitchen, she wasn't a nurse, and the sight of blood freaked her out. She'd been so distracted that she cut her finger while chopping vegetables. Kelsey had already motioned for Alana to get the first aid kit while she held Nikki's hand under the running water before wrapping a clean towel around it and applying pressure. Neither friend wanted to bring up what they believed was the cause of Nikki's inattention. They would save that conversation for another day when it was just the three of them. The cut turned out to be minor and had already stopped bleeding, but Kelsey still cleaned it and bandaged it up for her.

"I guess I wasn't focused on what I was doing," she said, avoiding eye contact with her friends.

"You can say that again." Kelsey smirked. She'd noticed Nikki watching Marcus and Meka all afternoon, and she thought the shit was funny. That could very well be her booed up with him by the pool, but she was playing.

Just then Marcus came rushing into the kitchen. Gavin had come outside to tell him that Nikki cut herself in the kitchen and was "bleeding all over the place," his exact words. Marcus damn near pushed Meka to the ground, attempting to come in to see about her. His reaction didn't go unnoticed by his date either. He pushed through like no one else was in the kitchen or even mattered, and he gently grabbed her hand.

"You okay, Li'l Bit?" he asked while inspecting the bandage on her finger.

"I'm just fine, but what do you care, Marcus?" she snapped before rudely snatching her hand away from his. Initially, Nikki warmed at his touch, and she was flattered that he came to check on her. Flattery soon turned to anger when she remembered how he had been treating her lately. For a moment they stood there mugging one another before she looked away. The kitchen had quickly become the place to be, and she was embarrassed by her sudden outburst. Relief came when she saw Eric being escorted by Kelsey's mother into the kitchen. He was late to the cookout, but he was right on time in her book.

"I'm so glad you're here," she sighed while walking over to him.

"Sorry I'm late. Is everything all right?" he asked, looking around curiously at the crowd of people in the kitchen.

"Yes, everything is fine now. I cut myself while chopping some veggies, but Kels fixed me up." She smiled up at him sweetly.

"Let me see," he said, grabbing her hand. His tone and facial expression showed he was just as concerned about her as Marcus had been.

The crowd had begun to disperse, but Marcus remained in place, watching the show Nikki's nigga was putting on. While he watched them, Meka was watching him, and if looks could kill, this nigga would have been dropped dead.

"Marcus, do you mind going outside to check the meat? O'Shea and Mr. James got my husband out there distracted playing dominoes, and I don't want the food to burn," she said, trying to get his crazy ass out of the kitchen and out of the trouble he was about to be in if he kept glaring at Nikki's date like that. Alana really didn't want to end up whipping his lady friend's ass if she decided to jump stupid with her brother-in-law or with Nikki. The girl seemed like she was just crazy enough to pop off.

"Yeah, I got you, sis," he said, finally able to look her way, but not before mugging the shit out of Eric and Nikki as they turned to walk toward the front of the house. When he turned around, he was face-to-face with Meka, who had her hand on her hip and fire in her eyes. "Why the fuck you looking at me like that? What?" he yelled angrily when she didn't respond quickly enough.

She jumped, and her eyes misted at his reaction. He was silently daring her to question him about his business, but she already knew what was up. "If you don't know, then I guess it's nothing, Marcus," she said dejectedly before turning and walking back outside. It didn't take a rocket scientist to know that Marcus felt a way about the female who had just exited the kitchen.

"Fuck," he hissed. He hadn't meant to get loud with her. It wasn't her fault that he practically pushed her off his lap when Gavin mentioned Nikki was hurt and bleeding. He turned to find his sister-in-law giving him a hateful look. "Don't start, Alana," he warned.

"Don't tell me not to start with you, Marcus Tate. I ain't scared of yo' big ass. You need to go apologize to that girl, and after you do that, you and Nikki need to figure out what the hell is going on between you two. The shit is ridiculous, and it's getting old," she fussed as Jakobi walked in holding a pan full of meat.

"Aye, what the hell you in here doing to my wife, nigga?" Jakobi mugged his brother before showering Alana with kisses until her screwed-up face was relaxed.

"It's nothing, baby, because your brother was just now on his way to fix what he messed up," she said, giving him the look again. She was glad that neither Eric nor Nikki had been paying attention, so they didn't notice Marcus's immature behavior.

"A'ight, Alana, damn. Just stop looking at me like that," he said, leaving out the back door. He found Meka sitting alone at the pool with her feet in the water. She had always been easygoing, and she usually went with the flow, but when they were inside the house, he saw something different in the way she looked at him. Like she wanted more from their involvement, and Marcus couldn't fuck with that at all. He owed her an apology for how he behaved inside, but that was all he owed her. After a few minutes of silence, Marcus finally spoke. "Look, I'm sorry. I shouldn't have talked to you like that," he said, playfully scooting closer to her.

"It's all good, Marcus," she said calmly as she patted his hand, which rested on her thigh. "I'm going to fix us a plate. I'll be right back." She wasn't really hungry anymore but needed a moment to gather herself before facing him again. It was taking everything in her not to cry right now. Her feelings were so hurt, but it wouldn't be a good look to let on that what he'd done bothered her as much as it had. The way he rushed to ol' girl's side told her all she needed to know, so there was no guessing how he felt about her. If they hadn't fucked around already, it was clear that they wanted to. The look in her eyes when Marcus touched her was very telling.

She didn't know exactly what she expected from Marcus, because he'd made her no promises and had been very clear on what they were doing with each other. He never gave any indication that he wanted anything more from her than to screw her whenever he felt like it. So, could she really be upset with him? Not really, but she just didn't understand how he could deal with her for so long and not develop any feelings for her or expect her to not fall in love with him.

Meka was so chill when she walked away that he was almost afraid to eat the food she brought back, for fear that she had slipped something in his shit. If he had not watched with his own eyes as she prepared it, there was no way he would've eaten anything off that plate. Once she was seated back at his side, he spoke again. "I know you said you wasn't mad and shit, but I just wanted to tell you again that I'm sorry. I ain't have no right to disrespect you like that. We cool?" he asked as he nudged her.

"Thank you, Marcus. I appreciate you saying that, and yes, we're cool." She smiled.

"Good," he said before kissing her cheek.

For the rest of the night, Marcus tried his best to keep his eyes and mind focused on the woman he was there with and not on the one who would surely invade his dreams later that night. The crazy part was that even though Nikki was there with dude, he felt her watching him all evening. He was positive that Meka picked up on it as well, based on all the eye rolling and teeth smacking she was doing. Eric, on the other hand, seemed oblivious, or maybe he just didn't care.

"Your family went all out with the fireworks today. Good thing they live so far out so the laws couldn't fuck with them," Meka said to Marcus on the ride home later that night.

"Yeah, we do it big like that every year," he reflected. The other couples stayed the night in one of the many guest rooms, but there was no way he was about to lie up with Meka around his people, so they were headed back to the city.

"Thanks for finally inviting me to hang with y'all. It was nice."

"It's nothing. You know me. I don't normally do the family thing with the females I deal with," he reminded her. It had been a long time since he'd brought a female around them. He'd learned a while back that females tended to get the wrong idea when you let them meet the family, and he would soon realize the mistake he made by taking Meka with him today.

"I know that, and that's why today meant so much to me. Really made me feel special, Marcus," she admitted with a sweet smile.

"Special?" he asked like he was offended that word even came from her mouth. "Come on now, Meka, you know me. Don't read more into it than what it is. I honestly just didn't want to go by myself." His response crushed her spirit and dropped her jaw. He figured that honesty would be the best way to go about things. He was quickly peeping game, and he didn't like where things were going.

She chuckled sarcastically, fed up with being treated like trash. "I'm thinking maybe you just didn't want that itty-bitty bougie bitch to be there with that fine-ass nigga and you not have a bad bitch on your arm," she spat jealously before she could catch herself. She hadn't taken her medication in two days, and it was showing. Had she been medicated, she would never have reacted the way she did earlier or right now.

"Call her out her name again and yo' ass gon' fuck around and come up missing." He seethed at her disrespect. She had the game fucked up if she thought he was gon' let her bad-mouth Nikki. Her flip comment also let him know that he wasn't tripping earlier. Meka was letting her real feelings for him show. She was so angry she didn't know what to do.

She was way off with her assumption though. The only reason he invited her ass was that he was sure that Nikki would be spending the day with her family like she did most holidays. Had he known she would be there, Meka wouldn't have been in attendance, and it didn't matter if Nikki was there with her man or not. He just didn't feel right being in the company of other women around her.

"Whatever, nigga," she countered with a wave of her hand.

"Be easy, baby. Yo' slip is showing." He shot her a warning look.

"Well, Smoove, so the fuck is yours," she said, rolling her eyes. She was so pissed that he was defending this girl. In her opinion, the bitch didn't have shit on her.

"You sho' right." He nodded, pulling into her driveway. He didn't even bother putting the car in park, because he didn't plan on staying. Marcus was really hoping that he didn't have to end up killing this girl, but things were not looking too good for her right now. One thing he wouldn't tolerate was a scorned woman coming back to cause problems for him, and it seemed like that's the exact shit Meka was on right now. Bitch was clearly unstable, coming sideways at a nigga like him.

"Oh, so now you ain't coming inside?" she asked, annoyed with him and upset with herself for her outburst.

"Slight change in plans." He shook his head, unbothered by her attitude. Their situation had officially run its course. She was no longer the laid-back, "go with the flow" chick he was used to. She was a woman who had caught feelings. Of all the drama he'd had with most of the females in his life, he could always count on Meka to keep calm and fuck him like no other woman ever had. Now that he was aware her feelings were involved, it was time to cut ties with her.

"Look, I'm sorry, Marcus. Forget everything I said. I guess my feelings were still a little hurt behind what happened earlier," she said, backtracking. She was horny as hell and pissed at herself for fucking up her dick appointment.

"It's all good, ma. I ain't even tripping." He shrugged.

"You sure you can't come inside for a bit? I can make it worth your while," she said seductively while gripping his limp dick through his jeans. It was humiliating to her that she had to beg him to stay after he was the one who played her.

"I'm sure you can, but I'm still gon' have to pass. I got moves to make," he said while removing her hand from his body. He was glad that his dick refused to react to her touch.

She sat there for a moment, silently pleading with him to look her way as he scrolled through his phone. Sadly he never obliged. "Okay, baby, just call me when you can come through." She grinned before removing herself from his whip. Just that quick she switched back to the happy-go-lucky girl he knew. However, no sooner than she made it to her door, she broke down crying when she turned to find that his rude ass didn't bother waiting to pull off until she made it inside. Straight bipolar shit.

Chapter 7

The Monday following the holiday, Marcus called Nikki up and asked her to meet him for lunch at the Kona Grill off the tollway so that they could talk. The incident at the barbeque was still fucking with him. He realized that he didn't handle the situation well and how wrong it had been for him to stop communicating with her without giving her an explanation. Granted, he thought it was fucked up that she was sending him mixed signals with the kiss, but he should have been man enough to tell her right then how he felt. They had become good friends, and she deserved better than to just be given the cold shoulder. That fact still didn't change his plan to tell her that they could no longer be friends. He was meeting her today because he felt that she had the right to know why things had to be this way.

His eyes roamed up and down her petite frame as she approached his table. Her look today was simple but cute as hell. Nikki wore a short-sleeved dark denim shirtdress with a pair of metallic, leather Tory Burch sandals. Her accessories consisted only of the silver crystal hoops in her ears and the black Celine bag she carried in the crook of her arm. He often wondered if she purposely wore things he'd purchased for her when she knew she was going to see him. Baby was makeup free with her short hair done up in soft waves and curls.

He stood and hugged her when she was within arm's reach. After planting a soft kiss on her forehead, he came around to hold her chair out for her. "Thank you for coming," he said after taking his seat.

"No problem. I figured we needed to talk after the ridiculous scene on Saturday," she sighed. Marcus was dressed relaxed and casual today. Why he felt the need to tease her along with all the other women in the restaurant by wearing those gray Balenciaga sweatpants was a mystery to her. Even she couldn't help but notice the nice fat print that sat there for the world to see. She never noticed things like that with other guys, but this was Marcus, so she paid attention to every single detail. A leather-trimmed white T-shirt and sneakers were of the same brand as his sweats and completed his sexy, laid-back look. His heavily lashed eyes were trained on her as she took in his handsome appearance. His waves and lineup were on point, his beard neatly trimmed. The man was so good-looking that it wasn't even fair. Single women, as well as those sitting with their men, couldn't help but steal glances at him, and it made her angry that she couldn't claim him as her own.

"First off, I want to apologize to you, Li'l Bit. Not just for what happened on Saturday but also for how I've been avoiding you lately. The only way to make things right is to be completely honest with you about how I feel, and hopefully, after that, you will understand why being friends isn't what's best for us."

"So you asked me here to tell me that you no longer want to be friends with me? What on earth did I do to deserve that from you, Marcus? I apologized to you for the whole kiss thing. I know I was out of line, but I just got caught up in the moment," she said on the verge of tears. For some reason, she was under the impression that he asked her here to apologize so that they could go back to how things were before. Nikki would rather have him as a friend than not have him at all. She was so blind and focused on the wrong things that she didn't realize if she confessed her true feelings and gave him a chance, all of this unnecessary drama could be avoided.

"That's what I'm trying to tell you. You ain't done shit to deserve this, but it's just the way things have to be," he stressed.

"Is this what you want or is this your girlfriend's doing? I noticed how she was looking at me that day. Is she threatened by our friendship?" she questioned.

"First of all, she ain't my girl, but we do fuck around from time to time. She knows her position, and she plays it. This is about you and me, Nikki, no one else. Now, from the moment I met you, I liked yo' ass. I don't even normally go for chicks like you, but I still wanted to get to know you, and I wanted you to get to know me. Because I wanted you so bad, I convinced myself that we could be friends and maybe you would one day be able to overlook my past and see me for who I really am. I was hoping that one day you would feel for me what I done always felt for you. I know now that was a mistake on my part."

"Marcus—"

"Just let me finish, please," he interrupted.

She nodded, giving him the floor. She couldn't believe he was laying his feelings out for her. Her heart was pounding like crazy, but she didn't know what to do or how to respond.

"We are from two very different worlds, but I need you to know that I don't feel bad about who or what I am. Everything that I've been through has made me the man I am, and I'm damn proud of that. I need to be with a woman who will rock with me regardless of my background. I can't keep pretending that I don't have feelings for you or acting like I'm cool with you going out with other people. I'm just not built like that, and I feel like a bitch for even trying to act like I was. At

the restaurant that day, I wanted to kill that nigga you
was with, and the same goes for when he showed up
to Shea's crib the other day. I want you for myself, but
because I know I can't have you, I'm going to back off
and accept it. With that being said, all this hanging out
shit is a wrap. It's been a minute, and I've gotten used
to not being around you so much, and I can't go back to
how we were before because it's just too confusing for
me. I feel like I been in a relationship, but I don't get the
feelings that I put out returned to me. I'm just asking
you to please try to understand and respect where I'm
coming from." His lips were pulled in a tight line, and
his face was pensive as he waited for her response.

"I do understand, Marcus, and I'm sorry. It was selfish of me to expect you to accept our friendship as is
without taking your feelings into consideration," she
agreed. What she was saying was not what was in her
heart, but she couldn't bring herself to tell him the truth.
Although she played it off a little better than he did, she
also had a hard time being around him so much knowing
how she really felt.

Why is this shit so easy for her? he thought as he gazed
into her beautiful eyes. Saying she understood so quickly
and not once copping to the feelings he felt she had for
him only confirmed what he knew to be true. Nikki cut
for him but didn't feel he was good enough for her, and
that realization made his decision all the easier. He had
never sold himself short with the ladies until he ran up
on her. What was the point of changing if the one you
changed for couldn't care less? He was done playing the
fool. He'd been fooling himself into thinking she would
ever see him as something more than a hood nigga who
was beneath her uppity ass.

"So when we run into each other do we act as if we're
enemies? It sounds like you want nothing more to do

with me, so I just want to know how I'm to behave when I see you," she said sarcastically. Although she was coming off as if she were cool with everything, he had no clue that she was practically dying inside.

"We speak. It ain't no ill feelings on my end. No need to be rude to each other, Nichole." He shrugged and picked up his menu. He needed a fucking drink in the worst way.

Nikki desperately wanted to tell him that she'd developed feelings for him too, but she had no clue why she couldn't just be upfront with him. Well, she had a few ideas of what it could be, but still, she refused to face her fears. Marcus was a player, and she didn't want to be hurt again in that way.

Also, she wondered how he would feel once he learned that she was a virgin. Would he still feel the same if he knew she wasn't fucking? Could he be satisfied with maintaining an exclusive relationship with her until they were ready to take things to the forever level? Could he even see a forever with her? Kendall had said he wanted it and look how that turned out for her. She just assumed that Marcus would be no different, or maybe even worse, and she just couldn't take that chance with him because she feared it would hurt too badly if things didn't work out.

This last month was agonizing without him, and they were just in the friend zone. She and Eric had become really close, but he didn't make her feel any better or think about Marcus any less. It wasn't cool, but Nikki found herself comparing Eric to Marcus in every way. Eric was handsome, too damn handsome and perfect in her opinion, but he was more on her level. Marcus had his own damn level, and his imperfections were what she was starting to like most about him. He was also very attractive and had a swagger that was on a million. Eric had a nice little swag as well, but there was just something extra special about Marcus Tate. He was older than her by four years, but his baby face and playfulness made him seem younger. She had no problem informing Eric about her plans to remain abstinent until marriage, and he was cool with it. Why couldn't she be open and honest with Marcus the same way?

They barely spoke as they ate, both lost in their thoughts of one another.

One down and one more to go. After lunch with Nikki, Marcus shot over to Meka's crib. It was time to have the talk with her. He had been stringing her along just like Nikki was doing to him, only he'd been doing it to Meka a whole lot longer. Somewhere along the way, things changed in their relationship, but he had been so far up Nikki's ass that he'd missed it. It was possible that she'd always hoped that more would come from dealing with him, but he was completely unaware.

"Hey, handsome," Meka sang as soon as she opened the door for him. He had to step back to make sure he was at the right house, because he'd never seen her look so rough. She was wearing boy shorts and a tan beater that had dried stains all over it. Bitch looked stressed out, and she reeked of alcohol. Marcus was speechless for a few seconds, taking in her appearance. With bags under her eyes, she looked as if she hadn't slept in days, but she was behaving as if everything were normal and the argument they'd had the other night had never occurred.

"Sup," he replied after clearing his throat and taking a seat on the sofa. "Where's Taylor?"

"With my sister," she answered. Meka wondered why he always asked about her daughter. She always made sure that her six-year-old was gone when he came through.

Actually, Tay was gone with family most times anyway. Meka never wanted to have children in the first place, but she let Damon talk her into it. He was madly in love with her and wanted nothing more than for her to have his baby. After multiple abortions, she reluctantly agreed to keep the baby after getting pregnant by him a fourth time. She wasn't in love with Damon, but he took excellent care of her, and she had no doubt that he would do the same for their child.

Of course, Meka loved her baby, but Damon loved her more, and when he saw how uninterested she was in being a mother, he took on most of the responsibility when it came to their child. She was fine with that because she was still able to rip and run the streets the same as she always had. However, all of that came to an abrupt halt after Damon died when Taylor was two years old. Although she knew Marcus was responsible for Damon's death, she really didn't care. She was looking for an excuse to leave anyway, so she played the part of the grieving girlfriend and collected the money that Damon left for her. She was nice enough to give a portion to his mother, but the stash that no one knew about from his safe, she kept for herself.

If at any time during their relationship Marcus would have told her to leave Damon to be with him, she would have done it without hesitation, even if it meant leaving her baby behind to be cared for by her father. He did a better job of it anyway. She knew it was fucked up, but by this time Marcus already had her heart. She had always managed to downplay it, but she was crazy in love with him.

Their affair had been going on for some time, and when Damon got wind of it, he was livid. Despite his frequent threats of what he would do to her and Marcus if he found out what the streets were saying was true, she was unable to stay away. Her man had his suspicions but no solid proof of her infidelity, only the word of a few hating-ass homeboys who had at one time or another tried to fuck her too.

He came for Marcus after intercepting a dick pic from him on her secret phone, but he wasn't successful in killing him. Marcus survived the shooting, and she knew it was over for her man after that. Weeks after his attempt on Marcus's life, Damon was found dead from an "apparent suicide." It was reported that he jumped to his death from the newly built Margaret Hunt Hill Bridge near downtown Dallas. Meka along with everyone else knew better than that. He loved himself and his baby too much to ever take his own life.

"You hungry?" she asked, moving toward the kitchen.

"Naw, I just came from having lunch with a friend." He wouldn't eat shit she cooked right now even if he were hungry. No telling when the last time was that she washed her ass, and he wouldn't want her anywhere near his food.

"Okay, how about something to drink?" she asked in her normal upbeat tone. She was biting the inside of her jaw to keep herself from questioning him further about who he went to lunch with.

"I'm straight. Come over here and sit with me. I got some shit I need to rap wit'chu about," he said in a serious tone.

"Is everything okay?" she asked, already dreading the conversation that was to come. She had a feeling it might have something to do with the way she reacted to the situation with ol' girl the other night. Whatever it was, the look on his face told her that she wouldn't like what he had to say.

"Just sit down, Tameka," he said with his palms pressed tightly together as he looked at her stoically. After she sat across from him, he took a deep breath and continued. "I came by to talk to you about us."

"What about us?" She tilted her head to the side with a smile like she was cute or some shit and wasn't sitting across from him looking like a damn clucker.

Marcus just shook his head and continued. "You and me?" He motioned between the two of them. "We done," he said straight up. No sparing her feelings, just straight to the point.

"Done? Are you serious right now?" she scoffed. It amazed her how cold he could be at times.

"Dead ass. We had a good thing going, but I think our situation or whatever you want to call it has run its course. Don't you want to have a real relationship one day? How long are you going to be cool with the way things are between us?" he wanted to know.

"I haven't really thought about it, but to answer your question, I do want a real relationship one day. Right now I'm fine with the way things are," she lied. She would tell him anything right now just to hold on to him for a little longer.

"Well, I'm not."

"Is that right?" She nodded with her lips pursed.

"Look, I didn't come here to hurt your feelings, but I just wanted to keep it a buck with you. We been at it for years, and I don't think it's right for me to keep fucking around with you knowing damn well that this is all it will ever be between us. I think you deserve more than a nigga coming through to fuck with you whenever. You need somebody to take you out and be willing to be a family with you and Taylor," he added, trying to soften the blow.

"But you ain't that nigga though is what you're telling me?" she asked bitterly.

"Come on, Meka. You know me better than that. I'll never be that nigga for any female."

"And you're sure about that?" she quizzed.

He nodded, but she doubted that he caught her drift. Meka felt that he would be that nigga for that stuck-up ho he was fawning over the other day. In her mind, this was all Nikki's fault. He'd linked up with her and now, all of a sudden, he had morals and cared about what she deserved from the next man. Marcus Tate had another think coming if he thought she was just going to accept this shit and move on quietly. *Fuck no! I got something for his ass.* "Well if that's how you feel then I guess there's really nothing more to say," she said, appearing unfazed.

"I guess not," he said, not really knowing how to take her attitude. All he knew was that this wasn't the last he would hear from Meka. This shit was far from over. He would mind his *P*s and *Q*s, but he decided to leave her with a little something to think about. Marcus stood up to address her directly as she moved toward the door to let him out. "You acting real cool, calm, and collected right now, but you let your true feelings show the other night, and I detect that you're feeling a way about how this all turned out. Am I right?"

No response.

"Yeah, I'm on to you. You need to tighten up, baby. Ass standing here looking like you going through some shit," he taunted while she stood there in shock. Moving into her personal space, he continued. "You acting all hard now, but the other night you behaved like a female in love with a man. Is that what it is? You in love with me, Tameka?" he asked low as he searched her eyes.

Her body grew tense, but she shook her head. Opening her mouth to answer the question would have led to her telling him the truth. *Yes, I love you, and I have for years!* that annoying voice in her head screamed.

"Right." He chuckled and nodded at the obvious lie. "Well, I'm gon' tell you like this, if you think of coming at me or crossing me in any way, you'll be dealt with accordingly. Don't let your feelings get you fucked off. Do you understand what I'm saying?"

"There's no need to threaten me, Marcus. I know better than anyone what you're capable of, but trust me, it ain't that serious on my end, boo. You have absolutely nothing to worry about." She shrugged. She was cool on the outside, but her heart was beating out of her chest. He pulled her closer, and she held her breath thinking he was about to kiss her, but he moved closer to her ear to speak.

"Don't say I didn't warn you, ma," he whispered, not believing a word she said. He knew she had her suspicions about him killing her baby daddy, but she didn't have proof. As far as everyone knew, Damon decided that he just couldn't deal with life anymore. She could try him if she wanted to, but the end result would leave Taylor without a mother, too, and that's all there was to it.

She was pissed that, despite her being afraid, the move made her panties wet. It was taking everything she had not to ask him if he wanted to take her on a couple of rounds for old times' sake. The nigga had just threatened her life, and she still wanted to fuck him. Bad.

Chapter 8

Sunday dinners at her parents' home were always a joyous occasion. Great food, family, reminiscing about the past, and catching up on current happenings. Today, however, Nikki wasn't feeling it. Because the weather was so lovely, the family decided to have dinner out back. Afterward, they retired to the theater room in her parents' home to watch a movie. It had been over a month since she'd last seen or talked to Marcus. She missed him terribly and hoped he was doing well. Eric was really a sweetheart, but it just hadn't clicked for them yet. They had even gone so far as to kiss a few times, but it was nowhere near as good as the kiss she shared with Marcus.

Junior had been doing well under Marcus's leadership at the shop and had quickly become his right hand. He was so excited about his job and often bragged about all the fun he was having traveling to tattoo conventions and all he was learning from Marcus. Her brother didn't know how she really felt about Marcus, so he didn't think it was a problem mentioning all the women they came into contact with on the regular. He never talked about Marcus hooking up with any of the women, but she could only imagine how Smoove was getting down.

"What the hell is your problem? You've been in a shitty mood since you showed up for dinner," Brandy said out of the blue, causing everyone to look in her direction, unsure of who she was talking to.

"Where did that come from? I haven't even said any-thing," Nikki asked defensively after realizing that she was the one her sister was charging up.

"Exactly. You're barely talking, and every time someone asks you something you're off in another world and don't even bother responding," Brandy said with an attitude. "You could have stayed home with all that," she added, rolling her eyes. She had no right to come at Nikki like that, but she was in a horrible mood herself and had been for days.

"Damn, Bran, chill. Seems like she has a lot on her mind, and you going off on her won't make things better," said Junior, coming to his baby sister's defense.

"No, what she needs to do is mind her business," Nikki said with an attitude that matched Brandy's. "Seems like you're the one with the problem seeing as how you're going off on me for no reason, Brandy," she said angrily.

"Hey, everyone chill. This is our family time, and I won't have it ruined with silly bickering, especially in front of my grandson. Come on, baby," Christine said as she scooped Alexander up in her arms and exited the theater with an attitude.

"Brandy Lynn, since you're the one who started this shit, go in there and apologize for upsetting my wife. Junior, go find something to do so that I can speak privately with Nichole," ordered their father.

Brandy left the room in a huff, feeling like her father was always taking his precious Nikki's side. She knew she was wrong in this instance, but she was in a funk as well, and at least she was participating in spending time with her loved ones with a smile on her face, unlike Nichole.

When his son was gone, Mr. Grant got up from his seat and moved to sit next to his youngest daughter.

"What's up, Dad?" Nikki asked. She came off low-spir-ited although she hadn't meant to sound that way.

"Tell Daddy what's wrong, sweetheart. Every time I've seen you lately you've had this joyless, faraway look in your eyes, and I don't like that shit," he said as he took her hand in his. He hated to see any of his children hurt, especially his sensitive baby girl. Nichole hadn't been herself lately, but what surprised him most was that she hadn't called or stopped by to talk to him about it. He was her go-to person, but for some reason, she was keeping him in the dark about what she was going through.

"I'm fine, Daddy, I promise," she replied.

"Nichole Elise Grant, since when do we lie to one another?" he asked, giving her a mean side-eye.

The hurt was apparent in her father's tone and instantly made her feel bad. "I'm sorry. I'm just dealing with something personal, and I'm not quite ready to discuss it yet," she answered and hoped he would understand. They had always been able to talk openly with one another, but she was still sorting out her feelings, and she didn't want to talk about what was bothering her.

"Did someone hurt you, baby girl?" he asked, searching her eyes for the truth. If anyone made that mistake, they would have him to deal with.

"No, it's nothing like that, Dad," she assured him.

"All right, Nichole, I'm willing to let this go for now, but when you're ready to talk I'll be here," he said, giving in for the time being.

"I know you will, Daddy, and I love you. You've always been there for me," she said as she wrapped her arms around him. She knew her father was worried, and she hadn't meant to do that to him.

"That's what fathers are for. I love you too, Nik Nak." Nicholas hoped that Eric wasn't the cause of the pain she was feeling. He needed to carve out some time to meet up with him to see what was up, since his daughter wanted to keep secrets.

***

"Eric, honey, I'm so glad to see you today," Janine Palmer said as she embraced her one and only son at the front door of her home on Swiss Avenue in historic East Dallas. The beautiful home had been in their family since the late seventies. When her parents passed on, the house was left to her. Her late husband, James, passed away when Eric was only sixteen, and since then it had just been the two of them.

"Hello, Mother. I was in the area and wanted to stop by to see you," he said, kissing her cheek.

"Well, I'm happy you're here. Come on in the kitchen with me. I was just about to have lunch, and there's plenty to share," she said.

"Looks like I stopped by right on time then, because I'm starving," he said excitedly as he hurried behind her.

They had her famous chicken salad sandwiches and pasta salad along with some bomb sweet tea that surely sent his blood sugar soaring. As they ate, she caught him up on her charity work and what she had going on in her life, and he did the same. When he didn't mention anything about a woman, she decided to get in his business.

"So, Christine tells me that you've been spending time with her daughter Nichole. How are things going with you two?" she asked, sounding optimistic.

"Yes, we've been hanging out, and we have a great time together, but don't go trying to marry me off just yet. We're just getting to know each other," he sighed.

"I know that, son, and I know that you get tired of me inquiring about your personal life. It's just that when I die, I want to go knowing that you're not alone and you have someone to take care of you."

"Hey, what's with the talk about dying? Are you okay, Mom? Is there something going on that you're not telling me?" He grabbed her hand and rubbed it, becoming concerned.

"No, honey, I'm fine. I didn't mean to scare you. I'm very healthy for someone my age, but I guess when you've dealt with death as much as I have, you come to realize that tomorrow isn't promised to any of us. Mostly everyone close to me has already passed on, and I just want you to be okay if the same should happen to me," she said sadly.

He got up from his seat to wrap his arms around her. She hated to run the fake guilt trip on her son, but she needed him to hurry up and find a wife. He was way behind, seeing as how he had yet to bring a female home to meet her, ever! A few of her old-fashioned friends posed questions about him from time to time and gave their unsolicited opinions on why he hadn't settled down just yet. In their eyes, a man as good-looking and accomplished as Eric not having a steady woman in his life was weird. She agreed with them to a certain extent, but she figured her son to just be playing the field for the time being. That wasn't unordinary for a man his age, but she had her own personal reasons for being worried. He had never been in a serious relationship, and she prayed every night that her son didn't pick up his father's bad habits.

"Don't worry, Mom. I'll be just fine, but I promise to put forth more effort in finding someone. I can't lie and say that Nichole is that someone, but I also can't say that she isn't," he admitted. Actually, he enjoyed spending time with her more than he had with any other woman, and that in itself was saying something.

"I don't care who she is, as long as she's good to you and I get grandbabies out of the deal," she said, laughing. These days Janine spent her time doing charity work and attending the events of the women in her social circle. She loved doing those things but would prefer loving on and chasing behind some grandchildren.

They enjoyed the rest of their lunch, but her words had Eric really thinking about things. He left his mother's home with a different frame of mind from when he had arrived. His mother was all alone besides having him to see about her, and with work, he wasn't able to spend as much time with her as he would like to. All the woman wanted was grandchildren, and with everything she'd done for him, the least he could do was make that happen for her.

He picked up the phone and dialed Nikki.

"Hello."

"Hey, pretty lady."

"Eric, how are you?"

"I'm good, but I'll be even better if you agree to have dinner with me tonight."

"I'd love to!"

She smiled through the phone, and that made him smile too. At times it still tripped him out how much he liked her. "Great. I know that you normally like to meet up when we go out, but I'd like to pick you up tonight. I want to show you that I'm serious about moving forward with you," he said. He was aware of her "no sex before marriage" rule, so he needed to speed things along.

"That's fine with me. I'll text you my address right now."

"You do that, and I'll pick you up at seven o'clock sharp."

"I look forward to it," she replied before disconnecting the call.

With a smile on her face, Nikki left the confines of her old room at her parents' house, where she had gone for some privacy to talk to Eric. She was now on her way to find Bran to apologize to her and see what was really up with her attitude earlier. She found her sister sitting alone in the den with a weary expression.

"Hey, Bran," she said as she studied her sister's beautiful face.

"Hey, Nik. Look, I'm sorry for giving you a hard time earlier. I was out of line," she sighed.

"I'm sorry too. I was in a pretty foul mood all day, so I understand you calling me out," she said, joining her on the ottoman. "But what's really going on? Is everything okay at work?" she asked, grabbing her sister's hand.

"Work is great. It's my love life that's a complete mess," she said as her eyes watered.

"Aw, don't cry, because then I'll cry. What happened? Have you started seeing someone new?" she asked, embracing her big sister. Since she was small, she had always looked up to Brandy and thought of her as one of the strongest people she knew. Brandy was usually the one providing her comfort and not the other way around. To see her so broken up was not something she was used to.

"No, there's no one new in my life. I'm still in love with Myron, so I haven't even been thinking about anyone else." She was really crying now.

"Have you told Myron how you feel?" Nikki asked her. Bran was always trying to play hard, but even before her confession, Nikki felt she still had strong feelings for her ex-husband. She really didn't understand why they got divorced in the first place. It was obvious to everyone around them that they were deeply in love and had been for years. It was never revealed if one them cheated or exactly what happened. All the family knew was that one day they were together and the next they weren't. It was all so unexpected.

"You know I'm too much of a chicken to do something like that, but it's too late anyway. Monica and I were at dinner the other night, and Myron was there with a date. It's not like I hadn't expected him to move on or anything, but to see him with someone else was so hard, Nik. It was so harddd," she cried before completely falling apart in her baby sister's arms.

As she cried her eyes out, Nikki could only hold her
while rocking back and forth. When she was finally able
to talk again, she said, "Nikki, I have loved this man since
I was seventeen years old, and I realized it was really
over when I saw him with that woman. I haven't even
thought about going out with anyone else yet. I feel like
I gave up on my marriage too quickly, and it has nothing
to do with seeing him the other night. I felt it when I
filed for divorce, but I was too stubborn to call it off. We
didn't have infidelity issues or anything like that. We had
growing pains from being together so long, and I felt like
he no longer understood me. Now I feel like I screwed it
all up," she said before she broke into another fit of tears.

"It's going to be okay, Bran, I promise. I really think
you should tell Myron how you feel, but until you're
ready to do that, I'm here for you whenever you need me,"
she assured her sister.

"So am I," a deep voice concurred from across the room.
They looked up and were both shocked to see Myron
standing there looking as if he was about to cry himself.
Hearing the last part of their conversation gave him hope
that he and Brandy could possibly work things out.

"Myron, what are you doing here?" Bran asked, trying
to clean herself up.

"I've been calling you for a few days and couldn't reach
you. When my mother said you were bringing Alex by
the other day, I came over, but by the time I made it
there you were already gone. I remembered the Sunday
dinners so I stopped by to see if you might be here. We
need to talk," he said with pleading eyes.

He hoped that she wouldn't turn him away like
she had done so many times since she filed for divorce.
They had been divorced for a year, but when he saw her
at the restaurant the other night, he still felt like he had
been caught doing some shit he didn't have no busi-

ness doing. His frat brothers were tired of him moping around sad about not being with Brandy, so they set him up on a blind date. It ended up being a total waste of time because all he could talk about was his son and his ex-wife. His date took the hint and politely told him that he needed to make sure he was over his ex before he went on any more dates. He honestly didn't know if that would ever happen. Brandy was who he wanted and would always want. It was in the middle of their conversation that he noticed Bran and her messy-ass friend Monica. He hated the look he saw on his ex-wife's face, but she ran out before he could go over to talk to her. He had been trying since then to contact Brandy.

"Are you good?" Nikki asked Brandy, who only nodded and had not once taken her eyes off Myron. "Okay, I'll give you two some privacy," she said before hugging her sister once more. She hugged Myron on her way out as well. "It's good to see you, brother," she said, smiling up at him.

"You too, sis." He smiled back before turning his eyes back to Brandy.

"So, what is it that you want to talk to me about, Myron?" Brandy asked after Nikki was gone. There was no disputing that Myron Tillman was a very attractive man. She hated that he was seeing her in this condition. She was sure she looked a hot mess, while he stood there looking like a chocolate god.

"I want to talk about what you saw the other night," he said, taking a few steps toward her.

"What about it? You were on a date. It's no big deal," she lied.

"Come on, Bran, you gotta quit acting like you don't give a damn and nothing matters to you. And for your information, it was a pretty big deal to me," he said, frustrated.

She didn't know what that meant, but she automatically assumed the worst. "So things are serious with you and that woman I saw you with? That's the big deal?" she asked, all the while willing herself not to break down crying.

"Hell no!" he said, now moving to stand directly in front of her. "The big deal to me was seeing you there. I didn't want to be there in the first place."

"So, why were you?" she asked with her arms folded across her chest.

He chuckled at her jealousy and took that as another sign that maybe there was still a chance for them. "Dame and Jay were tired of me whining about you, so they set me up on a blind date. It was a complete disaster because all I could talk about was you and our son," he said, touching her chin.

"I'm still in love with you, Myron," she blurted out before she lost her nerve.

"I never fell out of love with you, Bran. I'm always going to love you," he said, grabbing the back of her neck and pulling her into him. Myron's full lips covered hers for a deep, passionate kiss before he spoke again. "I should have fought harder for you. I never should have let you go," he said as he rested his forehead against hers.

"I shouldn't have asked you to. I'm so sorry about all this," she told him. She had been so stupid, but she planned to never let him go again.

"It's all good. Just as long as you promise to never leave me again, Brandy. My heart couldn't take it if that happened. I need you, baby, and I miss you so much," he said as he placed soft kisses on her neck. He wanted to move forward with Brandy, but they were also going to have to have a serious conversation about her man-hating friend Monica. She was probably happier than anyone when their marriage ended. That lady was manipulative and had placed all kinds of crazy ideas in his wife's head, and that's when their problems began.

"I promise I won't, baby, and I missed you more than you'll ever know," she admitted. She always had issues communicating her feelings to her husband, and that was one of their problems, but she would work on that starting right now. "My friendship with Monica is over," she said, shocking him.

"Really?" He tried playing it off and didn't want to show how happy he was to hear that.

"Yeah. I found out that she knew you would be there that night with that woman and purposely took me there. I had already been questioning our friendship and some of the things she'd said and done when you and I were together, so I confronted her that night. When I told her that I was still in love with you, she went off, telling me how stupid I was and how you were probably seeing ol' girl the whole time we were together. For the first time I saw her for who she really was, and I also recognized the part I let her play in the demise of our relationship. I'm sorry for allowing her to have so much of a say and influence in our marriage."

"I forgive you, Bug," he said, calling her by the nickname he'd given her when they were in high school. "Can I take you out tonight? Kind of like a first date." He knew they had a long road ahead of them to repair the damage that was done to their relationship, but he wanted to get started on fixing it right away.

"I'd love that, Myron," she said, wrapping her arms around his neck. "The only difference between now and our first date seventeen years ago is that you'll be getting lucky after this one," she said before passionately kissing the man she loved.

Chapter 9

Six Months Later

Love was definitely in the air tonight as the couples grooved to the old-school slow jams blasting through the speakers at the sweetheart dance. The invitation-only event was held at a private location hosted by Kelsey and O'Shea Lewis, with the proceeds from tonight going toward the Victoria Lewis Foundation for adopted and foster children throughout Dallas-Fort Worth.

It was a family affair, so tons of children were present for the festivities along with their parents, and they were having a blast. Kash was even acting like he had some sense for a change and could actually function without Alana. Everyone joked and teased Alana because they thought she was about to go into cardiac arrest when she saw her teenage son, Gavin, dancing with the girl he invited to the party. They kept a safe distance and didn't do anything inappropriate, but Alana still watched them like a hawk throughout the night. Zaschia just so happened to be Big B's baby sister, so Alana wasn't the only one keeping a close eye on the teenagers.

The smaller children eventually got pooped out from all the fun and were taken to the makeshift nursery that had been set up in the back for families with kids ages five and younger. Qualified caretakers, along with Kelsey and Alana's parents, were in charge of caring for the babies, and they had no problem doing so because it gave them an excuse to spend more time with their grandchildren.

Marcus and Nikki were in a better place these days. They spoke and remained civil whenever they ran into each other. Everyone was grateful for that, because it was hard the first few months or so with Nikki dating Eric and Marcus going back to doing his thing. Although they remained cool, their relationship was nothing close to the one they shared before.

While the other guys were paired up with their spouses, Marcus and Junior chose to come dateless. Surrounded by frilly pink, red, and white decorations, they kicked back and got their drink on without a care in the world. Junior had been hired on permanently and now worked full-time as the manager of Smoove Ink Dallas. Marcus was proud of all the progress he'd made. Having Junior there made his job a whole lot easier. The middle Grant child could no longer be considered a slacker, because although it had only been just shy of a year since he joined the team, it was the longest steady job he had ever held. He was now a hardworking man, and Marcus believed in Junior that same way that Jakobi had believed in him. Even though things would never be with him and Nikki, Junior had become like a brother to him. Marcus still thought about Li'l Bit from time to time, but it wasn't as bad as it was in the beginning.

As if he had thought her up, she entered the ballroom with her man, Eric. The two had been going strong for some time now, but there was something about their relationship that didn't sit well with Marcus. It wasn't his place to voice his concerns, so he kept his mouth closed. He just hoped she was happy.

The party was still going strong when Marcus got a text from Kelsey's mother, asking him to come to the nursery because his niece was awake and throwing a tantrum because she wanted him. Cheryl and Anita had both tried but were unable to calm her down and get her to go back to sleep. He excused himself from the table he and Junior had commandeered for the night to go see about his boo. YaYa immediately stopped acting up and smiled when she saw him walk in the room. Curly hair wild and free, with fresh tears streaming down her face, she was still the cutest little girl he'd ever seen.

"Uncle, I missed you!" she squealed like she hadn't just seen him about an hour ago. He couldn't do a thing but smile, while Ms. Anita rolled her eyes in annoyance.

"I missed you too, baby girl." He kissed her cheek, and just that fast all was well.

"Ain't that some shit. You see how your grandbaby do, Cheryl?" She turned to Mrs. Kim. "All that cutting up she was doing, and she take one look at his big, fine ass, and them tears dried right on up." Both ladies along with Marcus laughed. It wasn't hard to see who Kelsey got her mouth and sense of humor from.

Kiyarah led him to the play area in the corner where they talked and played for about twenty minutes before she was nodding off. He laid her back down in the large playpen next to her snoring-ass twin brother. He loved his nephews, but Miss Kiyarah Tate held a very special place in his heart, and it was clear to everyone that she loved her some Uncle Marcus. She resembled his mother, Marie, so much, which was probably why he'd grown so attached to her.

Once he made it back to the party, he wished he had stayed away just a little while longer. It was almost like Kiyarah knew he was going to need some love before coming back to the ballroom. It was surely one of the hardest scenes he had ever had to watch in his life. Pulling up to his childhood home, with Jakobi in the passenger seat, to find it engulfed in flames, knowing that his parents and little sisters were inside was the only thing that was harder to witness.

Eric was down on one knee, proposing to Nikki. His Nikki.

Uncertainty showed all over her face, and time stood still as he waited for her answer. He thought he was over it, over her. But seeing this shit made him realize he wasn't. Marcus had to refrain from intervening as he watched her nod, accepting the proposal and agreeing to share her life with another man.

From across the room, their eyes met, and he could have sworn he saw her head go from side to side as if she were saying no, but she didn't move so neither did he. It was almost as if she was asking him to do something. But what could he do, when she'd made it clear that she didn't want him? He was stuck. Holding her gaze for a few seconds longer, he finally looked away. As if she knew he needed it, Alana came to stand beside him, taking his hand in hers for a tight squeeze. He returned the gesture, letting her know that he was okay. He hung back and watched as the onlookers clapped and congratulated the couple on their engagement. When he felt the time was right, he excused himself once more to go offer his well-wishes to the couple.

"Eric, congratulations. You definitely got yourself a winner," Marcus said, shaking the man's hand.

"Thanks, Marcus. We really appreciate that," Eric replied nervously. He couldn't understand what the hell he was nervous about. She'd already said yes.

Marcus then turned to the woman of the hour. "Congratulations, Li'l Bit," he said before wrapping her up in a tight hug while planting a soft kiss on her forehead, letting his lips linger for a few seconds. "I'm really happy for you, baby," he was finally able to get out.

"Thank you, Marcus," she replied, her body shaking from the feel of his lips on her skin and the way his eyes bore into hers. The term of endearment definitely did a number on her pulse as well. Her heart was pounding, and the area between her legs was doing the same. Marcus was the only man to ever have that effect on her. Not even the man she'd just agreed to marry had been able to bring about those feelings in her, but this man standing before her could do so with just a look or a touch. For years she had denied her feelings and pushed him aside, waiting for something better, and now she wasn't so sure that someone better than him even existed for her. What had she been thinking? And why had she just agreed to marry someone else, someone she didn't love in that way?

Nikki was staring into the eyes of the man she loved at this very moment, and she didn't know what she should do. *Nothing, right?* She was with the man she was supposed to be with, a man more suited for her. Or was he? Just seeing Marcus and being this close to him was confusing her. As she watched him walk away, her father's advice from a while back came to mind: *"How you feel when you're in his presence will tell you if he's the one. All you'll be able to see is him, and you'll realize that there's no other place you'd rather be."* At that moment she knew that she had messed up terribly.

Marcus had long ago left the party, and Nikki was now relaxing in the gazebo out back alone. She was trying to figure out why the hell Eric had proposed to her in the first place. More importantly, why had she accepted? Sure they had become close, but to her, it was closer to a brother-sister relationship than husband and wife. Before she could ponder that thought any longer, she was joined by her besties.

"Hey, ladies," she greeted them in an unenthused tone.

"So how does it feel knowing you're about to join the marriage club?" Kelsey asked, trying to gain understanding. She didn't understand why their friend would say yes to a proposal from one man when she was clearly in love with another. If Kelsey knew nothing else, she knew love. She saw it with her best friends Alana and Jakobi, her own mother and father, and although Alana's parents had a hard time showing her love when she was younger, the love they had for one another was undeniable. Plus, the love between her and her husband, O'Shea, was special enough for someone to write a book about it. It was literally killing her being fake excited about her friend's engagement, and Alana felt the same way. She wanted Nikki for her brother-in-law because in her eyes they were meant to be.

"Honestly?"

"That's the only way we do it, Nikki," replied Kelsey.

"I'm still trying to figure it out. I'm not sure about anything that happened tonight," she said truthfully.

"Why the hell did you say yes if you're unsure about it, Nichole?" Alana asked a little louder than she intended.

"What was I supposed to do? He's my friend, and I wouldn't dare embarrass him by turning him down in front of all of those people," she sighed.

"So what do you plan to do now? I mean, there's no way that you can marry this man if you're feeling this way," said Kelsey.

"I know I can't, and I'll talk to him about it later," she assured her friends.

"Good. My next question to you is, what are you going to do about Marcus?" Alana asked, giving her the same look she did any time she mentioned Marcus. The look always said that she was aware of her friend's true feelings toward her brother. Just like all the other times, Nikki caught her drift.

"What am I supposed to do, Lana?" she asked. Her feelings for Marcus still scared her.

"The fuck you mean what are you supposed to do? Do you love him?" Kelsey damn near yelled. She was so tired of Nikki playing games, and unlike Alana, she couldn't continue to baby her or sugarcoat shit for her ass.

"I do," she said as a lone tear rolled down her cheek. The look in her eyes and the way her voice cracked told her friends how deep in love she really was. They both rushed to wrap their arms around her for a group hug. "What am I going to do? All this time I've pushed him away and made him feel as if he wasn't good enough for me. This man literally laid his feelings out for me, and I did nothing but reject and dismiss his words. I don't even feel like I deserve him at this point," she choked out. Now, she was hard down crying.

"Girl, hush. You deserve all the love your heart desires and then some, but I do think you owe it to Marcus to let him know how you feel. Despite what you might believe, I think he loves you too," said Alana.

"What about my other little secret?"

"I think that will make him love you even more." Alana smiled. "But I will tell you this, Nikki. You have to be willing to accept Marcus as is. He isn't perfect, but he is a good man and is loyal to those he loves. You will have to let go of your past opinions of him or what you think about the women he's been with and allow yourself to love the real Marcus Tate. The family man. A man who will go above and beyond for those who mean the most to him. He's a man with a troubled past, but he's a good man nonetheless. Plus he's a Tate boy, and they just don't make 'em like that no more, baby," Alana boasted, sticking up for the brother-in-law she'd grown to love like he was blood.

"He's definitely one of a kind, and that's why I fell in love with him." She no longer cared about the opinions of others or her own reservations when it came to Marcus. She loved him and would deny it no longer.

Before going to talk to Marcus, Nikki needed to address the situation with Eric. It was after one in the morning, and they were seated on the sofa in her spacious living room while the fire roared in the fireplace. Her feet were propped up in his lap as he gently massaged them.

"Nichole, what's wrong? You've been in your own little world since my proposal," he asked. He thought she would have been happier, but the way she'd been behaving since she said yes left him with an uneasy feeling. Her uncertainty was obvious. He only hoped he wasn't being as transparent as she was.

"Why did you do it, Eric?" Nikki asked him with her head tilted to the side.

"Why'd I do what, babe?" He played crazy.

"Eric Palmer, you know exactly what I'm talking about. Why the hell did you ask me to marry you?" she inquired, pushing his shoulder forcefully.

"Ouch! I asked you because I love you and I thought you loved me too," he replied, a bit taken aback by her question.

"I do love you, but not like that, and I don't think you feel that way about me either, Eric. So I'll ask you again. Why'd you do it?"

"I'm not getting any younger, Nichole, and I was thinking now was the time to get married and start a family. I thought you wanted the same thing," he replied. It hurt to hear her say she didn't love him that way, but he couldn't get mad, because she was right. He loved her, but he wasn't in love with her.

His reaction made her feel bad, and she realized that she could have worded that a bit differently. "I do want those things, Eric, but as your friend and someone who cares for you, I won't allow you to settle, and I won't do that to myself either. You're an amazing man, boo, and you deserve to marry someone you are madly in love with, someone you absolutely cannot live without. Now tell me what's really going on," she softly requested.

She'd drawn her own conclusions, but she wanted him to be the one to tell her what was real. He didn't respond but got up and headed to the bar to fix himself a shot of Patrón. She watched as he quickly downed it before immediately pouring another. "Talk to me, Eric. You can tell me anything, and you know that," she said, coming behind him to wrap her arms around his waist and resting her cheek against his muscular back. There was nothing sexual or romantic about their interaction, simply one friend being there for another.

"Nichole, don't do this to me," he groaned. He was relieved that she couldn't see his pained expression. For so long he'd put up this front, and he wasn't ready to be confronted about it. It was too much, because he really found it difficult to explain his situation to her.

"Eric, please," she pleaded.

"I can't."

"Yes, you can," she said as she forced him to turn to face her. She placed her palm against his cheek and looked into his eyes. "Tell me what I already know, Eric," she said, causing his eyes to widen in surprise.

On the way home, she really sat back and thought about her relationship with Eric, and something just didn't add up. Yes, they enjoyed each other's company and genuinely loved one another, but there was nothing romantic about it, at least not on her end. From the beginning, she prayed that those feelings would eventually come, but they never did. It was likely due to the fact that she was in love with Marcus, but there was still something with Eric that was off. She was the virgin, but he was the one who acted like he had never been with a woman before.

"How about you tell me what it is you think already know, Nichole."

"Okay. I know that you're a great friend who I love dearly. I also know that you love me, but . . . maybe I'm not exactly your flavor," she hinted. She prayed that she wasn't wrong and didn't offend him with her assumption.

"And what exactly is my flavor?" he asked, knowing that she was close to revealing his deepest, darkest secret.

"I want you to tell me. Tell me the truth, Eric. Tonight you asked me to marry you in front of all of my friends, so you owe it to me to keep it real." In the depths of his eyes, she could see the internal fight he was having with himself, and her heart went out to him as he struggled to get the words out.

"I . . . guess . . . I'm gay," he said but paused when he noticed the perplexed expression on her face. It was hard for him to explain, but he owed it to her to try. "Before you, I'd been with this guy, Rae, off and on since college. He is the only person, male or female, I've ever been with, but I ended things with him a few months before you and I started dating exclusively. You're legit the first woman I've ever dated or been sexually attracted to," he admitted before turning his face away from hers so that she wouldn't see his shame. It was the first time he had spoken those words to anyone. With the hardest part out of the way, he turned back to her and finished telling her about his relationship with Rae. He also explained that the attraction he had to her was the reason he'd become confused about his sexuality.

"Come here, boo. I think we're made for each other. We're both a complete mess," she joked while reaching out to him. He came to her willingly, needing to be held and comforted. "You know if we get married that confused mess won't cut it. You would have to give it up, because I've waited way too long to get my freak on," she said before they both cracked up laughing.

Once he got himself together, they were able to sit down and have a truthful discussion about everything, both apologizing to one another for letting things go so far and not being upfront and honest about their feelings and motives. Eric proposed to get them on the fast track to making some babies to appease his mother, while Nikki had just become content with the friendship they shared. While enjoying a bootleg version of Marcus, marriage had gone from her main priority to a distant memory.

"Can you imagine how shocked I was when you got down on one knee? How could you do that to me?" she asked, popping him on the back of his head playfully.

"I'm so sorry, Nichole, but I really thought I was doing the right thing," he said contritely.

"For who? Not for me and surely not for yourself," she said as she pulled back, looking at him like he was stupid.

"For my mom. Although I'm confused about things, the fact remains that I've slept with a man. Was in a full-blown relationship, ya know? Finding out about that will break her heart, Nichole, and I don't think I can do that to her," he said, shaking his head. He hated to disappoint his mother. She would never be able to understand him having feelings for a man.

"Eric, you have to find a way to tell her and live your truth. Doing anything other than that is cheating your mother and, most importantly, yourself. She loves you, and I truly believe she would want to see you happy," Nikki said.

"She desperately wants grandchildren, Nik. I'm the only one who can give her that," he sighed.

"Adopt or find a surrogate. There's more than one way to make her happy and still be happy yourself."

He nodded his agreement. "So, now that you know all my business, let me get in yours. What are you going to do about Marcus? I saw how that man looked at you tonight, and I also saw how you reacted to him. Shit had me kind of jealous," he teased but was very serious. The chemistry he witnessed between the two of them was palpable.

"I'm going to get my man is what I'm going to do," she said with an auspicious smile as she rested her head on his chest. "I just wanted to deal with our situation first." Nikki was so glad that she had finally made this decision, and she only hoped that Marcus still carried the same feelings for her and didn't turn her away like she'd done to him so many times.

"Thank you for not judging me and for being an amazing friend. Being with you had me questioning if I'm gay, bisexual, or all the way hetero," he laughed lightly. "I really do love you, Nichole," he said, pulling her in to kiss her cheek.

"I love you too, Eric," she said as they embraced.

Chapter 10

Marcus had just pulled into traffic after leaving the strip club. After hitting up Sensations with Junior for an hour, he was now on his way to the house. He wanted nothing more than to be alone right now, and he was having a hard time dealing with the fact that the woman he wanted was marrying another man. He just couldn't wrap his mind around that shit.

His racing thoughts and broken spirit didn't stop him from noticing the black Impala that had been following him for the last ten minutes. They were doing their best to go unnoticed, but Marcus had been in these streets long enough to know to stay alert and on his shit at all times. He used voice command in his car to dial Kobi while he removed his second gun from the middle console. This wasn't the first time in the last few weeks that he felt like he was being followed, and he was determined to deal with this shit tonight.

"Wussup?" Kobi answered, sounding as if he'd just lain down.

"Baby bro, was on my way home, and it seems that I've run into a little issue. Spotted a black Impala on my ass that's been with me since I hit Woodall Rodgers and—"

"I'm on my way," Kobi said, not allowing him to finish.

"No need for that. I'm strapped and ready for whatever these niggas think they got for me. Just wanted to tell you that I love you. Kiss Lana and my babies for me. Tell them I love them too just in case this shit goes left."

"Fuck all that, Marcus. Where are you?" his brother hissed into the phone, trying to keep his voice down so as not to wake his wife. He groaned in frustration when he realized that Marcus had already disconnected the call.

Marcus hated to do that to Jakobi, but he didn't want him mixed up in this shit. His brother had a wife and three children to live for, but as for himself, he didn't have shit to lose.

Nikki's face popped up in his mind, and thoughts of her remained with him until he pulled up to his spot about thirty minutes later. He gripped a nine in one hand, and another rested in the pocket of his hoodie, with fingers on both triggers. Refusing to go out like a ho, he was ready to take whoever was looking to do him harm down right along with him if he had to go. He was unaware of anyone having beef with him, so he had no clue who these niggas were. Any open conflicts he had before leaving the dope game behind had been handled with a conversation or a bullet, so all loose ends were clipped as far as he knew.

Finally, he saw the car that had been behind him pull up with the lights off and park down the road a ways, barely hidden amid some trees. They fell right into his trap, following him to where he laid his head, where no one would see or hear a thing. When he was confident that no one else was pulling up behind them, it was go time.

He jumped out of his truck, ready for whatever. He took his time, giving his would-be attackers a chance to catch up to him. Marcus pretended to stumble and sway as if he were intoxicated, but he managed to maintain his cool, although his heart was beating out of control. He heard at least two people behind him, and as soon as he felt they were close enough, he turned and fired, dropping the nigga on his left first with a clean head shot.

The masked man on his right seemed to be startled by his quick reaction and stalled for a millisecond too long, allowing Marcus to turn his gun on him, quickly lighting his ass up as well. Dude hit the ground with a thud, gun sliding across the concrete. He was glad that he'd chosen a home on the outskirts of town with the closest neighbor at least a half mile away so that no one would call the laws. One phone call and he would have this shit cleaned up in no time.

"Marcus, behind you!" a voice shouted out nearby.

Her shrill scream and the fact that she was this close to danger caused a fear that he'd never known to course through his body and damn near stop his heart. Fuck his life, he wasn't afraid to die, but the thought of her being hurt had him about to lose it. The fear in her tone shook him to the core, and by the time he turned to fire his gun, he felt a burning sensation in his right shoulder. A third man had come from out of nowhere, sending two shots his way. Luckily he was able to get a few off himself before going down.

Ignoring the danger, Nikki ran to Marcus's side. She had just pulled up and was startled by the sound of gunfire. She attempted to warn Marcus of the third gunman behind him, but it was too late. He was able to put the first two down, but that last man came out from the shadows unexpectedly. She suddenly realized that the man hadn't fired any more shots, and she thought that maybe he'd been hit.

Jakobi had pulled up right as Nikki ran toward his brother, catching the last man trying to get away. The masked man had a gunshot wound to his chest and abdomen and was stopped in his tracks with another shot to his left kneecap from Kobi's gun. As soon as dude hit the ground, Jakobi kicked his weapon out of reach. Right now all he wanted to do was disarm him and find out the reason they were coming for his family.

"Who the fuck are you and what business do you have with my brother?" Jakobi asked through clenched teeth as he ripped the ski mask from the man's face to see if he recognized him.

"I'on know what you talking about, nigga," the man stuttered right before going into a coughing fit with blood leaking from his mouth.

"You sure that's how you want to play it?" Kobi asked. The man only mean mugged him, refusing to give up any information. His defiance was admirable, but that wouldn't stop him from meeting his Maker today. "Suit yo'self, bitch nigga," Jakobi spat before sending him to the afterlife with two shots to the dome. He didn't know who the hell this man was or why he and his potnas had come for his brother, but he was determined to find out.

"Oh my God, Marcus," Nikki cried while searching his body to see where he had been shot. It looked to be the shoulder and leg.

"What the fuck are you doing here, Li'l Bit? That nigga could have shot yo' ass," he yelled as the pain in his shoulder intensified. It was then that he saw his brother walk over to him. The appearance of the youngest Tate brother told them who had stopped the last man from finishing him off. "Kobi, what the fuck, man? Get the hell out of here. I told yo' ass not to come over here," he shouted in frustration. His actions had taken so much from Jakobi, and he refused to cause any more chaos in his life. Not to mention the grief it would bring his family if he were hurt behind something that had nothing to do with him.

"I ain't going nowhere," Jakobi said, standing his ground. He was already on his burner phone, calling the cleanup crew. His brother had to know that he was on the way the second he hung up the phone on him. There was no fucking way it was going down like that.

"You need to go home to your wife and kids. Please, Kobi. I promise you I got this and I'm gon' be straight." When Jakobi made no move to leave, he became angrier. "Just go!" he shouted, causing Nikki to flinch.

"If it were me lying on that ground, would you leave?" he asked as they engaged in an intense staredown. "I fucking thought so," he added after Marcus failed to answer. Marcus was his lifeline and best friend, so there was no way he was abandoning him. Not now, not ever.

"Nikki, baby, you gotta go. I can't have you in the middle of this shit," he said, turning to face her after it became clear that his hardheaded brother wasn't leaving.

"I'm not leaving your side until I know that you're going to be okay," she said before removing her small jacket and applying pressure to the gunshot wound to his shoulder.

His brother had a doctor there within an hour. The bullet was removed from his shoulder, and he was stitched and bandaged up in record time. The doctor and nurse were paid to stay with Marcus around the clock until he was better. The bodies, along with any trace of what had occurred there tonight, had been removed and cleaned away, so the only thing left to do was find out who was behind the attempt on his life.

Nikki stayed glued to his side just like she promised. Having her near him was refreshing but confusing at the same time. He didn't want to love this girl, but she was making it difficult for him to feel any other way. He was thanking God that no harm had come to her in the midst of all the shooting, because he would never have forgiven himself if something had happened to her. He was still trying to figure out what the hell she was doing there at that time of night in the first place.

Hours later, the family was still fussing over Marcus, and all he wanted was for them to go home. He wasn't used to being the center of attention, and he didn't want them worrying about him. Alana had gone to check on the kids while Jakobi and Kelsey stayed behind, along with a few of his close friends. Although he was no longer in the streets, his loyal riders raced to the spot when they heard what happened to him. Situations like this could go either way, so they were glad that their former boss made it out alive. Marcus was still their dawg, so they were there and ready to put in work whenever he gave the word. Because of him and Jakobi, they had been eating on the streets of Dallas for years, so they were riding with them until the end. As soon as they found out who was behind this shit, there would be smoke in Dirty Dirty Dallas, or Triple D as the locals liked to call it.

Nikki stepped out to shower and change into the clothes Kelsey brought over for her. She handed over her bloody clothes to be disposed of but returned to his room a short time later. He wondered what her fiancé thought about her being there, seeing as how they had just gotten engaged the night before.

The two hadn't had a chance to say very much to each other since everything had gone down. He wanted to know how she was handling everything. It had to be traumatizing for someone as sheltered as her to witness a shooting like that. Marcus wondered how she felt about seeing him kill those men right in front of her. He needed to make sure she was okay.

Jakobi stepped out to make a call, and Kelsey followed so that she could call her husband, who was out of town for a game against Indiana, to give him an update on Marcus's condition. Finally alone, Nikki was about to say something to him but was interrupted when Alana walked into his bedroom with his niece and nephews. When he looked into Gavin's wet, reddened eyes, his heart damn near broke in two.

"Come on, G, I'm all right. Don't do that to me, nephew," he said, becoming choked up while giving Alana a look that was asking why she'd brought the kids there.

"I'm sorry, but they wouldn't let me leave without them," she explained. Gavin had insisted on coming to see his uncle, despite her telling him that Marcus was straight. He had to see him with his own eyes just to be sure. Even the twins showed out when she tried to leave, so she had no choice but to bring them along.

"I'm glad you're okay, Unc," he said, wiping his face with the back of his hand, attempting to get himself together. The young man had dealt with too much loss in his life, and losing his only uncle was something he didn't think he would be able to survive.

"Me too, Gavin. Thanks for coming to see about me," he said, giving his nephew a one-armed hug and a pound. "Gimme my baby," he said to Alana. YaYa was already reaching her arms out for him, demanding he pick her up.

"Marcus, your arm," Alana started to say.

"I'm fine, sis. I need some love from my favorite girl," he said while smiling at Kiyarah. He was surprised when Kash sat up in the double stroller and reached out for him as well.

"Uncle Mar, get me too," he requested, causing everyone in the room to look his way.

"Well, ain't this about a bitch. A nigga had to get shot for the tittie baby to finally warm up to me," he said, making everyone laugh. He played with his niece and nephew until his shoulder was on fire, and Alana removed them from his bed. She also called his nurse in to administer some pain medication. He really didn't want to take the medicine, but Alana and Kelsey insisted, convincing him that he needed it. Within fifteen minutes of receiving the injection, he was out.

He didn't realize how tired he was until he woke up and the room was dark with only a dim light on by the door. When he went to sleep, it was a little after noon, and now it was nightfall. He went to make a move and pain suddenly shot from his shoulder to his fingertips. The wound to his leg didn't bother him at all, but his shoulder was giving him the blues.

"Fuck," he cursed the pain.

"Do I need to get the nurse?" She was still afraid for him, and he heard it in her voice. Marcus turned to see Nikki curled up in a chair beside his bed.

"No, I'm good. Why you still here?" he asked. He didn't want to be happy that she was there, but he was. Distance and space were what he needed, and although he craved her presence, it irritated him at the same damn time. He had moved on, and her caring attitude was puzzling.

Nikki couldn't tell by his tone if he was just surprised that she was still there or if he didn't want her there at all, so she decided to ask. "Do you not want me here, Marcus?"

"I ain't say all that. I'm just saying that I'm good and you should probably go home and get some rest. I don't want you to feel obligated to be here with me," he replied, looking up to the ceiling.

"I've been resting just fine here," she replied while stretching her tiny body, drawing his eyes back to her. Like always, they traveled from her face down to her toned legs, which were clothed in some cute leggings, and then they slowly moved back up. This time she didn't pretend to not notice the way he assessed her. She simply embraced the feeling and the appreciation he apparently had for her small frame.

"I know last night was crazy, and I'm sorry you had to see that shit. How you coping with everything?" he asked, searching her face.

"I'm fine, and you don't owe me an apology. What happened wasn't your fault. I'm just happy that you made it through all that." She whispered the last part as she shook her head. Just the thought of him possibly dying out there was too much. It was crazy that she wasn't afraid or a crying, blubbering mess after seeing two people shot and killed, but she just felt it was either those men or Marcus and he did what he had to do.

"What were you doing out there that late anyway?" he asked.

"I needed to talk to you and what I had to say couldn't wait, so I drove over."

"What is it that you wanted to talk about?" he asked. He couldn't think of one single thing they needed to discuss, but apparently she thought there was and whatever it was was so important that it brought her to his home in the middle of the night.

"Us," was her simple answer.

"Us?"

"Yes, Marcus. I just wanted to be honest with you about some things and explain to you why I handled our situation the way I did so that maybe you'll have a better understanding," she said.

"You don't have to explain shit to me. Yo' nigga is the only one you owe an explanation about anything you've done, Nichole. Matter of fact, where the hell is your fiancé while you posted at my bedside keeping vigil over me? You should be at home with him and not here telling me about some shit that don't even matter anymore," he said bitterly.

"I'm exactly where I need to be," Nikki countered. She was trying not to cry, but he wasn't making things easy for her. If his goal was to hurt her, he was succeeding.

"I really don't know where you're coming from right now, but I'm tired and I just want to get some rest," he said as he rubbed his hand down his face. He wasn't trying to be a dick, but she was frustrating him. At the moment his mind was on finding out who tried to kill him, and this shit here was so fucking extra. She didn't want him. He had accepted that. Now she wanted to explain to him why she didn't want him? Nah, he was cool on all that. He didn't need to gain understanding. He just wanted to move the hell on.

"You can rest after I say what I need to say," she said with her voice raised. She was tired of being nice to him. After she spoke her piece she would leave, and not a minute before.

"Fine, Li'l Bit. G'on 'head," he relented with a dismissive wave of his hand.

Before she could speak, they were interrupted once more when his brother walked in the room. "My bad." Jakobi paused mid-stride, feeling that he stepped into the middle of a serious conversation. The tension in the room was thick, and both Nikki and his brother wore mean mugs on their faces. He had some information to share with his brother, but he didn't want to interrupt. "Do y'all need a minute?" he asked with his eyebrows raised.

"Naw, bro. The shit we kicking ain't even important. What's the word?" he asked, sensing that Jakobi had some leads for him. He didn't miss the defeated look on Nikki's face when he said that.

"I guess I'll step out and let you two talk. I'll be right back," she said while glaring at Marcus. She wasn't about to let him get rid of her with his stank attitude.

"So, what you got for me, bro?"

"Not much, but I got something. The names of two of the shooters," he told his brother.

Marcus studied the images on the phone but didn't recognize either face or name. Dutch had come through on that info, but he still had no clue who these niggas were or who they were affiliated with. And most importantly, why they were coming for him.

"What about the third guy?" Marcus asked.

"No ID on him just yet, but Dutch is working on it," his brother tried to reassure him.

"That's it?"

"Yeah, bro, that's it for now. Like I said, though, Dutch is on top of it."

"Damn, Kobi, I need to know who the fuck these people are," he stressed.

"I know. I'll let you know when he hits me with an update," said Kobi.

"Even though I'm in my own home, I feel like a sitting duck not knowing who's behind this shit."

"You straight, my nigga. Big B got your shit locked down, and his men are everywhere. Plus, I got something for you under your pillow just so you feel a little more at ease," Jakobi said.

"Thanks, baby bro, a nigga was feeling a little naked," he said before pumping his fist to his brother's. He removed the gun from the underneath the pillow and placed it on his lap under the blanket.

"What's up with Nikki? What she still doing here?"

"I have no clue. She say she needs to talk to me about something, but I ain't trying to go back there with her on that BFF shit. You remember how that ended. She need to say whatever she gotta say then go home to her nigga."

"Oh, you ain't heard, huh?"

"Heard what?" he asked right as Nikki walked back into his room.

"Look, I'm gon' head home and check on my family. I need to make sure Gavin is straight. He was pretty upset earlier," Jakobi said.

Jakobi never finished what he was about to tell his brother, and Marcus felt that he definitely knew some shit that he didn't. Hopefully, Nikki would fill him in on everything. "A'ight, tell G I'm good and I'll call him first thing in the morning." He hated that his nephew had to see him shot up and fucked up. His family was the main reason he got out of the game. The other reason was standing at the foot of his bed, looking like a sad puppy, and he didn't like being the reason for her long face. Despite how bad she aggravated him, he couldn't deny that he still had very strong feelings for her. Seeing that nigga propose to her brought everything back to the forefront.

"Will do," replied Jakobi before going over to give Nikki a hug good-bye and exiting the room.

"So, what's up? Go ahead and say what you need to say," Marcus rushed her once they were alone again.

"Like I said before, I wanted to talk to you about us," she said timidly.

"There is no us, ma. You made sure of that shit," he chuckled sarcastically before he could catch himself.

"There has always been an 'us,' Marcus, so stop being a jerk and listen!" she said, bucking back defiantly and wiping the smile off his face.

"You got that, Li'l Bit. My bad," Marcus relented. He was surprised and a little turned on by how angry she was. This was the first time he'd ever even heard her raise her voice.

"The first night I met you I was attracted to you. Like, crazy attracted to you, but I was scared of the feelings I had so I pushed them and you away. I'd never experienced anything like it before." He didn't respond but just stared at her, his gaze on her intense as she continued. "I did everything that I could think of to make you go away, but you wouldn't let up, and in some ways I didn't want you to. I know it wasn't right, but I wanted you to keep coming for me even though I never planned to give you a chance. Then you came up with this brilliant idea for us to just be friends and practically forced me to get to know you. On one hand, it was great, because I got to spend time with you without having to admit my true feelings. Things on my end couldn't have been better. You, on the other hand, got the short end of the stick because I refused to be honest with you about how I felt. I apologize for the way I behaved toward you. Making you feel as if you weren't on my level or that you weren't good enough. I really think it's me who's not good enough for you. I was too focused on your past and worrying about what others would think of our relationship instead of following my heart. It wasn't right, and I'm sorry, Marcus," she said sincerely.

Kelsey had talked to her so badly last night after she shared her true feelings for Marcus. She couldn't even argue with her friend because everything she said was the truth. She had been playing games with Marcus while waiting for what she thought was a better man to come along, and he deserved better than that.

"Why the hell are you telling me all this now though, Nikki? You got a whole fucking fiancé now so none of this even matters." The frustration was evident in his tone and demeanor. He didn't really know how to feel about her confessing her feelings to him. Maybe she was just clearing her conscience before she officially moved on and got married.

"I'm not engaged, Marcus." She flashed her left ring finger, which was bare.

"You're not?" he asked, remembering his brother eluding to something like that when they were talking.

"No," she said while shaking her head. She was hoping that telling him all this would prompt him to confess his feelings as well and accept her back into his life. As what, she didn't exactly know. She wanted to be his woman, but she didn't know if he had the same feelings toward her.

"Look, I appreciate you telling me all this, and you're right, I was feeling you, and you did have a nigga feeling like he was beneath you and shit, but I'm over it. Ain't no hard feelings on this side, ma," he said, fronting. He'd wanted this for as long as he'd known her, and now it seemed too little too late.

"So if I told you I wanted to be with you, you wouldn't care? Being with me is not something you want?" she asked, already knowing the answer. The tears were threatening to spill from her eyes.

"It's not that I don't care, Nikki. I just don't feel the same about you anymore." He shrugged.

She couldn't believe what she was hearing. He didn't want her anymore, and it was all too much to accept. Nikki was in full panic mode. "Marcus, what if I told you that the reason I was running so hard from you was that I've never been with a man before and my attraction to you had me considering going there with you despite my plans to wait until marriage? That wouldn't change your mind either?" she asked. She was damn near begging at this point, but there was no shame on her side.

Marcus almost choked when he realized what she was telling him. "What do you mean you've never been with a man before?" he asked for clarification.

"I've never had sex, Marcus," she said softly with her head down.

"Hell naw. You better hold your fucking head up," he demanded. "Why you saying that like it's a bad thing, Li'l Bit? You should be proud of that." He had never come across a female her age who was a virgin, and personally, he thought she was dope, but she seemed to think differently.

"Proud, huh?" she scoffed. "Do you know how many times I've been dumped? How many dudes tried to game me into letting them be my first? Or how about the guy I planned to marry cheating on me and getting another woman pregnant? Honestly, I just didn't think you would be any different from those guys. I didn't think you would stick around after you found out," she admitted.

"I hate that you didn't give me a chance to show you I would've. And any man in your past who couldn't respect and appreciate the gift you were offering wasn't worth your time anyway."

Speechless, Nikki gazed at him in astonishment. She hated that she had taken him through all this nonsense. Maybe if she had just been honest with him in the beginning, things could have worked out differently. She'd completely misjudged Marcus, and now there was a strong possibility that they would never get a chance to see how great things could be between them.

"That's not the reason you're no longer engaged is it?" he asked, slick and being nosy.

"No, that is a whole other issue. Eric and I are still close, but our relationship was more like brother and sister. He had his reasons for proposing, and I had my reasons for accepting. I didn't want to embarrass him by turning him down in front of all those people. Also, I knew I couldn't go through with marrying him feeling the way I do about you."

"Well, I'm glad we had this chance to talk, and I understand why things went down the way they did between us, but—"

"I want to be with you, Marcus, and I want you to want to be with me too," she cut in before he could finish his statement.

"Nichole." He groaned her name with his head in his hands. He had waited years to hear her speak those words, but now that she had, he couldn't fuck with it. "I can't do it, ma," he said as devastation registered on her face. "I got some real shit going on in my life right now, and I don't know where it's coming from. There is no way you can be in the middle of that. I won't let that happen."

"But Marcus—"

"Besides, I already told you that I don't feel the same way about you. It took me a minute, but I'm over it. I'm over you, and I think you should go," he said with a straight face. He couldn't risk her being hurt because of some unknown beef of his. He had to send her away, even though doing so was causing his heart to break a second time. This time was even harder than the first because he now knew how she felt about him. If being in love with someone was this difficult, he wasn't sure he wanted it anyway. Shit was too fucking complicated.

"Please, Marcus. You're doing exactly what I was afraid of from the beginning," she cried.

"Too much shit has happened, and look how long it took you to tell me how you felt, Li'l Bit. You didn't trust me with this information in the beginning, and I'm thinking that was probably for the best." It was so hard for him to hurt her, but it was necessary. Her safety was a priority, and he was sure that her heart would heal in time. "Now can you please leave? I'm tired, and I'm done with this conversation," he said with fake contempt.

She was shocked by the words he spoke. Never had he handled her that way, and it fucked her up. Refusing to allow him to disrespect her any further, she snatched her purse from the chair and stormed out of his room. She cried the whole way home, and her heartache was way worse than it was when she found out that Kendall had betrayed her. Nikki felt the sting of Marcus's rejection in every part of her body, but the pain it caused in her chest was so unbearable that she doubted she would ever get over it. It was so bad that she had to pull over twice to get herself together. With no one to blame but herself, she wished that she had the courage to be upfront with Marcus from the beginning, but she hadn't, and now she was here: all alone and hurt, again.

Chapter 11

Marcus had been released from his doctor's care three weeks ago, but he was still in severe pain. The pain from his gunshot wounds was nonexistent, but the hurt from not being able to be with Nikki was the worst shit ever. To find out that she wanted him and always had was music to his ears and the worst thing ever all at the same damn time. The torture he was dealing with was becoming too much. He was snapping at his staff and being rude to everyone he came in contact with. Marcus was known as a fun-loving, cool person, so his recent change in attitude was shocking to most. Unable to tolerate him any longer, Amina pulled him to the side to tell him about himself. He had no response for her after she got him together because everything she said was on point. After staying home for a few days to get his mind right, he felt he was finally ready to get back to business. Nikki crossed his mind frequently, but he was able to put his feelings aside and focus on his businesses. In addition to the tattoo shops, he'd recently invested in his potnas Jahshua and Boo's home-building company. With Junior on his team, he was able to focus more time on different areas of his brand.

Apparently, since everything had gone down, Nikki had talked to Alana and told her how she poured out her heart to him only to be rejected. Alana, in turn, complained to her husband, who called and cursed him out because he was getting harassed by his wife. When he explained to Jakobi his reason behind doing what he did, his brother completely understood. However, that didn't stop his sister-in-law from showing up to the shop to give him a piece of her mind. He took it all in stride because he felt he was doing the right thing and he knew Alana was just looking out for her friend. They were still no closer to finding out who was behind the shooting, so everyone was still on high alert. Unbeknownst to Nikki, he had one of Big B's men tailing her to ensure her safety. When your enemy couldn't get to you, they would go after the ones you loved, and he wasn't taking a chance with her life. It didn't matter to him that they weren't together.

He was in his office going over some paperwork when Junior came knocking. "Hey, boss, you have a visitor," he informed him.

"Who is—" he started, but stopped when he saw the tall, dark, older man standing behind his shop manager. The resemblance between the two couldn't be missed, but Li'l Bit looked even more like him.

"Dad, this is Marcus. Marcus, this is my father, Nicholas Grant Sr.," Junior said.

Marcus immediately stood and extended his hand. "Mr. Grant, it's nice to finally meet you."

"Same here, Marcus. I've heard a lot about you from my son as well as from my daughter," he informed him.

"Is that right?" he asked as he raked his hand down his thick beard.

"It is," he said, glancing at his son. It was clear that he wanted this conversation to be private, so Marcus spoke up.

"Junior, will you excuse us for a moment?" he asked.

"Of course. I'll be in my office looking over the applicants for the Oklahoma City location," Junior said then left.

"So, Mr. Grant, what brings you by today? You trying to get tatted up?" he asked with a smirk. Marcus hoped that this old-school nigga wasn't here on no bullshit trying to check him about his daughter. He did what he had to do where she was concerned, and he didn't give a damn what anyone thought about it. He would try his best to remain respectful, but he was still a hood nigga, which meant he was uncheckable. Fuck what you heard.

"First of all, I wanted to thank you for what you've done for my son. He's doing really well and seems to be happy working for you," old school pointed out.

"No need to thank me. Initially, I did what I did as a favor for Li'l Bit, but Junior has turned out to be a great help to me and a much-needed addition to the team," he replied honestly.

"That's good to hear. Now, moving on to the second reason I stopped by to see you today, Li'l Bit, as you referred to her a moment ago," he said, cutting to the chase quickly.

"What about her?"

"She came to see me recently, and she was extremely upset and heartbroken. And one thing I don't like to see is my baby girl in pain, Marcus," Mr. Grant said with a serious mean mug, hands in his pockets, standing tall.

"Hurting her wasn't my intention. I only did what I did to protect your daughter," Marcus replied, unfazed by old school's glare. He was sure his stance was meant to intimidate. Too bad for this nigga, Marcus wasn't easily shaken.

"I figured as much," Mr. Grant stated, backing down a little.

"When she came to see you did she tell you that I'd been shot recently?"

"She did."

"Now how would you feel if your baby girl was hurt when those niggas ran up on me? She was there, you know?" Marcus told him. "I still don't even know who they were or why they came at me."

Marcus didn't know how much of the story Nikki told her father, so he didn't mention shooting the men. They would never be found or heard from again, so he wasn't worried about getting caught up anyway.

"I understand what you're saying, young man. Her safety is important to me as well, but she's hurting, and I don't know what to do about it. I'm not used to not being able to step in and make things better for my baby, and that's hard for me," he admitted. His daughter was used to getting what she wanted, and she wanted Marcus. That she was being denied was extremely hard for her. "You're the only one who can fix this."

Marcus hated to hear that she was having such a hard time with this, but he was stuck between doing what he thought was right and what his heart craved. He needed her like he needed his next breath, but what the fuck was he supposed to do? Risking her life was not an option for him. "I don't know what to do either," he said, defeated, as he dropped his head. Raising it back up, he spoke again, "I care too much about her to put her at risk that way," he confessed.

"The only thing I can suggest to you is that you let her make the decision. She's aware of the danger, but she still wants to be with you. Allow her to choose you, despite it all, just like her mother made a choice to be with me despite the bullshit I was into when we met. I have faith that you'll make sure she's protected," Mr. Grant said. He was aware that Marcus had one of his men following Nikki. After learning of the shooting, he put someone on Nikki himself, but they quickly found that Marcus had her covered already.

"I would do everything in my power to keep her safe, but shit happens, and I can't deal with that possibility. I would turn this city upside down if she were hurt."

"I'm sure everything will work out. I have a name for you. The third shooter," he said, surprising the hell out of Marcus. "Does the name Ricky LeBlanc ring a bell?" Nicholas had his people comb through Marcus's life until they found the link between him and the men who tried to kill him.

Immediately Marcus knew who was behind the failed attempt on his life, and he was having a hard time processing it. He needed to get with Jakobi ASAP. "You mind me asking you how you got hold of this info?" Dutch hadn't even been able to get back to him with his name yet. They were waiting for his prints to come back from a connect Dutch had in law enforcement, but so far they'd had no hits.

"The how doesn't really matter, Marcus. Like I said, I don't like to see my baby girl hurting, so I had my people do a little digging. Handle your business with your friend, and I also expect you to handle things with my daughter," Mr. Grant said before walking out like a boss.

Nicholas Grant was with the shits, and Marcus was sure that his darling Nikki had no idea what her father was really capable of. He wasted no time getting Jakobi on the line to discuss his plan with him. Not the type to rub shit in, his brother didn't bother saying "I told you so" when he was told who his brother suspected was behind all this bullshit.

Meka hadn't heard from her homeboy Ricky in weeks, and she was starting to get worried. She picked up the phone and dialed his number for what seemed like the millionth time. Unlike the other times when she only got the voicemail, the message stated the phone was disconnected. She thought that maybe he had left town again. Having been in seclusion for so long, she hadn't had her ear to the streets to see what they were saying. Her close friends had long since quit coming around because of her mental state and the constant drinking.

Marcus had been true to his word and didn't come back around to fuck with her. That was well over six months ago, but she always held on to the hope that he would come back like he always did. For a while after his departure she was suicidal. Before long her suicidal thoughts turned homicidal. She wanted Marcus dead but had no way of getting at him. These days she hardly left the house and was severely depressed. Damon's mother came over a few months back and packed up all of Taylor's belongings, telling her that she would keep her until she got her shit together. On the cool, she didn't give a damn that her baby was gone.

Ricky, a longtime friend of Damon's, stopped by to check on her after hearing from various friends that she'd officially lost her mind. Actually, his dog ass was hoping to catch her at a vulnerable time to see if she would finally let him fuck. Meka was very particular, and only a select few had been blessed enough to have her, but it was rumored that she had the best pussy on the planet. You had to be stupid paid and willing to break crazy bread just to get close to her. Marcus was the only man she dealt with who didn't have to pay to play and was the only one she developed any feelings for beyond sex.

The first afternoon that Ricky showed up to her spot just so happened to be his lucky day. Meka was feeling charitable, and after breaking him off with the most bomb shot he'd ever had, she ended up telling him about getting played by Marcus as they downed a bottle of mango Cîroc. She also let it slip that Marcus was responsible for Damon's death. Ricky hated that he was on the run from some niggas he'd robbed when his best friend was murdered. Meka also lied and told him that Marcus had gotten physical with her on more than one occasion. That pissed him off even more, and when he learned from one of his boys how paid Marcus was, he decided that he and his crew would rob him before taking his life. Fuck the fact that he'd just fucked his dead homie's girl. These new niggas were backward as hell. Be on some straight Bobby Womack shit and wife yo' bitch after you die. That shit was acceptable in Ricky's mind, but there was no way he could let the nigga get away with killing his homeboy, right? If you're going to be devoted and ride for your potna, be one hundred with the shit. Don't pick and choose which situations require loyalty.

Just like she knew he would, Ricky approached Meka about the lick. She was with it but warned him that Marcus and Jakobi were not the type of niggas they would just be able to pull up on, on some stick-up shit. Their plan had to be A1 if they wanted to make it out alive. She tried to stress to him that the Tate boys were the type to shoot first and ask questions later.

Ricky seemed to take her warning seriously, and up until three weeks ago, he had stopped by to fuck and drink with her just about every day. His sudden disappearance had her thinking that he'd gone through with the robbery and murder plot then skated off with the bread. She had more than enough money, but she was still pissed at the thought of Ricky cutting her out. Meka had no idea that every man involved in the attempt on Marcus's life were considered missing by family and the authorities.

Relaxing in a tub full of hot, soapy water was soothing and helped to calm her already-fried nerves. With her eyes closed, she could have sworn she smelled Marcus's Clive Christian cologne. Knowing she was only imagining things, she smiled at the memory of his glorious scent. The reminiscing had her missing the way he could fuck her into a coma, and her hands automatically went below to grip her sex. He used to love watching her touch herself. *Damn, I miss him.*

"Mmm," she moaned as she pictured him hovering over her, watching her with lust-filled eyes the way he did when she played with her pussy for him until she squirted. He loved to see that shit. She made tiny circles on her swollen clit with thoughts of her former cut buddy dancing in her mind. It didn't take long for her dam to blow, and she wished like hell he was there to give her what she really wanted.

Moments after she climaxed and her breathing was almost back to normal, she opened her eyes to see him standing in the doorway of her bathroom. The sight of Marcus caused her to involuntarily release her bladder in the water. She blinked several times to make sure she wasn't seeing things. He had to have watched her get herself off, and the look on his face said he was anything but turned on. He seemed to be disgusted at the sight of her. Any other time she would have been jumping for joy seeing him standing there, but the look on his face was sinister, and she already knew he wasn't there on no sexual shit.

"I warned you not to try me, Tameka," he said, shaking his head at her.

"I don't know what you're talking about, Marcus," she lied in a shaky voice.

"Jamil Crosby, Michael Spencer, and Ricky LeBlanc."

"I swear I tried to call it off, Marcus, but they didn't listen," she tried explaining. If he knew their names, she had no further doubts regarding the fate of her lover and his friends. She silently prayed her end hadn't come as well. A lone tear escaped her eye as the reality of what she'd done set in.

"If you hadn't planted the seeds in their heads, them niggas never would have come for me," he said calmly while sitting at the edge of the garden tub. He should have listened to Jakobi and quit fucking with her bitch ass years ago, but he didn't, and now they were here. She fucked up royally when she sent them niggas at him, and just thinking that Nikki could have been hurt in the process of her getting her revenge pissed him off even more, making it all the easier for him to do what he came to do tonight. "The woman I love was there that night when them niggas ran up on me. They could have killed her," he spat angrily.

"Love?" she whispered in shock. She didn't think he was capable of loving a woman, and that it wasn't her he was in love with was a hard pill to swallow. "Why couldn't you love me, Marcus? I've loved you forever," she shouted as tears rolled down her face. With the situation she found herself in, worrying about him loving someone else should have been the least of her worries, but she was crazy as fuck, so she wasn't thinking straight.

"I just couldn't. How was I supposed to do that when you don't even love your damn self?" he asked.

More tears came from hearing the truth in his words. As beautiful as she was, she didn't love herself. For the love of money, she'd sell herself to the highest bidder and had let men use and abuse her body and mind for years. No woman with self-love would have allowed that. She had no respect for herself, so he had none for her. "Are you going to kill me?"

"Naw, I ain't gon' kill you, Meka," he said truthfully. He noticed the tension leave her body as if she was relieved to hear him say that. "You gon' kill yourself," he informed her coolly, enjoying the sight of her eyes almost popping out of her head in fear.

"Wha . . . what?" she stammered.

"You heard me. I'm not gon' kill you, bitch. You gon' kill yo' gotdamn self. You did that when you plotted on me with them niggas after I gave yo' hoe ass fair warning," he informed her before setting a bottle of pills in front of her.

She noticed for the first time that he was wearing gloves, and she assumed it was because he didn't want there to be any trace of him being in her place tonight. Even his shoes were covered. At this point, all she could do was cry, because she had fucked up and she was going to pay for it with her life. Her not leaving well enough alone had resulted in the death of Ricky, and she couldn't take it back. Blaming her behavior on her mental state or being drunk wouldn't do, because the plan was discussed days later while she was medicated and sober. She hadn't even bothered to tell him that she had lied about a lot of the shit she'd said about Marcus. She was just so angry at the time, and the thought of him dying really didn't matter to her. Right now, though, she'd give anything to take that shit back.

Marcus had his gun with the silencer screwed on sitting in his lap just in case she tried some funny shit. He had no qualms about popping her ass. He watched as she emptied half of the pills into her hand then proceeded to snatch the bottle of water that he had extended toward her. Meka tossed the pills in her mouth before she gulped down a large portion of the water to wash them down, causing some of it to spill from the side of her mouth. She repeated the process once more, and all of the pills were down.

Tears ran down her face as she thought about how for all of her daughter's life she had put anything and everything above her. At that moment, Meka wanted a second chance to be a mother to Taylor, the mother Damon wanted her to be. Why couldn't she have just loved Damon? He was good to her, and she shitted on him every chance she got. He was dead, and that was on her. She fucked his best friend, and because of her he was also dead. Meka's lesson before she crossed over was if you can't be with the one you love, love who the fuck you're with.

Marcus sat there for almost an hour before she was out, her head slumped against the side of the tub. Still, he waited a while longer. After feeling for a pulse and finding none, his job was complete. He walked away not feeling an ounce of remorse about what he had done.

Nikki sat at her desk, admiring the lovely view she had of the city of Dallas. It was nearing sunset, and the sky was painted in different hues of oranges, pinks, and blues, but not even her beautiful surroundings could lift her spirits today. She'd completed her work over an hour ago, but she still couldn't bring herself to get up and go home. Never in her life could she remember being this down and lonely. Eric offered to come spend the night and keep her company, but she'd declined. The only man she wanted comfort from had made it clear that he didn't have feelings for her any longer. She wanted to cry every time she thought about it.

Deciding that she had stalled long enough, she began packing up her belongings to head home for the day. Right when she was about to pick up her purse, the voice of her secretary, Grace, came over the intercom.

"Ms. Grant, I have a Marcus Tate here to see you. He doesn't have an appointment but insists on seeing you anyway." Grace spoke in a tone Nikki wasn't used to hearing. *Is she trying to sound sexy?* Marcus's good looks clearly had the sixty-year-old woman hot and bothered. Nikki would have laughed if she weren't so nervous.

"That's fine, Grace. You can send him in, and you're free to leave for the day," Nikki said, trying her best to sound unfazed by his presence.

The rapid beating of her heart and her clammy hands told of the excitement as well as the dread she felt at seeing him again. As she began straightening out her clothes, she wondered what his visit was pertaining to. Of course, he walked in looking like he'd just stepped off the pages of a fashion magazine. When their eyes met, she stopped breathing for a moment, completely caught up in gazing into those ebony-brown irises of his. *Get yourself together, Nichole.* Before she could ask him the reason for his visit, he spoke up.

"So, that's how you do, Nichole? You don't get your way, so you go and tell your daddy on a nigga?" he asked with disdain.

"Tell my daddy on you? What the hell are you talking about, Marcus?" she asked, taken aback and confused by what he was saying.

"So you trying to tell me that you had no idea your father showed up to my shop trying to check me about hurting your feelings?" he asked her as he walked around to stand on the side of the desk where she sat.

"No, he didn't," she gasped, placing her hands over her eyes in embarrassment. "I can't believe he did that. I saw him on Saturday, and I admit that I let him know everything that happened, because that's just the type of relationship we share, but I promise I had no idea that he would come to see you about it. I'm so sorry, Marcus, and I promise you that I didn't ask him to come talk to you," she said, finally able to raise her head and face him. He already thought of her as a spoiled princess, and her father coming to her aid believing Marcus had wronged her probably only reinforced those thoughts.

Surprisingly, he smiled. "Don't even trip. He did it because he cares about you and he doesn't want to see you upset," he said before taking a seat on the edge of her desk. For a moment they just stared into each other's eyes. Marcus broke eye contact first and looked down at his hands before he spoke again. "I care about you too, Li'l Bit," he said, locking eyes with her once again.

"What are you saying? I thought—"

"I'm saying that I care about you, and I'm sorry about the way I handled things when you told me how you felt that night," he said.

"You care about me, but you don't want a relationship with me, right?" she asked, trying to gauge where the conversation was going.

"That's what I said, but I wasn't being honest with you or with myself. I said what I said to make you stay away. I thought I was protecting you. It would kill me if anything were to happen to you behind this street shit," he said, grabbing her hands from her lap.

"Were you able to find out who was behind everything?"

He nodded, and she knew him well enough to know that he'd taken care of whoever it was.

"Even if I hadn't, I would still be here right now. Your father said something that made sense to me. He told me that I should let you make the decision whether you wanted to be involved with me despite the shit I had going on. He was confident that I wouldn't let anything happen to his baby girl." He smiled.

"I trust that too, and that's why I wasn't afraid. I see how you are with your family, and I have no doubt that you'll protect me just the same."

"That small possibility of you being hurt still scares the shit out of me, but the thought of being without you is even scarier," he confessed.

With those words, she was out of her seat and wrapping her arms tightly around his neck. When his strong arms engulfed her body, she felt she had died and gone to heaven.

"What about that other issue I told you about?" she asked with her forehead pressed into his chest.

"Stop thinking of it as an issue, Li'l Bit. I'm willing to wait," he told her without hesitation.

"I'm not sure if I can though," she said, making him laugh. He took it as a joke, but she was serious as hell. She was going to have to stay prayed up around this man because he would have her breaking all of her rules. His hand came to her chin and lifted her face, forcing her to make eye contact with him.

"Sure you can," he said before giving her a closed-mouth kiss that caused electricity to course through both their bodies. There was no tongue involved, but this kiss was just as potent as the one they shared in the parking lot of Smoove Ink that night. She felt the intensity of this one from the top of her head to the bottom of her feet and through each and every nerve ending in her body.

"I missed you so much, Smoove," she whispered against his lips, causing him to throw his head back in laughter.

"I missed you too, Li'l Bit," he replied before kissing her again.

Chapter 12

Junior had his back turned filing some paperwork when Amina walked into his office. For a moment she stood there, silently taking him in. Junior was so damn fine to her, and if Marcus didn't have that stupid shop rule about fraternizing, his ass could definitely get it. Baby had the whole artist vibe going, and it was very becoming on him. You could just look at him and tell he was creative. He had some beautiful, long, curly hair that many women would kill for. On any given day you could catch him wearing it wildly all over his head or maybe pulled up top in a bun. She was absolutely obsessed with his mane and often imagined herself in bed with him, running her fingers through it. To top off all that fineness he was also a card-carrying member of the beard gang. Nigga could easily have been club president. His reminded her of the rapper Stalley's beard: full with a nice length and shaped properly. *Damn,* she thought as she switched hips and placed her daughter, Brielle, on her other side. After getting her look on real good, she finally spoke.

"I'm glad I caught you before you left."

Junior turned around quickly to face her. He was slipping and forgot to lock up after she left an hour ago. All of the artists had left for the day, so they were in the shop alone. "Girl, what's wrong with you? You can't be sneaking up on folk like that," he said, letting his eyes linger on her a second too long.

"Sorry," she replied with a smile, peeping the way he was checking her out. "I came back to get my cell phone. I left it plugged up at my desk, and I wasn't trying to be without it all night," she informed him.

"Okay, go on and grab it, because I'm about to shut everything down and get up out of here," he said, trying to avoid making eye contact with her. He had been attracted to Amina from the moment he saw her, but he wouldn't dare go against the rules. He loved his job and didn't want to do anything to break Marcus's trust in him. "Hey, li'l mama," he said, speaking to her beautiful baby girl. She immediately started babbling and reaching for him. "Can I?" he asked, getting permission to hold her baby.

"Sure. I'm surprised she even went to you. My baby is not friendly at all," she said. He laughed, but Amina was really shocked because Brielle was very particular and didn't fool with many people. Her own father couldn't even pick her up without her throwing a fit. That was likely due to her witnessing him beat her ass in front of the baby on numerous occasions. She was only two years old, but she would scream bloody murder anytime Darius raised his voice because she knew that soon after he did, her mother would be screaming and crying as well.

About a year ago Amina had finally had enough and left her on-again, off-again boyfriend, but he did everything in his power to make her life a living hell since then. The restraining order she had against him did little to deter him and seemed to only encourage him to come around more.

"What you talking about, li'l girl?" Junior asked Brielle, who was talking nonstop about nothing in particular.

"Wha'chu talking a . . . bout?" She repeated his words with her little head tilted to the side like she was checking him. He and Amina both laughed.

Junior thought Brielle was beautiful just like her mother. It was a shame that she had a wack-ass daddy who continued to cause them problems.

Junior went around the shop making sure every room was clean and the computers were shut down, all while holding Bri in his arms. When he finally reached the front door, Amina stretched out her arms for the baby, but he stepped back, not quite ready to hand her over.

"I got her. Let me walk y'all to the car," he said as he closed and locked the door before pulling the gate down. On the way to her car, he fussed at her for being out in the middle of the night with the baby, and she gave him a brief update on what was going on with school. For the last few years, she had been studying part-time to become a paralegal. Dealing with Darius caused her to take frequent breaks from school, but she was finally nearing the finish line.

"Just one more semester and I'll be done. I'm not going to lie though. I'll miss working at the shop with y'all." In addition to working for Marcus, she also held down an internship at a law firm. She'd done such a good job that they offered her a position before she was even finished with school, and she'd happily accepted.

"We'll miss you around here too, but we're proud of you. Not only are you almost done with school, but you done basically held down two jobs all while taking damn good care of your baby. That's quite an accomplishment," he said, giving her props.

"Thanks, Junior," she said shyly. She took Brielle from his arms to secure her in her seat.

"I guess I'll see you when you come back to work next week."

It was her only weekend off this month, and she planned to enjoy it with her daughter. "Yep, I'll see you bright and early Monday morning." She smiled sweetly before hopping in her ride and pulling off.

Junior had to make sure he stayed focused and away from Amina because she would have him breaking shop policy, which would, in turn, cost him his job, and he couldn't let that happen. He didn't have a steady girlfriend at the moment, but he did have a few ladies he liked to spend time with. They were more than enough to keep him entertained and keep his mind off the pretty Ghanaian girl.

Amina only made it about a mile down the road before her car started to shake and make an awful noise. She could tell that it was about to cut off at any moment. She kept up with the maintenance on her vehicle and had just had a tune-up last month, so she couldn't begin to think of what could be wrong with it. Luckily she pulled off to the side of road right before the car died.

Through the rearview mirror, she saw that Brielle was already sound asleep in her car seat. After attempting a few times to restart the car, she gave up and dialed her best friend Cree's number to see if she could come and pick her up. She got no answer. She could think of no one else to call, so she reluctantly dialed up Junior. He shouldn't be too far away, she figured, so it wouldn't take him long to get to her.

"Yeah."

His voice was super sexy over the phone. She got sidetracked envisioning late-night phone conversations as that deep voice caressed her eardrums. It had been a minute since she had thoughts of another man since breaking things off with Brielle's father, but she had always felt a connection with Junior. *Focus, Amina.*

"Hey, Junior, it's Amina. I'm sorry to bother you, but my car broke down not too far from the shop, and I have no clue what's wrong with it. Do you mind coming back to give me a ride to the house? I can have my car towed to my mechanic tomorrow morning." She hated to call him, but besides Cree she had no one else. Her mother was home in West Africa with family until next month, so she couldn't do a thing for her right now.

"I don't mind at all. Where are you exactly?" he asked. It was late, and he didn't like the thought of her sitting on the side of the road with Brielle. After she gave him her location, he busted a U-turn and sped back in the direction he'd just come from.

Amina was so glad that Bri had gone to sleep on the short ride. It was way past her bedtime, and the last thing she needed was to be out here stranded with a fussy toddler. She played around on her phone while she waited for Junior to arrive. It wasn't long before she saw headlights as a car pulled up behind her. She put her phone away and proceeded to grab her purse and backpack as well as Brielle's diaper bag from the front seat before stepping out of the car.

"Man, you got here quick," she said as he approached her car. She opened the back door to get Bri and her car seat, and that's when she heard his voice.

"You should have known that I wouldn't be too far behind."

That sinister tone caused her entire body to tense up as she realized who was standing behind her. She was inwardly chastising herself for getting out of the car without confirming that it was indeed Junior who had pulled up. Too many things had been happening lately for her to have been so careless.

"Darius, what do you want? Why can't you just leave us alone?" she asked with an attitude. Despite her challenging tone, her entire body trembled with fear as she turned to face him. She was scared to death with no escape. Her baby girl was in the car, and there was no way she would run and leave her with this monster.

"You just don't get it. I ain't ever gon' leave you alone. This shit here is forever, Amina, so you may as well get used to it. I love you, and you love me. I don't know why yo' fat ass wanna play games and try to keep my baby from me!" he shouted.

"Are you trying to go to jail, Darius? The restraining order says that you're not supposed to come near us at all," she reminded him. She wasn't fazed by his name-calling because she was used to it. They met when she was teaching dance, and at that time she was video vixen fine, but after she got pregnant she gained a lot of weight, and he never missed an opportunity to let her know he wasn't pleased with the way she looked now. Too bad for him she loved the hell out of her new body. Of everything he took from her, her confidence was something that surprisingly remained.

"How the fuck a piece of paper from some bullshit judge gon' tell me I can't be within a hunnid feet of my woman and my baby? Go put your shit in the car, and I'll get the baby," he ordered, taking a step toward the back door.

"No! Dee, please just leave me alone!" she cried. This man was standing here talking like everything was all good. The only way she was going to that car was swinging, kicking, and screaming. Never would she willingly go anywhere with his deranged ass, and she didn't hesitate to tell him so. "I ain't getting in that car with you, Darius," she said defiantly.

"You gon' get in the car on your own, or I'm gon' beat yo' mu'fuckin' ass and make you get in," he growled as he moved toward her. A sound coming from behind them stopped him dead in his tracks.

"Amina, get Bri and go get in my car," Junior instructed calmly. He'd spotted them from the other side of the road so he sped up and hit a quick U-turn, being sure to hit his lights so they wouldn't notice him pulling up. Junior seemed to have come from out of nowhere, and he didn't have to tell her twice. Amina hurried to retrieve her baby from the back seat.

"Bitch, what the fuck you think you doing? You take my baby anywhere near that nigga or his car and I'll kill you!" Darius shouted, halting her movements.

"Nigga, you ain't about to do a gotdamn thing. Amina! Get the baby and get in the car," Junior repeated sternly.

After making eye contact with Junior, she ran to the other side and did as he said. She moved quick and removed the entire seat from the back with Bri still asleep inside. Darius went to rush her but was halted by a shocking blow to his face followed by a series of powerful combinations from Junior. He didn't stop until Darius was on the ground, howling in pain just like a punk-ass nigga. He could beat the shit out of a woman all day but didn't have shit for a real man when it came down to it.

"Nigga, this shit is between me and my girl. It ain't got a mu'fuckin' thing to do with you," Darius yelled. Since they had broken up, he hadn't seen his baby mama with another guy, and in his mind, that meant she wasn't over him. He recognized dude as someone who worked at the shop and also as the man he saw holding his baby in the parking lot as he waited for Amina to leave work. If he found out that she was fucking this nigga, he was killing them both. If he couldn't have her, no one could. Since there was no way that he could live without her, he would have to kill himself as well. He fucked up when he stepped out of his ride without his hammer. If he had his gun on him, he would have ended it all tonight. "The fuck you think you are dipping in business that don't pertain to you?" he said, still on the ground.

"Don't worry about who the fuck I am. You just stay away from Amina and Brielle. If not, you gon' have some serious fucking problems on your hands."

Junior was beyond pissed at how terrified she was of this nigga. She was visibly shaking as she removed Brielle from the car. He was surprised she was able to get the baby to his whip without dropping her due to how badly her body shook. This nigga laid out on the ground at his feet was not right in the head, and Junior could see that with his own eyes. He wasn't going to quit until either he was dead or Amina was, and Junior was determined not to let the latter happen.

"You gon' see me again, nigga. Believe that," Darius promised.

"I'm looking forward to it, bitch," Junior growled venomously. If Amina and Brielle weren't only feet away and they weren't on this busy road, he would have taken Darius off the set, but he had something for his ass the next time he saw him.

"I'ma see you too, Amina. I love you, baby," Darius shouted, locking eyes with her through the window.

Crying silently in the front seat, Amina waited for Junior to join her in the car. She could tell he was pissed off, and she felt terrible for dragging him into her mess. "Junior, I'm so sorry. I didn't mean to get you involved in this. I don't know why he won't just go away and let me be," she cried as they pulled off.

"Chill, you don't have anything to apologize for. It's not your fault that his ass is crazy. Does he know where you live?" he asked, wondering if it was safe for her to go home tonight. She nodded.

Amina lived in constant fear every day of her life. She'd moved numerous times, but Darius somehow always found out where she was. She barely got rest because he would show up out of the blue some nights, banging on the door and demanding entry. Thoughts of Darius breaking in to take her baby girl away had her anxious and on edge every day. It was a miracle that she'd made it through school this past year, because the stress from the situation she was in was weighing heavily on her.

"I'm putting you two up in a hotel for a few days, at least until we get this figured out," he told her.

"I can't let you do that, Junior. We'll be fine, I promise," she declined, shaking her head. Honestly, she didn't know if they would be okay. Darius was getting crazier by the day, and she never knew when he was going to show up or what he was going to do next. She really wished she had taken Marcus up on that offer to get her a gun and shooting lessons at the range, because she was tired of living in fear and getting caught slipping by this nigga. Two weeks ago he roughed her up at the car wash and only stopped when a few bystanders decided to intervene on her behalf. She was sick of depending on other people to look out for her. It wasn't that she didn't appreciate the concern and help she received from others, but she just wanted to be able to protect herself and her baby on her own. She felt it was her responsibility to do it and no one else's.

"I wasn't asking, Amina. That nigga gone in the head, and he is liable to do anything at this point. Marcus would do the same thing if he were here, so let me do this for you. I'll get with the boss tonight and see about getting you moved somewhere safer," he said, glancing back at a sleeping Brielle. He was glad she slept through all the drama, and he wanted her mother to have that same peace when she slept tonight.

After she finally agreed, he stopped by her place so that she could grab some things for her and the baby before they headed to the hotel. He called Marcus on the way over to let him know what happened.

Amina and Brielle had retreated to the master bath in their room at the Omni, so Junior pulled out his laptop to try to get some work done. Amina tried to convince him that she would be fine and that it was okay for him to go home, but he refused to leave. He just couldn't leave them alone after everything that had occurred tonight.

When the girls emerged from the bathroom ready for bed, he tried to focus on Brielle and not on the silk pajama shorts set her mama was wearing. There was no denying that her ass was fine. She stood at about five feet seven inches, and he guessed her to be around a size fourteen, with big, juicy legs, plump breasts, and a nice fat ass. Baby was the shit. Amina had the body of a real woman, and she embraced it proudly. There were some men who preferred their women on the slimmer side, but Junior didn't really have a preference, nor did he dis-criminate. He'd dated all different types of women, but he could honestly say he had never been more attracted to any woman than he was to Amina. If their situation were different, he would go after her, no questions asked.

Amina put Brielle down so that she could pull back the covers for them to get in bed, but the baby ran over and climbed onto the couch with him. Junior put his work aside and let her cuddle up in his lap. "She really likes you," she said with a broad smile.

"Why is that so surprising? I'm a likable dude," he joked.

"I wasn't saying it like that. She's just normally not this friendly with people. I guess you all right though," she teased, making him laugh. "Come on, Bri. Come to bed with Mommy." Brielle didn't comply with her mother's request but instead snuggled up closer to Junior.

"She's fine with me. I'll be up for a while. When she falls asleep I'll put her in bed with you," he promised.

"You sure?"

"Of course. Go on and get some rest," he assured her. Amina bent down to press a kiss against Brielle's fore-head. Her closeness and the smell of her Victoria's Secret coconut milk body wash had him wanting a kiss as well. As if she'd read his mind, she turned to him and gently kissed his cheek before moving back to the bed. It was a harmless peck but the sweetest thing at the same time. He watched as she dropped to her knees at the edge of the bed and prayed silently. Even Brielle bowed her head and closed her eyes. *A praying woman?* Now that was a beautiful sight to see. When she was done, she climbed in the bed alone.

"Junior, thank you for everything you did for us tonight. I don't know what would have happened if you hadn't shown up," she acknowledged.

"You're welcome, Amina," he managed to get out. The look in her eyes had him questioning if she was just grateful to him for looking out for her or if she was feeling him. He could deal with being sweet on her, but knowing she harbored the same affections for him would make resisting her harder. "What kind of boss would I be if I didn't look out for my employees?" he said like it was no big deal.

"Oh, so you're just doing this because I work for you and for no other reason?" she asked, not really buying what he was trying to say.

"No doubt. There could never be another reason, Amina," he said, letting her know in so many words that he would never go there with her. He had to be very clear on his intentions.

"You sho right," she said before turning away from him. "Good night, boss." He wasn't fooling her with that "I would do this for any of my employees" mess. She knew what was up, and it was only a matter of time before he knew it too.

"Good night," he said low and regretfully.

He hoped that he hadn't hurt her feelings, but he wasn't trying to let Marcus down. So many times in his

life he fucked off opportunities that he had all because
he was lost and confused. School was easy for him, so he
could have at least finished that, but he quit. His father
had hooked him up with countless jobs through his many
connections, and each time Junior would fuck off, end
up being let go, and no doubt embarrass his father in the
process. Most times he didn't even try. Still, his dad continued to encourage him to find a career that would make
him happy, as well as allow him to provide for himself.

Being the manager of a tattoo shop may not have been
a big deal to others, but to him it was everything. He
loved what he did. Marcus gave him the opportunity to
lead when everyone else felt that he was capable of running nothing more than his mouth. Over the last year and
a half, he had shown up and found what he was supposed
to be doing with his life. Marcus did that for him, and
he would be forever grateful to him. He would never go
behind his back to be with Amina, no matter how much
he was digging her.

By the time they got up and moving around the following morning, Marcus was already knocking on the
door to their hotel room. He made some late-night calls
and was able to find her a place out of the way with more
security. At that very moment her things were being
moved from her apartment and placed in storage, and
her new place was being furnished. She wouldn't need
security for long because Marcus planned to go holla at
her ho-ass baby daddy real soon. He'd had enough of that
nigga harassing her, and it seemed that he had officially
pissed Junior off too.

"What's up, man," Junior said as he opened the door,
holding Brielle in one arm and dapping Marcus up with
the other.

"Nothing much. Where's Mina?" he asked, looking
around.

"She's still in the bathroom getting herself together," he replied, trying to ignore the suspicious look he was getting from Marcus. "You can chill with the looks, boss man. It's not like that between us. She slept in the bed with the baby, and I took the couch. I just didn't feel like leaving them alone last night was the right thing to do," he assured Marcus.

"My bad, just making sure. I can tell y'all are feeling each other, but it's just bad for business. You understand?" Marcus really wanted to make an exception for them, but it wouldn't look good for him to do that. If he let them get away with the shit, he had to allow everyone to do it.

"Yeah, I get it, and I promise that you don't have anything to worry about. Check it though," he said as he took a seat at the table across from his mentor. He made sure the shower was still going before he spoke. "This nigga who's bothering her is nuts for real, bruh. If she hadn't thought to call me to come get her, there ain't no telling what his ass would have done to her and Bri," he said, pulling the baby closer to him. "You should have seen the look in his eyes. I tried to beat his fucking face in, and if they hadn't been with me, I would have," he said truthfully.

"I know the feeling, because I been wanting to fuck that nigga up. He'll be seeing me soon, though," Marcus said, looking Junior dead in his eyes.

"Just make sure I'm there when you pull up on his ass," he said seriously. He wanted in on this one. Junior already knew how his boy got down. If Marcus was coming to see you, then you were in a world of trouble, and the likelihood of you making it out alive was slim to none. Junior had never killed a man before, but Darius's bitch ass was on his list and would be dealt with real soon.

"You sure you want to do that?" asked Marcus.

"Absolutely," he answered as Amina emerged from the bathroom fully dressed. Her mechanic had informed them that morning that her car stopped because it had been tampered with. They had no doubt that Darius was behind it all. It was the perfect way for him to catch her by herself. What he hadn't counted on was her calling Junior to come get her. He'd looked like he wanted to kill her, and now that Junior had beaten his ass they felt he would really go off the deep end.

Chapter 13

Nikki rushed to her car in the parking garage at work, determined to make it to the nail salon on time for her appointment with Mae. Tonight was date night, and she didn't want to keep Marcus waiting. They had been an official couple for a few months, and things couldn't be better. If she had known that this was how things would be when they got together, she would have told Marcus upfront about her feelings and given him a chance. She felt that they wasted so much time apart due to her fears and hang-ups.

Honestly, this was the best relationship she had ever been in, and Marcus treated her like a queen. That he was cool with waiting for marriage to have sex was a shock to her at first, and at times she let her mind wander, and her insecurities kicked in. She often thought that maybe he kept some chicks on the side to satisfy his needs until they made it to that point in their relationship, and that thinking only made her more paranoid. Deep down she knew that Marcus wouldn't do anything to hurt her, but it was hard not to think otherwise considering his history with women. They hadn't spoken the words "I love you" to one another just yet, but she did indeed love Marcus, and his actions told her that he felt the same way about her. She knew she had to quit tripping if she wanted things to work out between them.

As she sat in the massage chair with her feet soaking in the water, she smiled, thinking about her boo. Tonight was

a surprise date that he had put together, and she was looking forward to what the night would bring. For Marcus to
be such a thug, he also had a romantic side that she appreciated. It might sound crazy considering her upbringing
and uppity attitude, but she was drawn to his street side
even more. Maybe the old adage of good girls liking bad
boys wasn't entirely false. There was just something about
the way he took control and was all man at all times that
turned her on. Not having sex wasn't an issue for him, but
when she was with him, she honestly didn't know how
long she would be able to deny herself intimacy with him.
It was all she thought about most days, and she knew that
she needed to get herself together and refocus on more
important things.

Just then a text came through from her man, and her
lips immediately morphed into the most glorious smile.

Future Husband: It's been two days, and I'm missing
you like crazy. Can't wait to see tonight.

My Dream: Miss you too, and I'm looking forward to
tonight as well. At the nail shop nw.

Future Husband: Baby, please don't be late.

My Dream: I won't be late, Marcus.

Future Husband: I'm saying tho, you have been known
to be late a time or two! And don't give me that look lmao.

My Dream: Whatever Marcus. I'll be there, and I'll be
on time!

Mae had just finished up her pedicure, and all she had
to do was let her nails dry, then she'd be out of there. In
the meantime, she hopped on the group text with her two
besties to see what they had going on. Alana informed
them that she was thinking about taking time off work to
go back to school for her master's degree. Kelsey, in turn,
shared with them that she and her husband, O'Shea, just
found out they were expecting another baby. This would
make three for them. OJ, their oldest, was five, and

their baby girl, Kinsley, was three. Nikki updated them on work and how things were going with Marcus. She expressed to them how happy he made her. The women were so excited about all the new things happening in their lives and scheduled a lunch date for early next week. It was hard getting everyone together because they all had so much going on, so they agreed to set some time aside to spend with each other.

Paying more attention to the next text she received from Marcus caused her to walk directly into a hard, muscular chest as she made her way out of the nail shop. Nikki unconsciously gripped the strong shoulders of the man to steady herself so that she wouldn't hit the concrete and embarrass herself in front of all the people moving about the busy shopping center.

"I'm so sor—" she started to say but was at a loss for words when she looked up and discovered that the man she had run into was none other than her ex-boyfriend Kendall. She immediately removed her hands from his body like he was on fire and took a few steps back. He was much finer now than he was back in the day. The baby face was no more and held a more mature but equally handsome quality. And his smile, goodness gracious. *Why the hell am I standing here gawking at this man when I have one who's even finer than he is?* she thought, quickly pulling herself together. "Kendall, what are you doing here?" she was finally able to ask.

"Well, I was heading into the barber shop over there before you ran into me and almost knocked me down," he joked while giving her the once-over.

His eyes roaming all over her body was making her uneasy, definitely not the same feeling she got when Marcus looked at her the same way. "Sorry about that. I was so into this phone that I wasn't paying much attention," she admitted while she held up her cell phone.

"I see," he replied, still giving her that look. "How have you been, Nichole?"

"I've been well, and you?" she answered, trying her best to sound unfazed by his presence.

"Working and enjoying life," he said simply.

"Well, it was good seeing you, but I must get going," she said, wanting to get far away from him. She could tell from the look in his eyes that he was liking what he saw, and she didn't need those types of problems. He even had the nerve to lick his lips.

"Hold up, Nik, let me get your number real quick, and maybe I can take you out to lunch so that we can catch up. Moms was just asking about you the other day," he told her.

"How is she?" she asked to be polite. She really didn't care for his mother, and the feeling was mutual. That lady didn't think anyone was good enough for her precious Kendall, and she didn't hesitate to let Nikki know that every chance she got.

"She's good. Talking about retiring soon," he informed her.

"Cool. Be sure to tell her I said hello. I really need to get going," she said quickly.

"What about your number? Lunch? Catching up?" he asked, smiling his smile.

"I don't know if that's a good idea, Kendall. I'm seeing someone, and I don't think he would appreciate me going on dates with my ex-boyfriend," she replied. She really thought she would be able to get away without actually giving him her contact information. There was absolutely no reason for Kendall to be calling her, and they really didn't need to catch up on anything. She had her closure, and he was the past. No need to backtrack, right?

"Girl, I didn't ask you out on a date," he said cockily, making her laugh. "Seriously, I'm talking about catching up as friends. We grew up together so I'm sure your man wouldn't mind. I'm in a serious relationship myself, so I promise to be on my best behavior while you're in my company," he said convincingly.

"Fine, Kendall, give me your phone," she sighed. As she handed him back his phone after entering her contact information, her own phone began to ring.

Kendall didn't miss how her eyes lit up when she realized who was calling her. She was looking real good to him, and he had always thought of her as the one who got away. He regretted cheating on her back in college. It turned out that the woman he was in love with who claimed to be carrying his seed was sleeping with damn near every brother on campus, and her baby ended up being someone else's. He missed the special friendship he shared with Nikki, and he wondered if she was still a virgin. If she was, he would love the chance to make things work with her and be her first lover. He wasn't necessarily ready to get married, but even after all this time she was definitely someone he could see himself being with. Lunch was the perfect excuse to spend time with her and see how serious she was with whomever it was she was dating. The way she smiled when she answered the phone told him that maybe he was a day late and a dollar short, but he still planned to shoot his shot.

"Hey, baby," she flirted as if Kendall weren't even standing there. Honestly, she almost forgot all about him when she saw Marcus's number on the screen. Holding her phone away from her face so that her man couldn't hear her, she turned back to Kendall and spoke, "It was good seeing you, but I have to go," she whispered.

She didn't even give him a chance to respond before she moved quickly toward her car while chatting with her man on the phone. He just stood there staring at her

petite frame as she sashayed away. Her ass had filled
out a little more since college, and her breasts sat up
high and looked firm. She used to be rail thin and had
inexperience written all over her. Nikki seemed to have
tapped into her sexy side over the years, because she had
a mature and alluring swag about herself that she hadn't
had back then. He was hoping to spend time with her and
get to know the new and improved Nichole Grant.

"Babe, who you talking to?" asked Marcus.

"Oh um, I ran into an old friend as I was leaving the
nail shop, and we were talking for a few minutes." She
felt maybe she was being a little dishonest by not telling
Marcus that the old friend she ran into was actually her
ex, but she didn't want him to feel a way about her being
friendly with Kendall. Her man had a bad temper, and
she didn't want him getting upset over nothing. It probably wouldn't matter that Kendall was adamant that he
wasn't trying to come at her that way and she definitely
had no thoughts of him as more than a friend. Marcus
still wouldn't like it, so she would keep running into him
to herself for now.

"I thought you would have been on your way home by
now."

"Where are you?" she asked him as she looked around
the shopping center. The sounds of traffic and people
in the background sounded very similar to where she was
at the moment. She didn't see him or his truck, so she felt
she was just being a little paranoid.

"Just left from making a deposit at the bank," he
answered truthfully. His truck was being detailed in the
parking lot of his shop, so he was driving Amina's car at
the moment. He didn't tell her that he was at the Chase
Bank that was located in the same shopping center where
she got her nails done because he didn't want her to think
he was spying on her. He couldn't believe his eyes when

he saw her take the man's phone and seemingly enter her number into it. Maybe he was reading too much into things, and it was just a friend. The fact that she didn't mention it was a guy shouldn't have been a big deal, but for some reason it was. "Well, I'll let you go, and I'll see you in a few," he said flatly.

"Is everything okay, babe?" she asked, picking up on the change in his attitude.

"I'm good. Just can't wait to see you, that's all," he said, sounding a bit more upbeat but still not himself.

"I'm in the car now, and don't worry, my outfit for tonight has already been picked out, so all I have to do when I get home is shower and do my makeup. I had my hair hooked up at Alley Katz after work yesterday, so I'm good in that area as well. I told you I was going to be on time, babe," she promised.

"Okay, I'll see you at seven, Li'l Bit."

"I'll be ready and waiting," she said, smiling into the phone.

"Bet," he said before disconnecting the call.

Although Marcus was feeling a way about the exchange he witnessed between his woman and the mystery man two days ago, he was able to put his feelings aside and show her a good time on their date that night. Being with her always lifted his spirits, and even though in this instance she was the cause of the doubts he was having, he was able to shake it off after being in her presence for a while. He recalled how bomb she looked when he picked her up that night, and as promised she was ready to go when he arrived.

Since the night was all about wining and dining his lady, he ditched his Tahoe and pushed his matte black BMW i8 instead. After dinner at Truluck's, they shared a horse and carriage ride through the West End and uptown. He'd never known that romance without sex was even possible. He was getting to know her on a whole other level, and he was enjoying every minute of it.

Marcus knew more about her than any other woman he had ever been with. Before, he was never interested in knowing a woman beyond the bedroom, but with Nikki things were different. Their connection was a deeply spiritual one, and he couldn't wait to one day make her his wife.

Glancing over at her as she sat in the passenger seat, he admired the cute sundress she wore today. She was so damn beautiful to him with her tiny ass. Right now they were on the way to her parents' home for dinner. He had gotten pretty cool with her father, but this would be his first time meeting Christine Grant.

"What are you looking at?" she asked, grinning from ear to ear. Marcus had a way of looking at her that made her feel like she was the most beautiful woman in the world.

"I'm looking at your pretty ass," he replied, smiling back at her.

"You're looking pretty handsome yourself this afternoon, Marcus Tate," she complimented him. "Are you nervous about meeting my mother?"

"Not at all. Your pops is cool, so I gotta believe that he married someone just as laid-back and chill as he is. Besides, I figure that if I was able to win your father over, then your moms should be a piece of cake. We all know how your father feels about his baby girl. I thought I was gon' have to beat yo' daddy's ass the first time we met. Coming up in my shit, trying to check a real nigga," he joked, making her laugh out loud.

"Wait until I tell my father what you said. He gon' jack your butt up," she threatened playfully.

"Woman, I ain't scared of yo' daddy," he laughed. "Nah, for real. You better not tell him that shit. I believe that man is an undercover gangster or some shit. He liable to send some shooters my way," he half joked.

"No way. Nicholas Grant Sr. is a fine, upstanding citizen. Wouldn't hurt a fly," she said proudly and believing every word she spoke. Almost. Nikki recalled a conversation she had with her father a while back and him mentioning something about his life before he met her mother. He said he had been into some bad things, and she wondered exactly what he meant by that. At the time she thought he was referring to normal teenage rebellious shenanigans, but now she wasn't so sure.

Although her father was a respected businessman, she'd noticed over the years that not all of his friends fit into that category. A few friends he'd known since childhood still came around to this day, and just by looking at them you could tell that they were straight OG status. There wasn't a thing corporate about them, but to her father, they were some of his very best friends. They were godfathers to her and her siblings. Her mother was even close with them. If her father hadn't turned his life around like he said he did when he met her mother, she had no doubt that he would have been right along with them doing whatever it was men like them did.

"I know, baby. I'm fucking with you," he said before leaning over to kiss her cheek. His lady loved her father to death. She felt that he could do no wrong, and the man felt the same way about her. Marcus didn't care what she said, though. Her father was more than just an entertainment attorney. Marcus saw past all that kind and loving shit, too. It took a boss to recognize one, and if her father wasn't currently affiliated with the game, there was no doubt in his mind that he had been at one point in his life.

"Nice house," Marcus said once they were out of the car and headed to the front door of her parents' home.

"Says the man who just purchased a mini mansion to live in all by himself," she pointed out. She was in love with Marcus's new home, and lately she'd been spending a lot of time there.

"Shit, my spot is nothing compared to this," he said as he marveled at the enormous French country–style mansion that sat on the sprawling estate.

He purchased his home with her in mind and added certain touches that she mentioned wanting in her own home. Nowadays he planned his life to include her, and he hoped that one day soon they would be married and living in the house that she said she loved so much every time she visited. At times he questioned whether he was moving too fast with thoughts of the future, but ultimately he didn't think so. It had been four years since they first met, and they had become good friends before taking their relationship to the next level. They were practically dating one another then, because not much was different now that they were together, besides putting a label on what they shared and him getting to hold and kiss her whenever he wanted.

"Well, hello you two," said a smiling Brandy as she opened the front door to let them inside.

"Hey, Bran," Nikki greeted her sister.

"Nice to see you again," Marcus replied as they entered the humongous home. He was a little taken aback by Brandy's cheerful attitude. She was smiling at him and everything. The few times they had been in one another's presence, Nikki's oldest sibling hadn't exactly been welcoming in his opinion.

"What?" she asked when she noticed him eyeing her strangely.

"Nothing," he lied.

"Seriously, what is it?" Brandy smiled at him curiously.

"You're being nice," he said, looking back and forth from her to Nikki. They both laughed. "What? I didn't think you liked me, so you threw me off smiling and being all friendly and shit." He shrugged.

"Believe it or not, Marcus, I'm actually a smiling and friendly person. Hang around us long enough and you'll see that we are all very protective of our Nikki." She winked before hugging her baby sister. "Every guy she dates gets put through the ringer, so chill out, my brother. You made it through," she added, making him laugh.

"Boss man, what's good," Junior called out as he descended the staircase. Like always, dude was suited and booted in designer clothes.

"Junior, what's up, my dude?" Marcus responded cheerfully. The two men then shared a quick handshake and shoulder bump.

"I think everyone is waiting on us in the dining room, so let's head that way, because a brother is starving," he said, rubbing his stomach.

"Your behind is always starving, boy," Brandy said, shaking her head at him.

"Come on, babe," Nikki said, grabbing Marcus's hand to lead him into the dining area. "I'm kinda hungry too, and I hope Mom made a pecan pie," she said with her mouth already salivating at the thought of having a slice.

"You know she did. She makes you one every week," Brandy said while playfully rolling her eyes at her baby sister. She was glad to see Nikki so happy, and she knew that Marcus was the cause of it. Up until this point, she acted indifferent with Marcus the few times she was around him because she didn't want her little sister to be hurt by him in any way. She couldn't care less about his background or his reputation in the streets. Her only concern was that her sister be with someone who loved her and treated her right, and it seemed Marcus Tate was indeed that guy. "Oh, don't let me forget to give you those Louboutins you've been crying about not being able to find for the last month. I found them in your size online, and they just came in the other day," she turned and said to Nikki. She knew this news would make her sister happy.

"Bran, no. You didn't!" She ran up, hugging her sister tight and not trying to hide her excitement. "You're the best big sister in the world. Thank you," she said, grinning. The smile was wiped off her face when they entered the dining area to find Mrs. Palmer already seated at the table. She immediately became uncomfortable because when she spoke with Eric yesterday, he informed her that he still hadn't told his mother that they were no longer seeing each other, nor had he confessed to her that he was gay, or confused as he called it.

"Nikki, sweetie, there you are," her mother said sweetly as she made her way over to greet her youngest child and her handsome boyfriend. "And you must be Marcus. I've heard so much about you. It's nice to finally meet you," she said while smiling what could only be described as a smile of approval as she checked him out. She was looking into the eyes of her daughter's husband. She could just feel it.

"It's nice meeting you too, Mrs. Grant," Marcus replied as he took the hand she extended and placed a light kiss to her knuckles.

"Marcus, back up off my lady," Mr. Grant joked, causing everyone in the room to laugh. "How have you been, son?" he asked.

"Well, sir, and you?" he replied while shaking her father's hand.

"Oh you know, just working and spending as much time as I can with this beautiful queen here," he said, pressing a kiss to his wife's temple. "How are things going with the shops?"

"Better than ever. Thanks to your son's hard work, our Oklahoma City shop is set to open in two weeks. The grand opening is going to be huge, and the after-party that follows will be even bigger. If y'all don't have plans, I would love it if you came, at least for the grand opening." He really wanted them to be there because he and Nikki had set up something special for Junior as a way to congratulate him on his success over the last year. It would be even better if his entire family was there to support him.

"Sounds like fun," Mrs. Grant said, clasping her hands together in excitement.

"Oh, it's going to be perfect. I'm so proud of you." Nikki smiled lovingly at her man.

"Thank you, baby," he replied, pulling her closer to his side.

"All right, we'll work out the details later, but for now let's eat," Mr. Grant said as he pulled out the chair for his wife before taking his seat at the head of the table.

Marcus held out Nikki's chair before taking a seat between her and Mrs. Palmer. He had no clue what the lady's problem was, but she had been standoffish since they entered the room. Since making things official with Nikki, he had been in Eric's presence a lot, and dude was really good people. Just by looking at or talking to him, you wouldn't even know that he was into dudes. He wasn't flamboyant or no shit like that, so he came off as just one of the guys. His lifestyle choices were his business as far as Marcus was concerned. As long as he didn't have any romantic feelings toward his lady, they would have no problems.

Before they said grace and dug into the delectable spread, Nikki took the time to introduce Marcus to Myron, Brandy's ex and soon-to-be husband again, as well as their adorable son, Alexander, and Janine Palmer.

Mrs. Palmer was civil, but Nikki could tell that she felt a way about her being there with another man, and she thought the woman was going to fall out of her seat when she introduced Marcus as her boyfriend.

While helping bring out the dessert, Christine informed Nikki that she thought that by now Eric would have told his mother that they were no longer engaged. Her mother didn't know all the specifics or why things didn't work out, but it had been months, so when Janine practically invited herself to their Sunday dinner, she didn't think it was such a big deal. Now her mother regretted it because she could tell that her friend was bothered by it all.

The table was covered in what could only be described as a down-South feast, and Marcus wasted no time digging in. The food tasted just as good as it looked and Marcus enjoyed getting to know everyone. It was obvious that Nikki was the baby of the family, because despite her age, they all still doted on and fussed over her. It was a trip because he did the same and spoiled her like crazy. To his way of thinking, there was no use breaking tradition.

Marcus also loved the fact that although they had money, Mrs. Grant prepared the meals for her family and kept up her home on her own for the most part, only having a cleaning service come through twice per month. She didn't want or need too much outside help taking care of her family. Nikki was proud of that and wanted to run her own home the same way when she was married, minus the maid service. This was definitely a family he could see himself marrying into.

Chapter 14

"How could you do this to my baby? I really thought you were different, Nichole. Here he is thinking things are going good with you and you're being dishonest and parading around with another man behind his back," spat Mrs. Palmer disgustedly.

"Mrs. Palmer . . ." she started but was unable to find the right words to say without outing her good friend to his mother. She had just come in from the restroom and was on her way through the kitchen to rejoin her family back out near the lake. Mrs. Palmer was waiting for her and went off as soon as she entered the room. "Eric and I have been over for months now. We are still really good friends, so he's already aware that I'm seeing someone else. I'm not exactly sure why he's led you to believe otherwise, but that's a conversation that you should be having with him, not me," Nikki said as politely as she could. Old-school folk sure thought they could walk around checking folks all willy-nilly. The nerve.

"For months?" she questioned with confusion written all over her face.

"Yes, ma'am," Nikki answered, feeling bad for the older woman. She felt especially bad for Eric and wished that he could find the courage to talk to his mother and be honest with her about what he was dealing with.

"Nichole, please forgive me for approaching you without having all the facts. It seems that my son and I have some things that we need to discuss," she said regretfully.

"Do you mind telling your parents good-bye for me? I hate to be rude and just leave, but I need to speak with Eric right away."

"Of course, Mrs. Palmer. I'm sorry that you found out about us like this."

"That's okay, sweetheart. Again, I apologize for speaking to you that way. I was out of line, and I hope you'll forgive me," she said before leaving. It was obvious that this news troubled her greatly.

Nikki quickly sent a text to Eric, giving him a heads-up about her conversation with his mother.

Wifey: Ran into your mom at my parents' today. Marcus was with me. Awkward! Janine confronted me about cheating on you so I had no choice but to tell her we were no longer dating. Didn't tell her why but of course she was upset and plans to come talk to you. Call me so that I can give you the full scoop. Love you. P.S. Your mother is low-key scary! #Yikes

By the time she and Marcus left her parents' home she still hadn't heard back from him. It was weird because he would normally respond to her right away, and with something this important she was expecting him to call instead of text so that he could get the full story. Nikki hoped he wasn't upset that she told his mother they broke up, but she really didn't have a choice. She planned to give him until the next day, and if she didn't hear from him, she was going to stop by his place.

Knock. Knock. Knock.

After trying unsuccessfully to reach Eric, Nikki showed up unannounced to his home around four o'clock the following afternoon to check on him. Something just wasn't sitting right with her, so she had to make sure he was okay. Marcus insisted on accompanying her today, and she was happy that he had. Eric had to be home because his car was there in the driveway and they could hear his dog Bevo barking like crazy on the other side of the door. On the way over she'd alternated between calling his house and cell phones but hadn't got an answer. They had been at the door for a few minutes when it became evident that no one was going to open up. Nikki then took it upon herself to use the key he'd given her to gain entry into his place.

His home was eerily quiet but spotless as usual. Bevo ran back to the living room where she stood with Marcus. He was no longer barking but was now whining incessantly while nudging at her legs, directing her toward the back of the house. She wanted to follow him, but the fear of what she would find held her in place. Marcus sensed her apprehension and ordered her to stay put while he checked the back of the house. He already had his gun at his side as he followed closely behind Eric's coal black Great Dane.

"Shit! Nichole, call 911!"

The urgency in Marcus's tone caused her to sprint toward the master bedroom. "Oh my God!" she screamed when she came to the door and her eyes took in the horrific scene before her.

Marcus tried his best to shield her, but it was too late. She'd already seen too much. There on his king-sized bed lay Eric with coagulated blood pooled beneath his head on top of the stark white bedding. Lying beside him was a fair-skinned gentleman she'd only seen in pictures. Rae. Marcus made another attempt to remove her from the room while he used her phone to call for help. As she fought against him to get to her friend, Nikki's mind was racing, trying to figure out exactly what had happened here. Looking from Eric then back to his friend, she noticed the gun that must have fallen from his lover's hand now resting on the floor with his hand hanging off the foot of the bed directly above it. The gunshot wound to the man's head was visible, but she really couldn't make out where exactly Eric had been hit because there was so much blood.

Bevo stood at his owner's feet as they dangled off the side of the bed, and he began nudging his legs. Hearing the agonizing gasp that suddenly came from him gave her strength to break free from Marcus. "Baby, he's still breathing!" she yelled, rushing over to Eric. They hadn't checked either man for signs of life and had only assumed they were both dead. They damn sure looked to be, and there was no telling how long they'd been there without medical assistance.

Everything was a blur after that. She could hear Marcus yelling to the dispatcher that one of the victims was still breathing and asking for an ambulance to be sent. She held Eric in her arms as she begged him to breathe and stay with her. The police and ambulance arrived minutes later, although it felt like an eternity to Nikki. Homicide detectives took statements from both her and Marcus before releasing them to go to the hospital to check on their friend's status.

Unfortunately, Rae wasn't lucky enough to leave in an ambulance but was instead stuffed in a body bag, placed in the back of a white van, and hauled off to the morgue. He had one gunshot wound to the temple, and Eric was shot once in the chest and in the face. It was obvious to everyone on the scene that this was an attempted murder-suicide. Even Nikki and Marcus thought so, but she wondered what had occurred to make Rae go off the deep end. According to her last conversation with Eric, he and Rae ended things on a good note, and there was no animosity between the two.

Nikki tried to reach Janine by phone but was unsuccessful. Telling someone that their child had been shot and might not make it wasn't something that should be sent via text, so she called her mother instead to tell her what happened, hoping maybe she would have better luck reaching Mrs. Palmer.

The entire crew was present in the emergency room waiting area, and it took every single one of them to keep Nikki from blowing up on the staff when she couldn't get an update on his status. She was beside herself with worry and needed to know what was going on with her friend.

"Nik, I think we should just come back tomorrow. We won't be able to see him tonight, and you need to go home and rest. Hopefully, when we come back, he'll be awake and able to take visitors," Alana said, rubbing her back. Nikki nodded her agreement.

"I wonder where the fuck his mother is. How could she not be here right now?" Kelsey asked with disbelief. Nikki's parents had even shown up, but Mrs. Palmer was still nowhere to be found. Christine said she sounded normal over the phone and didn't seem upset at learning that her only child had been wounded in a terrible shooting in his home. His life was hanging in the balance, and his own mother hadn't bothered to come check on him. Something was definitely going on, and Nikki wanted to know what the hell it was.

Marcus was en route to Wizard's to shoot some pool and have a few drinks with Jakobi, Big B, and Junior. It had been a minute since he had time to hang with just the fellas. Between his businesses and having a high-maintenance girlfriend, he was always on the move. Then this shit with Eric was adding to his stress level. When his woman stressed, it caused him to stress, and it pissed him off that there was nothing he could do to make her feel better about things. He needed a couple rounds of brown liquor, preferably Hennessy, and a few hours of chill time with the fellas, then he would be back on it.

He also wanted to take this opportunity to see where Junior's head was at. They'd handled that issue with Amina's ex, Darius, a while back and never spoke about it again after the deed was done. He was positive that Junior had never done anything like that, and although he seemed cool about everything, Marcus wanted to make sure he was straight.

"My niggas, what's good," Marcus greeted them as he walked up on his boys. Big B, Kobi, and Junior were already on their second round of pool and drinks.

"'Bout time yo' ass showed up," his brother said.

"My bad, bro. Too many things going on at once," he replied.

"Tell me about it," Junior added. He'd been so busy lately that he didn't know whether he was coming or going most days.

"What's up with you, Junior? We ain't really had a chance to chop it up after that shit with ol' boy," Marcus probed. Jakobi was the only one of them who hadn't been in on it, but he knew what was up because his brother didn't keep secrets from him.

"Shit, I'm straight, bruh. Haven't given dude a second thought," he replied honestly. He figured his boss thought he was losing sleep over what they'd done, but that wasn't the case. If he had it to do again, nothing would have changed.

"I'm just making sure. I don't want you to trip over that bitch-ass nigga. It was either Amina or him, and we did what we had to do."

"I'm already knowing. If you ask me, the nigga got off easy. I really wanted to handle his ass," he fumed.

"Don't trip. His dumb ass made it easy for us." Marcus shrugged.

Marcus then proceeded to update them on what was going on with Eric. Learning that he had been shot was a shocker to them but not more shocking than finding out he was gay. Of course, Marcus had known for months, but he wasn't the type to gossip. Eric was a man's man. He played basketball with them some Saturdays and even hit the bar with the crew from time to time. The ladies swarmed him everywhere they went, and he seemed to like the attention. Nothing about that nigga said he liked dudes. Nothing at all. They now understood why it was so easy for Marcus to welcome him into their circle. At first, it was puzzling to them, seeing a hothead like Marcus Tate be so unbothered by a man previously engaged to his woman, even though it was for less than twenty-four hours. He didn't see Eric as a threat, so he was straight.

"How is my sister holding up?" Junior asked. He was sorry to hear that Eric had been hurt, and he was sure Nikki was going through it.

"She's a mess, man. This shit is so fucked up. The girls are up there at the hospital with her right now. I was thinking I needed a break from it all, but now all I want to do is go back up there and see about her," he stressed, not liking the thought of not being there when she needed him.

Junior just nodded. He appreciated how hard Marcus went for his sister. He was glad that she had someone to hold her down, but he still needed to go over and check on her himself. They were close, and he wanted to be there for her too.

Chapter 15

"Why you always gotta talk so much shit?" Alana questioned, rolling her eyes at Kelsey.

"Aww, don't get ya big-ass drawers in a bind. You know it wouldn't be right if I wasn't talking a little shit, best frannn." Kelsey blew a kiss at her and winked as she scooped up the cards that lay in the middle of the table.

"Lana, after all this time you should be used to it. Look at me. I've been dealing with her trash-talking, cocky, competitive ass all my life. Surely you can put up with it for just one night," O'Shea said, wearing a playful smirk.

"Really, Shea? That's what we doing now?" Kelsey pouted.

"Come on, Cocoa, you know I'm just fucking around. You know I like that trash talk," he sweet-talked his wife.

"You know I know, daddy," she flirted back, looking at him as if he were the only person in the room.

"Get a fucking room." Alana feigned disgust while everyone laughed.

It was couples' night at the Tate compound, and Kelsey and O'Shea were kicking Alana's and Jakobi's butts at spades. The Lewises didn't have shit for them when they were playing dominoes earlier, but now that they were playing spades, which was Kelsey and Shea's game, Kelsey was talking more shit than a little bit. Marcus and Nikki were hugged up, sitting at the bar and watching them go back and forth, and they seemed to find the constant banter hilarious.

This was a fairly new tradition for the group and only
the second time that they had gathered together for it.
Now that Nikki was seeing Marcus they decided to make
this a monthly affair. They played games, ate delicious
food, and had powerful discussions. They talked about
everything: politics, relationships, religion, and the
increase in police shootings of unarmed black men.
Nothing was off-limits. With all they had going on in
their individual lives, this time together helped everyone
stay connected.

Tonight's topic ended up being sex. Nikki was unsure
of how they got there, because one moment they were
talking about going to see R. Kelly when he came to
Dallas, and the next minute they were having a full-blown
conversation about that bump and grind. She didn't have
anything to offer as far as personal experience, but she'd
educated herself extensively on the subject and was able
to make some key points that they all found interesting.

Nikki was glad to have such an awesome group of
friends. They allowed her to ask questions without
judgment or making her feel silly, and she appreciated
that. Marcus was fascinated by her innocence, and he
was glad to see her smiling for a change. It took a lot
of convincing to drag her from Eric's hospital room to
hang with them tonight, and she was glad that they had.
Chilling with them took her mind off of imagining the
worst when it came to her friend. It had been days, and
he was still in a coma, fighting for his life.

The couples had moved to the theater room for a
movie, and as usual, she was seated on Marcus's lap as he
gently stroked up and down her back. His touch was so
comforting to her and was intimate without being sexual.
In fact, they were always touching each other. Nikki
craved his warmth and scent twenty-four hours a day.
It seemed he felt the same way, seeing as how his face

was buried in the crook of her neck, inhaling her at that very moment. When the movie was over, they picked up exactly where they left off on the topic of sex.

"If this question is too personal let me know," Jakobi started to ask Nikki.

"What made me decide to wait for marriage to have sex, right?" she said with a knowing smile.

"Yeah. I mean you just don't see that a lot these days. I'm sure you get tired of folks asking you that shit though," he said, feeling kind of bad for singling her out.

"Yes, I do get that question a lot, but I don't mind. It's nice to be able to share my perspective with others. To answer your question, it started for me in church. I remember being about fourteen years old, and my pastor preached a sermon on sexual immorality, adultery, and premarital sex. Reverend Simmons put the fear of God in me, and I was afraid to let a boy look at me let alone touch me. I was convinced that if I did, I was going to burn in hell," she said, making everyone laugh.

"Anyway, about two weeks after that sermon we were at church for Wednesday night Bible Study, and I was stopped by one of the deacons who asked me to knock on the door to Reverend Simmons's office and have him to come to the sanctuary. They were trying to figure out something that had to do with the developers and the new church they were building right across the street. I was in a rush to get back to my friends, and I somehow forgot my manners. I opened the door to the reverend's office without knocking and found Ms. Llewellyn bent over with Reverend Simmons giving her the business from behind," she said, making everyone in the room gasp. "I took off running up out of there so fast," she said, mentally recalling how she felt seeing them engaged in the sexual act.

"That's fucked up," Kelsey said, not hiding her disgust.

"Right, Kels! I was traumatized. I'd never seen anyone having sex before, but that wasn't the only thing that bothered me. What bothered me most was that this man could preach one thing, telling us how to live our lives, but he was doing the complete opposite. His wife was just doors down leading a women's group, and there he was doing that. After that, I wanted to know if the things that Reverend Simmons claimed were true, so I started reading the Bible. I was doing my own research because I no longer trusted what I was learning from my parents and my pastor. Sure enough, I found what I was looking for and came to the conclusion that although what the reverend said was true, he was having a hard time practicing what he preached. That one incident piqued my interest, so I kept researching. Not just scriptures either. You would not believe how many books I've read on sex and celibacy," she giggled.

"Yup, got a whole collection of nasty books in that library of hers," Marcus said to her with a side-eyed glance.

"Hush up!" she admonished, swatting at him playfully. "After all that reading I keep coming to the same conclusion. Sex is a beautiful thing that has been made dirty by immoral people. I understand we all sin and fall short, and although Reverend Simmons turned out to be a complete fraud, the words he spoke were gospel. I knew then that I didn't want any man besides my husband to experience me in that way. My body was made for his pleasure, no one else's. It should only be loved, caressed, and appreciated by the mister to my missus. At least that's the way I see it," she added as she looked into her man's eyes dreamily, envisioning them loving, caressing, and appreciating one another. The smirk on his face told her that he was imagining those same things.

"Damn," O'Shea replied thoughtfully.

"Damn is right," Jakobi concurred. He admired Nikki for her choice, and he figured his brother did too. Marcus's eyes roamed her face the entire time she spoke, and he could see that his feelings for her ran deep as hell.

"Nik, tell them what you told me about soul ties," Alana said. "No lie, that shit had me praying for a week straight," she said without a hint of humor in her voice.

"Fuck yeah," agreed Kelsey.

"The hell is a soul tie?" asked O'Shea.

"It's like a spiritual or emotional connection you have to someone after you've had sex with them. It can even be a close relationship, but most people relate soul ties with sex. Even after you've moved on, part of them is with you and you with them, essentially making you feel incomplete. Imagine having soul ties to every single person you've slept with. The transfer of one's filthy, evil energy mingling in you because you became one flesh with them at some point. Body fluids and feelings aren't the only things exchanged when you lay with someone," she schooled them.

"I feel like I need to go take a fucking shower," Marcus said, making everyone laugh. "Seriously though, that shit make a nigga feel dirty as hell." He'd fucked so many women he'd lost count, and he couldn't imagine being tied to them in any way.

"Don't trip, baby. Soul ties can be broken with prayer and forgiveness, so you're fine," she said, kissing his cheek.

"I need to be on the prayer hotline then," he joked but was serious at the same time.

For a moment they all sat quietly, more than likely trying to remember every person they'd been intimate with. Nikki sat contemplating and inwardly chastising herself because she realized the mess she had created for herself.

"You okay, boo?" Alana asked. The women were now in the kitchen putting away the food, and she seemed a bit out of it.

"Yeah, I'm cool. Just thinking about Eric," she replied. Not only was she thinking about Eric, but she was also thinking of the secret she'd been keeping from her friends. Alana loved Marcus like he was her blood brother and so did Kelsey, so there was no way that she could tell them what she had been up to. Hell, she didn't fully understand it herself, so explaining it to someone else would be nearly impossible.

"That was a pretty deep discussion tonight. They in there looking crazy as hell trying to remember every ratchet ho they ever smashed," Kelsey laughed.

"Hell yeah," Alana said, joining in. "Shit, y'all know my past so ain't no use in me fronting. I was praying my ass off when Nik first broke that shit down to me. I'm so glad I found my baby love. His is the only soul I want tied to mine," she said seriously.

"You sho know what to say," Jakobi said, walking up behind her and wrapping his arms around her waist. Alana turned in his arms to face him and offered her lips to her husband for a passionate kiss.

"Gotdamn, you two niggas never stop," Marcus teased as he walked in behind his brother.

"You got a lot of nerve saying that shit with the way you have your hands all over Nikki. It's like you have to be touching her at all times," countered Jakobi.

"You ain't lying about that," he said while pulling his woman in for a hug. "You good, baby?" he asked. Her mood had changed. She didn't seem upset, just different. And distant.

"Yes, I'm fine. You ready to go? I wanted to stop by to see Eric before I head home," she replied with a small smile.

"You going home tonight?" he asked, surprised.

"Yeah," she answered but offered no further explanation.

"A'ight," he replied before kissing her forehead. She had been staying with him a lot lately, and he figured she would tonight as well, so he was surprised that she wanted to go home.

He really hoped everything was okay between them, because lately she had him wondering if a relationship with him was something she really wanted. He understood she was worried about Eric, but he had a feeling that something else was bothering her. Recently he'd noticed her pulling back a little and not spending as much time with him. He figured it was due to an increase in her workload but found out that might not be the case.

Hoping to make her day, he showed up at her job with lunch for her last Thursday but was told she'd taken off and would be out of the office for the remainder of the day. He tried reaching her right away but didn't get an answer. No call back or text. She didn't contact him until later that evening, and when he asked how her day had been, she said she'd been busy at work and was just getting home.

He held off on confronting her, thinking he was just being paranoid. Something was definitely up with her, and although he was itching to find out what it was, he knew that whatever was up would surely be revealed with time. He just hoped no one died when it was all said and done. He'd waited a long time to give his heart away, and he would allow no one to play with it.

Chapter 16

"With the success of the Oklahoma City shop opening, I was thinking we could do an anniversary party for the Texas shops. We had a gang of people come out for that party in the city, and I feel like that's one of the reasons business has been booming out there. We're doing well in Texas too, but we could always be doing better," Junior said to Marcus as they sat talking at the front desk of the shop.

"You know, that don't sound like a bad idea. We had a grand opening and party for each shop out here, but it didn't have shit on that party that you put together in Oklahoma. Shit was all the way live, bruh," Marcus said, dapping Junior up.

Nikki was standing between his legs with her back to him, waiting for her girls to arrive so that they could hit the mall. Her man had just handed over his black card so that she could get whatever she wanted while she was there. She'd finally stopped refusing to let him pay for things for her, figuring it was better to just accept it than to continue to argue with him. He knew she was independent and had more than enough money to splurge on herself, but he liked to do nice things for her, so she let him.

"Hey, party people," a cheerful Alana sang as she danced through the door with Kelsey by her side getting bumped by her swaying hips.

"Lana, I'ma fuck you up if you don't quit playing. Get yo' dancing ass on somewhere, shit," fussed a pregnant Kelsey. Of course, everyone laughed.

"Damn, best friend, your ass must be having a girl this go-round because you weren't mean at all when you were carrying OJ. Folk can't even breathe wrong these days without you fussing. I don't see how Shea is putting up with you."

"He has his ways of shutting me up when I get worked up and fussy," she countered, sticking her tongue out at Alana.

"I bet he does. Damn freaks," Alana laughed. "You ready, Nik Nak?"

"Yes, ma'am, I am," Nikki said before turning to peck Marcus's lips a few times.

"Where are you ladies headed to?" Amina asked as she walked back out front with Bri beside her. She had gone to the nursery in the back a while ago to put her daughter down for a nap, but Brielle wasn't having it. She fussed and fought until her mother finally gave up. Brielle thought she was slick. Amina knew she was just trying to get back out front because she knew Junior was out there.

"About to go shut this mu'fuckin' mall down," Kelsey said excitedly. Her baby bump was finally visible, and she was too cute.

"You trying to roll?" Alana asked, smiling brightly. She loved her some Amina and admired how determined the young lady was to make something of herself. She and Alana's li'l boo, Cree, were best friends, so they saw each other a lot.

"Maybe next time. I'll be here working and studying for the rest of my shift if I can ever get this one here to lie down," she said, referring to Brielle, who was now hanging on to Junior's pant leg. Like he always did, he picked her up, allowing her to rest her head on his chest.

"I can't believe her li'l mean ass even likes you, Junior," Kelsey pointed out.

"Yeah, this my li'l roll dawg right here, huh, Bri Bri," he spoke to the baby, who nodded her head before wrapping her arms around his neck.

Amina loved the love that Bri had for Junior. He, Marcus, and Kobi were the only positive male figures in her life, because her daddy wasn't worth shit. She was so happy with her new place and even happier that Darius had no clue where she was. After she changed her number on his ass, she knew it would be only a matter of time before he showed up to the shop. There was no doubt that all hell would break loose on that day. Junior had already beaten his ass, and she knew that Marcus was dying to catch a fade with him too.

"I'll call you later, honey," Nikki said to Marcus with a final parting kiss.

"A'ight, y'all be careful," replied Marcus before the ladies took off for their shopping spree.

Five minutes passed before the door chimed and in walked a thick-ass, fair-skinned chick who commanded the attention of every single man in the shop. Some females too. Ol' girl was just that bad: average height, thick legs, stupid juicy booty, no waist, and 34DD breasts that had to have been enhanced. Wavy Peruvian hair hung down to her ass, and her face was made up perfectly. Baby girl was big fine. Marcus got his look on real quick then turned his attention back to the paperwork on the desk. He didn't want or need those problems, so he left the task of checking her in to Amina.

"Good afternoon. How may we help you?" she asked cheerfully.

"Sorry, but I didn't come to get a tattoo. I'm actually here to see this handsome guy right here." She smirked, nodding her head toward Junior, who was already mugging the hell out of her. Amina was surprisingly able to keep her smile intact despite how perturbed she was.

"Hey, you," the woman said, stepping in front of Junior, who still held Brielle in his arms. She went to hug him, but Bri pushed against the woman's chest, preventing her from effectively doing her thing. Marcus snickered, and Amina smiled inwardly at Bri's cock-blocking ass.

"Let me take her in the back," Amina said, attempting to remove her child from his arms. She didn't want her baby anywhere near this woman, and it seemed like Bri wasn't having it either.

"Nah, she's fine," he held his hand up and blocked her mother from taking her. "I'll put her down for her nap when I come back. Leah, let me talk at you outside for a minute," he turned and spoke to the woman. Junior had no clue how she found out where he was working, because when she asked, he made it clear that it wasn't any of her business. The most he told her was that he was working at a tattoo shop. He didn't want anyone he was fooling with showing up to the shop on no bullshit. Leah was known for acting an ass, so he surely didn't want her coming around.

With her head down, she reluctantly followed him out front. She should have known that coming there was a mistake.

"Did this fool just punk me for my own child?" a dumbfounded Amina asked Marcus, who was still snickering.

"Sure did. Hell, Bri wasn't gon' let you take her away from Junior no way. She done got attached to that nigga. Seems like you done got attached to him too," he pointed out as he watched her watch Junior and his lady friend through the window. "Y'all bet' not forget the rules, man. I have them in place for a reason. Imagine if y'all was in a relationship and her big, fine ass walked in here looking for Junior. You would act a fool, and shit like that cannot happen here. I know how y'all feel, but if I let y'all make it, then everybody else gon' think I'm playing favorites," he explained.

"Marcus, I've never lied to you, and I don't plan on starting today. I cut for Junior, but he's already made it clear to me that, as the manager, he has to lead by example and it wouldn't be a good look for him to become involved with an employee. I completely understand where he's coming from, so one thing you won't ever have to worry about is me causing any drama just because I done caught feelings. Keep in mind that I won't be working here much longer though, and when the time comes I'll go for what I know." She winked, making Marcus laugh.

"Do yo' thing, ma," Marcus encouraged her. "Aye, but did you see how Brielle pushed that ho back? Baby girl wasn't having that shit," Marcus said, causing her to fall out laughing.

"That's my boo right there. She got her mama's back," she said, glancing at Brielle, who was still looking at the bitch like she was crazy.

Amina stood there thinking about her love life. She hadn't heard from Darius in a minute, so she finally got up enough courage to give a dude her phone number a few days ago. It was only something to do to pass the time until she could see if anything would develop between her and Junior. She made it clear to the guy she was talking to that she wasn't looking for anything other than friendship at the moment, and he said he was cool with that. The most they had done was text and talk on the phone a few times, but tomorrow they were going on an actual date, and she was nervous as hell. "I got a date tomorrow, boss," she said out of nowhere.

"How the hell you was just talking about you feeling this man but you going on a date with another nigga?" he asked, looking at her like she was stupid.

"I do like him, but I'm not about to sit around twiddling my thumbs while he does his thing either," she scoffed, motioning toward where Junior stood with ol' girl. Marcus simply nodded his head in understanding.

"Well, I'ma need to meet this nigga first before y'all go out. I swear I don't want to end up fucking nobody up for getting out of line," he fussed. Amina had become like a little sister to him, and he didn't want to see her hurt any more than she had been already.

"I was gon' have him come by here later on anyway. I need you to meet him and give him the stamp of approval before I go anywhere with his ass. The last thing I need is a repeat of Darius."

"Fuck no! That nigga was crazy," Marcus agreed.

"No, that nigga is crazy," she corrected him.

"You know what I meant. Fuckin' lunatic," he laughed, attempting to play it off as Junior walked back in the shop minus big fine.

"What's so funny?" he asked.

"Nothing, bruh. Just chopping it up with Mina about this li'l date she got tomorrow," Marcus said, putting her on the spot.

"Oh yeah?" Junior didn't attempt to hide his displeasure at hearing that she was going on a date with someone else. His eyes shot to her, but she was focused on Marcus with her mouth hanging open. She was looking like she wanted to strangle him, so she didn't notice the scowl that graced Junior's face.

"Yeah, it's not a big deal though," she told him when she finally looked his way. Marcus had completely thrown her under the bus, and she wanted to curse his ass out. She knew then not to tell his messy ass anything else.

"Whatever," Junior said with a bit too much attitude. He needed to check himself quickly. "I'll be back. I'm going to lay her down," he said, walking away as Brielle dozed off in his arms.

"You are such a fucking hater," Amina fussed at Marcus, who was cracking up laughing.

"Don't get mad at me, player." He continued laughing while blocking her playful hits.

Junior was pissed but attempted to play it off. Could he really be mad at Amina? No, but it didn't stop him from being heated anyhow. He had just kicked Leah's hardheaded ass to the curb. She thought she would surprise him by showing up to take him to lunch, but she ended up talking herself out of some regular dick. He wasn't beat for the drama, and women who did random popups were full of drama, so it was best that he nipped that in the bud right then. She called herself questioning him about the baby he was holding and whether she was his. He didn't bother denying it, so she automatically assumed that Amina was his baby mama. It didn't matter to him what the fuck she thought was going on because whatever they had was a wrap after today, so he didn't owe her ass an explanation.

"Hey," Amina said, coming to stand near the crib beside him as he stared down at a sleeping Brielle.

"Say, man, I ain't really cool with that date shit, but I know I don't have a say in the matter. I also know that I don't have a right to make this request, but I need to put it out there anyway," he said, turning to face her. He didn't feel the need to front or pretend that he didn't have feelings for her. He was sure she was already aware of it anyway. She was also aware that there was no way they could date each other, so he didn't want to stand in the way of her meeting someone else.

"What is it?" she asked. She only suspected he had feelings for her, but he'd confirmed her suspicions with his remark, and the realization caused her heart to warm with relief.

"I'm not her father, and I may be way out of line, but I'm not comfortable with random niggas being around her," he said, looking down at Brielle. He and Bri had formed a tight bond over the last few months, and he couldn't stand the thought of her being anywhere near whatever dude her mother was seeing. It was already tough enough thinking of Amina being in the company of another man.

"You know me better than that, Junior. I would never bring someone I just met around my baby," she assured him. She didn't get offended by his request and was flattered that he was so protective of her daughter. That he cared for her baby only made her fall for him even more.

"And no fucking kissing on the first date," he added on his way out of the room, causing a broad smile to appear on her face.

He's jealous. Too cute.

Chapter 17

After two whole weeks, Nikki's prayers were answered when Eric finally woke up from his coma. It had been touch and go there for a minute, but he was able to pull through. The bullet from the gunshot to his face had gone in one cheek then out the other, so despite the bandages on his face and some bruising, he still looked the same. The chest tube had been removed so slowly, but surely he was improving.

Between juggling work and her relationship, she still managed to visit him nearly every day. When things got too hectic for her, and she was unable to sit with him, Marcus would stop by and check on him for her. Her man being there for her friend meant the world to her. He didn't have to go out of his way, but he did it to make her happy and lighten the load she was carrying. This was the same man she chose over him, yet he never felt threatened or treated Eric badly.

"Hey, Nik," Eric groggily called out, getting her attention. He had been asleep for a while and was just waking up.

"Hey, boo. How you feeling?" she asked, looking him over in concern.

"Shot the hell up," he joked.

She laughed along with him. It was good to see that he still had his sense of humor. He still hadn't said much about what happened the night of the shooting, but she did notice that he wasn't sleeping well. This prompted her to approach the physician about prescribing something to assist with that, but Eric refused to take the medication, stating he didn't need it. He wouldn't admit it, but she knew he was having nightmares, so she didn't see why he was declining to take something that would help him rest. She'd been here with him a few times when he had them, and she had to practically shake him awake because he thrashed about so violently.

Thing was, he claimed he didn't remember anything at all about the shooting, but she didn't necessarily believe him. Rae's death had officially been ruled a suicide, and the police stated the crime scene indicated that Rae shot him before turning the gun on himself. Eric refused to speak on it when she asked about it. He said he wasn't quite ready to talk about what happened, so she didn't push. After minutes of silence, he began to speak.

"I don't think I would have ever told my mother the truth," Eric said. "Not because I didn't care about Rae, but because he just wasn't the person I was meant to be with. Deep down I think always knew that. I'm realizing that this was all my fault. My actions are what sent Rae over the edge." The entire time he talked he looked down at his hands as if he was reflecting on some things.

"How can you say that? You can't blame yourself for another person's selfish actions," Nikki said, taking his hand in hers as he finally made eye contact with her.

"Of course he's not completely blameless, but if I hadn't kept our relationship hidden all these years, then things probably would have turned out differently. Maybe then—" His words were halted by the sight of his mother entering his hospital room.

Nikki felt Eric tense up, and he squeezed her hand so tightly that it hurt. His reaction to seeing his own mother surprised her but also further let her know that something wasn't right with them. Even Nikki felt a way about her being there, seeing as how she hadn't come by to see

him at all since he'd been hospitalized. It also occurred to
her that he hadn't even asked for his mother. She didn't
bring it up because she didn't want to hurt him by telling
him that his mother had not been there for him. What
she did know was that he was shaken seeing Janine there.

"How are you, son?" She directed her question to Eric
as she stood at the foot of the bed.

"Fine, and you?" he asked flatly.

"Just fine, honey. I've been worried about you."

"Is that so?" He smirked while looking from her to
Nikki then back to her.

They engaged in a stare down for a while, and Nikki
thought the entire scene was weird. The tension in the
room was too thick, and she was uncomfortable. "Do you
want me to give you a minute with your mother?" she
asked Eric.

"No."

"Yes."

They spoke simultaneously. His grip on her tightened.
"Stay," he said without turning to look at her. It was
settled. She wasn't going anywhere. Eric needed her.

"Nichole, sweetheart, how have you been?" Janine
finally addressed her with a smile that didn't quite reach
her eyes.

"I've been well." She kept it short and sweet.

"And how is that handsome boyfriend of yours?"

"He's good," Nikki answered, not feeling the vibe she
was getting from Mrs. Palmer. She couldn't figure out
what this lady's deal was, but thankfully Janine didn't
stay very long. She asked a few questions about his
condition and how long doctors expected him to remain
in the hospital. Eric gave her short answers and told her
he didn't remember a thing about what happened to him
that night. After she got that bit of information, she was
out of there. No sooner than she dotted the door, Eric
blew out a loud breath of relief. Nikki decided then that

it was time to confront him. Her gut told her that something was amiss, but the bomb he proceeded to drop on her was shocking and unexpected.

A Few Weeks Earlier

"Here, hold this for me," Eric requested, handing Rae the bags from Neiman Marcus. He needed a free hand to reach for his cell phone, which was vibrating in his pocket. When he fished it out, he saw that he had several missed calls from his mother as well as a text from Nikki.

Rae had shown up to his place a week ago begging and pleading for them to talk. A lot of time had passed, and he had been cool since they split, so Eric didn't think he was on no slick shit, so he agreed to hear what he had to say. He messed up and slept with him that same night, and now Rae foolishly thought they were back together. The first couple of days were cool, and it was nice chilling with him like old times, but Eric didn't want to go backward. He knew he was going to have to break the news to Rae sooner rather than later. They'd been shopping at North Park for the last few hours and were finally about to head to his place, so he figured tonight was as good a time as any to let him know what was up.

"Fuck!" he hissed after reading the text from Nikki. He should have already come clean and told his mother the truth, but he just couldn't fucking do it. He couldn't be mad at his boo for revealing the truth about them breaking up, and he hated that he put her in a position to be confronted by his mother.

"What's going on?" Rae asked when he noticed Eric's face was screwed up after looking at his phone.

"I need to drop you by my place then step out to see my mother for a minute."

"Why? We had plans, Eric," Rae responded with an attitude.

"Just come on. I don't have time for your shit right now," he snapped.

Rae stood pouting for about thirty seconds before he decided to join him. In the car, he suggested, "Since you're already going to see your mom, I think today is a good day to tell her about us."

"No, Rae, it's not," Eric shut him down.

"Well, when will be a good time?"

"Whenever I get ready is when," he snapped, turning toward Rae at a red light. He was tired of him always thinking he was running the show.

"It's always going to be this way. I told you before that I was done with this hiding shit, and how I let you reel me back in is a mystery to me. Ass probably only wanted me because you heard I was dealing with my ex again. I should have just stayed with Kalvin. At least he's out and not scared of what his fucking mother thinks," he spat.

"Fuck you, Rae, with your dumb, delusional ass. Talking about I reeled you back in. This time it was you who showed your desperate ass up on my doorstep, not the other way around. Get that shit right! Not to mention I was in a whole relationship while you were over there being Kal's side bitch, so please come correct. I can't believe you would throw Kalvin up in my face. Fuck you and him! Feel free to bounce if that's what you want. The hell am I saying? We're not even fucking together, so do your thing," Eric chuckled sarcastically.

Rae was a manipulative person, and normally his mentioning Kalvin would make Eric cave, but not this time. He knew in the beginning that Eric wasn't comfortable with the way he was or the feelings he had for him. It was a process for him, but Rae trying to rush him through it only added to his reluctance to come out to everyone. He didn't grow up the same way Rae had. He didn't have parents who would love you regardless of the choices you made in life. He didn't feel that being gay was a choice, but you couldn't tell Janine Palmer otherwise.

"I want to be with you, Eric, but this is too much. I forgave you for that fake-ass relationship you called yourself being in with Nikki, but something has to give. You can't hide who you are forever."

"You knew off the muscle that I didn't want to come out because I expressed that to you over and over when we met. I only planned on doing it when we were together because I cared about you, but all you ever do is complain. It's always about you and what you want. Fuck my mom's feelings though, right?" he shouted. Thankfully Rae had no response this time. Eric guessed the truth was all it took to shut him up. All Eric wanted at the moment was some quiet time so that he could have his mind right for this meeting with his mother.

When they arrived at the house, Eric went right for the shower so that he could freshen up before going to see his mother. As usual, Rae sat there sulking and pouting, looking for attention. At the moment Eric couldn't care less, having no time to pacify him. Now more than ever he was sure Rae wasn't the one for him, and he was glad that he hadn't come out to his mother just yet. He knew it was something that had to be done, but having Rae as the man at his side wasn't appealing at all. It was time to stop playing this back-and-forth game and let him go on about his business for good. Eric was confident that he could find love again after Rae was gone. He knew his mother would not approve of his lifestyle, but he prayed that she would still want to be in his life after it was all said and done.

"Babe, what's up with the fundraiser next month?" Rae shouted from the other side of the bathroom door. He was used to Eric getting in his feelings, so he didn't take it personally or seriously when he said they weren't back

together. It had been their routine for years. "Have you decided if you're going?" He was really hoping that by this time Eric would have already talked to his mother and this would be sort of a coming-out party for them.

"I'm taking Nikki," he answered in annoyance. He couldn't figure out why this man was still talking to him.

"So your beard is going with you, huh?" He was really hoping that this time would be different and Eric would finally do all the things he promised he would through-out their relationship. His efforts this go-round had been piss poor, and Rae was far from pleased.

"Ha-ha," Eric said sarcastically as he emerged from the bathroom with a thick black towel wrapped around his waist. "Don't talk about her that way. Not my fucking beard, she's my friend, and she was going to the fundraiser anyway for work, but because Marcus will be in Houston, he asked me to take her. At least with her I'll have a good time, and I won't have to listen to you whining all night long," he added. It was definitely a wrap for this shit. Rae probably didn't notice that all of his belongings had already been removed from Eric's place and were being shipped to his home as they spoke.

"Oh, let me stop. I forgot how sensitive you can get behind Miss Priss. If I didn't know any better, I would think you were actually in love with her." Rae shook his head in disgust.

"How I feel about her is none of your concern, but you know what? I wish I would have left you with Kalvin that first time you left. I don't know what I was thinking asking you for another chance. I'm thinking now that maybe you were right. At the time I only wanted you because you were with someone else. I'm cool on that shit now, so take your mooching ass back over there with him. I'm done with the game playing and bullshit, Rae. Straight up," he said with finality.

"Hell no! I'll go tell your mother about us myself if I have to. You think you can just say it's over and that will be it? I've invested too much time and energy into this, and you want to just end it? No way, Eric," Rae fumed. Eric's words seemed different from all the other times. Rae could tell he was really serious about not dealing with him any longer.

"Look, I don't give a damn who you tell. I'm just as tired of living a lie as you are, but I'm finally realizing the real reason I haven't been able to tell my mother the truth. It's you. You're the reason. I could never take you home to her because she would be able to sniff your petty, money-hungry ass out within minutes of meeting you," he said hatefully. How dare he threaten to go to his mother about something like this? Rae saying that shit really showed what type of person he was.

Rae didn't work and never planned to. Kalvin took good care of him, and when things ended between them, Eric came along and took over the responsibility. That was one of the many reasons that Rae wanted to be with him. He actually had love for him, but he felt the same way for his ex. If Kalvin hadn't moved on to someone else, he would have gladly gone back. He made it clear to Rae this time that when he left, there was no coming back, so in a sense Eric was his only option. Now here he was saying he didn't want him either. That just wasn't going to work for Rae.

Eric removed the towel from his body so that he could get dressed. It took him a couple seconds to realize that Rae hadn't responded to the cold words he spoke. After pulling up his boxer briefs, he turned around and discovered the reason Rae was mute. The man he used to love, the man who claimed to still be in love with him, had a gun pointed at him with tears rolling down his face.

"What the fuck are you doing?" he shouted, jumping back and throwing his hands up in surrender.

"I'm doing what I should have done a long time ago. Eric, you're a fucking joke. I'm tired of this shit, so I might as well put us both out of our misery. You were never going to tell your mother the truth. This shit would have gone on for years if I let it," he said as more tears came. He'd been depressed, miserable, and suicidal for years. He couldn't take being all alone and expected to provide for himself. He'd rather die.

"I guess the apple didn't fall too far from the tree," Janine said disgustedly as she entered the room, catching both men off guard. Her son stood there half naked with the man she saw him with earlier pointing a gun at him. At least his ass has clothes on, she thought. She would have died if she walked in on them doing the do. Janine spotted them as they were turning onto his street earlier, not even noticing her at the stop sign. She made the block and pulled up to her son's house just as they walked inside, holding hands. She drove down a few houses to park then took a moment to process everything she'd seen. After sitting for about fifteen minutes, she made her way to Eric's place to confront him.

"Mother!" he called out in shock. The embarrassment of having her see him like this with a man showed all over his face. "It's not what it looks like," he attempted to explain, both hands out in front of him.

"It's not like what? You are gay, aren't you, son?" Unable to answer, he just hung his head in shame. "I mean you're standing here in your underwear with another man, and you seem pretty comfortable with that. So tell me exactly what it's like," she said with her hand up to her ear, awaiting an explanation. Still, he said nothing.

"Even with a fucking gun pointed at you, you won't tell her. Clearly, she already knows what's going on, Eric!"

screamed Rae, who up to that point had remained quiet
and hadn't taken the gun off of Eric.

He just stood there with his eyes fixed on his mother,
shaking and full of regret. This wasn't the way she was
supposed to find out. He should have had the balls to be
honest with her as soon as Nikki broke things off. Hell,
he should have done it way before then. Now he was
standing there looking just as crazy as Rae's messy,
dramatic ass.

"You are so weak, and you make me sick!" cried Rae.

"Well, he got it honest. Just like his father, he probably
would have gone to the grave with this secret," she told
Rae matter-of-factly. "Is that what your plan was, son?
Were you ever going to tell me?"

"I was going to tell you, eventually. You have no idea
how hard this is for me." He finally found his voice with
tears streaming down his face. Janine kept right on
talking, not caring one bit about the turmoil her son was
experiencing right in front of her.

"I always had a feeling about you, but I prayed that
this filthy spirit be removed from you. When you started
seeing Nichole, I thought there was hope for you. Turns
out it was all a front so that you could sneak around
with your little boyfriend." She nodded toward Rae.
"You see, young man, his father was a sissy too. He just
hid it well," she told Rae and laughed as surprise registered on the faces of both men. "All those years I spent
with a man who didn't even want to touch me because
he preferred the company of men. What a fucking waste.
I took care of his ass though," she laughed wickedly.

She'd slowly poisoned her husband over the years
by lacing his food and drinks with cyanide. It drove
her crazy finding out a few years after marrying Eric's
father that he was gay. He'd only married her to please
his parents, who would never approve of him being

with a man. She stayed with him for the money and also because the thought of failing at marriage and having everyone say "I told you so" wasn't an option. So, they put on a big front for their families and friends while secretly hating each other. Watching him slowly deteriorate right before her eyes was retribution enough for her. Eric was the best thing to come from being with that man, and now here he was carrying on the same way his father had.

"I love you, Mom, and I don't want this to change our relationship or the way you see me as a man," he said solemnly. The look on her face was one of pure repulsion without a trace of pity. Learning the truth about him had already changed how his mother saw him. Like she said, he was just like his father. If Nikki would have agreed to go through with marrying him, he wondered how long he could have suppressed the urges he had to be with a man. Would he have remained faithful to her or would he have been a chip off the old block and dipped behind his wife's back? He honestly couldn't say. "I just need you to say you still love me," he choked out.

"You are no longer my son. I do not love you. I could never love you after this. I refuse to let you embarrass me the way Reese did all those years!" she screamed hatefully.

Hearing those words, Eric knew that he would never be able to have a relationship with his mother again. She hated him just like she'd hated his father. He felt sick to his stomach even saying what he was about to say because it went against who he was, but he would say it just to not have his mother looking at him the way she was right now. "Look, Rae and I are over. I can change. I felt an attraction with Nikki, and I'm sure I can find it with another woman. I can be who it is you want me to be," he said, attempting to bargain for her love.

"I've heard enough of this family drama," yelled Rae, his breaking point officially reached. He was sick of them talking as if he weren't even in the room. This man was sitting here trying to tell his mother that he wouldn't be gay anymore just to please her, like it was something that was just going to go away. Eric forgot all about the gun Rae was pointing at him until he heard a loud pop followed by a burning sensation to his face. Then another pop sounded before a bullet entered his chest, sending him flying back onto the bed. Janine didn't even flinch when it happened.

"You can go now," Rae told her as he sat down next to Eric's body on the bed. He needed to finish this, but he didn't want her evil ass there when he did it. She nodded, knowing the young man was about to kill himself, and she did nothing to stop him. His death wouldn't mean a thing to her, but before leaving, she wanted to have one last word with Eric.

"Well, son, I came here thinking I was going to have to take care of you like I took care of your father, but it seems your man has saved me the trouble," she said before walking out of the room. Her voice held no emotion as she spoke to him. It was like she wanted him to die knowing she didn't give a fuck about him. Tears fell rapidly from his eyes as his life slowly slipped away.

Rae's next move was an easy one. The decision was not hard at all. Life without Eric or Kalvin wasn't a life worth living, and he didn't plan to try. With the gun in his hand, he placed it against his temple and pulled the trigger, effectively ending his own life. Before everything went completely black, he thought maybe they would be meeting soon in the hereafter. Sadly, that wouldn't be happening today, because his partner would live to see another day. Unfortunately for Rae, it was a done deal.

"Are you serious right now?" an appalled Nikki asked.

"Wouldn't play around about something like this, Nichole," he answered in a serious tone.

"You're telling me that she just left you for dead?"

"That's exactly what I'm saying," he told her as his eyes watered a little.

When Eric first began detailing the events of that day, the crew had just entered his hospital room, and instead of asking them to step out while he and Nikki talked, he continued. They'd heard everything. The part that was most shocking was his mother's reaction and confession. Was her plan to really harm Eric? There was no way that what he was saying could be true. Nikki felt something was off with Mrs. Palmer, but this was absurd.

"Eric, are you sure this wasn't just in your mind? I mean your mom couldn't have—"

"Nichole, it happened, baby girl. She left me there to die, and she also told me in so many words that she killed my father. And for her to say that she had come there that day to do the same thing to me was too much. I didn't want to believe the words that came out of her mouth, but she left me no choice. Growing up, I knew how she felt about my dad, but I never knew why. I surely didn't think she could ever hate me the same way. She walked away like it was nothing." He shook his head.

"My goodness. I'm so sorry," she said, hugging him tight. Everyone looked on in disbelief, not knowing what to say.

"What are you going to do about your mom?" Alana asked. She was thinking the lady was psycho and needed to be locked up for what she'd done to his father.

"I don't plan to do anything. I just don't want her around me ever again," he said sadly. He was crushed that she made the choice to walk away from him that day, but he didn't want anything to do with her after this. Her love for him was conditional, and he didn't want it.

Straight or gay, he deserved his mother's unconditional love. His father had his ways, but his mother was the evil one in his eyes.

"Well, you have us, so you'll be just fine." Kelsey hugged him while everyone in the room agreed with her statement. Eric had been through so much, and he was happy to have a great support system. He would miss his mother, but he knew they could never go back to the way things were before.

Chapter 18

"I need to talk to you," Nikki heard her father say before she could make it to the front door of her parents' home. She had come to see her mother and drop off some things to her that she'd been putting off for the last few weeks. She had no idea that her father was home, and surprisingly her mother didn't mention it to her.

"Hey, Daddy. I didn't know you were here," she said, hugging him. "Is what you need to talk to me about important? I was on my way to meet a friend for lunch, and I don't want to be rude by showing up late." She smiled. He didn't smile back, which was very odd. Nervous, she began chewing on her bottom lip. Her father's tone and the way he was looking at her had her feeling uneasy.

"Kendall can wait," her father said with his brow raised.

"What?" she stammered as she stepped back, caught off guard by his words.

"I said Kendall can wait. That is who you're going to see, right?" he challenged.

"Daddy, it's not like that," she explained with a weak smile.

"It's not like what? Are you or are you not preparing to go on a lunch date with someone other than your boyfriend?" her father questioned with his voice raised.

"It's not a date," Nikki defended herself.

"Does Marcus know about it?" he countered.

"No, but—"

"But nothing, Nichole. If it's not a date, then there is no need for you to be so secretive. I ran into Kendall's father at the lodge, and imagine my surprise when he told me how happy he was that you and his trifling-ass son have been spending time together again. You need to tell me what the hell is going on and you tell me right damn now," he demanded.

"Daddyyy," she whined.

"Nichole Elise Grant." He raised his voice, causing her tears to immediately spill from her eyes.

This was not how their relationship worked. Her father didn't yell at his baby girl, and she didn't keep secrets from him, so she spilled the beans. She and Kendall had indeed been spending time together. It didn't take long for her to pick up that Kendall wanted more than a friendship with her, but not even that stopped her from seeing him. She was dead wrong for even entertaining his cheating ass when she had a perfectly good man already, but she couldn't help it.

His rejection of her years back affected her more than she let on, and seeing him again, knowing that he wanted her but couldn't have her, gave her the confidence that she'd lost back then. Today she was meeting Kendall for lunch, and it would be for the last time. Having gotten her little revenge, or whatever it was, she felt now it was time to focus her full attention on what she was building with Marcus, which was what she should have been doing in the first place. Trying to get back at Kendall's tired ass was a complete waste of her time.

Nikki never realized how corny and boring Kendall was until she started hanging out with him again. Maybe she was into corny and boring men before, but Marcus came in and brought excitement and fun to her life. Whatever he was was what she now liked, and it was time for her to quit playing games. Besides, if her man caught wind of what she'd been up to, he was going to, in his words, "fuck somebody up," and she didn't want that somebody to be her. She was in love with Marcus and couldn't figure out why she was even giving Kendall the time of day. Nothing had happened between them, but the mere fact that she was seeing him behind her man's back was cause for concern.

By the time she was done telling her father everything, she was hard down crying. Her father didn't even bother comforting her as she cried, and that hurt more than anything.

"Nichole, why are you trying to sabotage things with Marcus?"

"Is that what you think?" she asked, looking up at him pitifully.

"I know for a fact that's what you're doing. All the years I've heard you talk about wanting to find a man who loves you with all his heart, a man who takes care of you, a man who you can take care of, and one who respects your decision to wait for marriage to have sex. The moment you find it, you jeopardize it for Kendall's dusty ass. Marcus has practically jumped through hoops to be with you, and this is how you repay him?" her father said as he looked at her as if he didn't even recognize her. For the first time ever Nicholas Grant was disappointed in his daughter, and she could see it all over him. He was struggling right before her eyes, and seeing that had her struggling as well.

Kendall had done her dirty when they were together. His betrayal made her feel inadequate. Although it was she who begged Marcus to give their relationship a try, she was never really fully invested in what they shared, but she didn't know why. Maybe it was the fear of things turning out the way they had with her and Kendall. She loved Marcus ten times more than she ever loved Kendall, and if he ever betrayed her that way, she would probably die from the pain. It hurt to even think about it. She let his past with women make her insecure in their relationship even though she felt in her heart that Marcus had been true to her.

"I was only meeting with him today to end things, Daddy, I promise."

"Nichole, Marcus already knows about Kendall. I talked to him earlier." Her father broke the news to her regretfully.

Her heart began thundering wildly in her chest at hearing those words. "Wh . . . what do you mean he knows? Daddy, you didn't," she said as a fear she had never known crept into her bones. She couldn't lose Marcus behind this. The thought of it alone caused her to become nauseous.

"Of course I didn't, Nichole, but he called to give me a heads-up so that I wouldn't come to see him, trying to fix this for you after learning that things were over between you two," he said, feeling sorry for his daughter as he watched the words that left his mouth break her heart.

"Over? He said that?" she asked as she broke down.

"I hope you're able to fix this, baby girl," her father said, walking away. She made this mess, and she would have to fix it on her own. This wasn't something he would be able to make right for her. He had love for Marcus, and in the short time he had known him, he felt as if he had gained another son. Marcus reminded him so much of himself at that age, and the genuine love he had for his daughter was more than he could ask for. Nicholas just couldn't understand what possessed his daughter to do what she'd done, but he prayed that it wasn't so bad that they couldn't work through it. He'd already planned to confront his daughter and put a stop to whatever was going on after speaking with Kendall's father, but when

Marcus called that morning, he knew that things were beyond his control.

"What the hell have I done?" she asked herself out loud as tears of regret soaked her face. She didn't bother showing up to the lunch Kendall had planned for them. Not only that, she never even called to cancel, and when he tried reaching out to her, she rejected each call before finally blocking him altogether. Her focus was on what the hell she was going to tell Marcus to make him stay.

The days turned into weeks, and the weeks soon accumulated to two months since Marcus ended things. She'd tried everything to get him to talk to her and just hear her out, but nothing worked. Every single day she dialed his number at least twenty times, and she planned to keep on doing that until he talked to her. Her body was in physical as well as emotional pain, and she had no one to blame for it but herself. Her actions had caused her to lose the only man she had ever truly loved.

What she felt for Marcus was the realest thing she had ever known, and she had to find some way to get it back. She had stopped by his house a few times, but he refused to open up for her. Every time he forced her to walk away only fueled her need to return and try again. She refused to give him time to find someone else. He was a good catch, and any woman would appreciate the man he was. She slipped up a few times and had taken him for granted, but she would do everything in her power to make things right.

On the bright side, the situation with her father was better, and she was relieved because she would lose her mind if all three of the men in her life were upset with her at the same time. Junior was still pissed with her for what she'd done, and he was giving her the cold shoulder just the same as Marcus was. It turned out that he and Marcus were chilling at the sports bar after work one evening and happened to run into Kendall.

Junior never really cared for the man and wanted nothing more than to beat his ass for what he had done to his sister years ago. Before he had the chance to rub it in Kendall's face by introducing Marcus as Nikki's boyfriend, dude started bragging about all the time he had been spending with his sister and how happy he was that she forgave him. The man even went so far as making vows to Junior, saying how he wasn't going to hurt her and how he was going to do right by her this go-round.

Junior told his father that he had never seen Marcus look so defeated, and just when he thought his boy was about to beat Kendall's ass, he downed his drink, slammed the glass down on the bar, causing it to shatter, then left without saying a word. He was officially done, and Junior could see it all over his face that night. His baby sister clearly hadn't received the memo.

In between lightweight stalking Marcus, she focused all of her remaining energy on work, avoiding her family and friends for the most part. Fortunately, Alana wasn't upset with her for what had gone down with Marcus. She was just surprised that Nikki was creeping around the way she was. It was completely out of character for her, and both of her friends told her so. They, along with Eric, agreed with her father's take on things. They all felt that she was intentionally sabotaging her relationship with Marcus. Subconsciously that's exactly what she'd done. There was no other way to explain her behavior over the last few months. Though it wasn't intentional, she'd messed things up with Marcus before he had the chance to do her dirty. Nikki decided not to focus on why she'd been dishonest and instead channel her energy into doing what was necessary to get her man back.

It was Friday, and she had the next three days off. Having nothing to occupy her time, she found herself getting in the car and driving to Smoove Ink. She couldn't call ahead to make sure Marcus was there because they had been screening his calls. Giving Junior a call wasn't even an option because he still wasn't speaking to her. She hated that she was out here acting like some lunatic girlfriend, but she couldn't help it.

As soon as she stepped foot in the shop, she became the center of attention. The way everyone was looking at her had Nikki thinking that maybe Marcus had banned her from the shop and had given strict instructions to escort her from the premises if she showed her face there. All eyes were on her, and when she looked down at her attire, she suddenly knew the real reason. Coming here was an impulsive act, and at the time the only thing on her mind was seeing Marcus, so she wasn't worried about changing her clothes. Suddenly she wished that she would have thought this whole thing through.

She had been lounging around the house after getting her hair and nails done, wearing her favorite pair of denim booty shorts and a cobalt blue short-sleeved crop-top shirt. The matching wedged heels she was wearing only fueled the looks of lust she received from the men in the shop because they had her legs looking long and luscious. Immediately she became self-conscious and wanted to run up out of there. This was never an outfit that she would wear in public, but for some reason she liked to dress sexy at home. Not even Marcus had seen her in anything this revealing. Before she could turn to leave, she heard her brother's voice.

"Nichole, what the hell are you doing here, and what the fuck do you have on?" Junior hissed through clenched teeth as he mean mugged every single nigga who was eye fucking his baby sister.

"I came to see Marcus. I really need to talk to him, Junior," she pleaded pathetically. Instantly she forgot all about her clothing.

"Well, he's not here right now, and I don't think he would want to see you anyway. Come on," he said, pulling her by the arm like a parent dragging their child along, preparing to beat the hell out of them.

"Let me go," she yelled, snatching away from her brother once they were in the parking lot located on the side of the building.

"What the hell has gotten into you? First you pull that shit with Kendall, and then you show up to this man's place of business, dressed like a fucking thot in front of his employees. I promise you that behaving this way will not get you the results you want. I feel like I don't even know my own sister right now," he said, pinching the bridge of his nose in frustration. His words sliced through her and she couldn't stop the tears that came. These days all she did was cry.

"I'm acting this way because I've never been in love like this, Junior. Hell, I don't think I knew what love was until I met Marcus. I know that everything that happened was my fault, but it's driving me crazy not being with him. I hate that he won't talk to me. That mess with Kendall meant nothing. I only did it to dangle in his face what he missed out on and to gain back the confidence he snatched away from me all those years ago. It took seeing him again to realize how much that betrayal really messed me up. I swear I never meant for things to go as far as they did," she sobbed.

"What's all that shit he was saying about you forgiving him and giving him another chance?" Junior questioned.

"I had to forgive him, Junior, so that I could move on with my life and with Marcus. I don't know where he came up with that other stuff. I never gave him any indication that we could be more than friends. The day that Dad confronted me, I was on my way to see him to let him know that we couldn't hang out anymore, but it

was too late because you ran into him the night before. I
know that seeing him behind Marcus's back was wrong,
and I really wish I hadn't even entertained it." She sniffed
remorsefully.

"I know you're going through a lot, sis. Just give him a
little more time. He'll come around," Junior said, trying
to reassure her. He only hoped what he was saying was
true, because it seemed to him that Marcus was done
with her. Junior just couldn't bring himself to hurt his
sister's feelings like that.

"You really think so?"

"Yeah, I do. And go put on some gotdamn clothes. I was
about to beat everybody's ass up in that shop for staring
at your damn-near-naked ass," he said, making her laugh.
"I'm serious. Shit ain't funny, Nichole," he said, glaring at
her.

"Brother, you know I have to really be going through
it for me to walk out the house looking like this. I'm just
glad Marcus wasn't here," she said, placing her hands
over her face in shame.

"I done already seen yo' li'l ass," Marcus said from
behind where they stood.

He pulled up just as Junior was dragging her out of
the shop, but they were so busy going back and forth that
they hadn't noticed him. He couldn't lie, his baby was
looking good. He had never seen her dressed like that,
and he was lightweight upset that anybody besides him
had the pleasure of seeing her that way.

The shoes she wore were sexy as hell, accentuating her
legs and calf muscles. Her thighs, stomach, and arms
were tight, toned, and looked silky smooth. It was as if
she'd just dipped her chocolate body in coconut oil or
some shit, and he could just imagine himself licking her
from head to toe. She was fresh faced with no makeup,
and her short hair was hooked up as usual. He had no

idea how he made it two whole months without touching her or seeing her beautiful face.

It was difficult, but he had to teach her ass a lesson. He wasn't some weak-ass nigga to be played with or taken for granted. He knew her well enough to know that nothing sexual had gone on with her and her ex, but that still didn't excuse her lying and sneaking around. When that nigga said that shit in that bar that night, it took every ounce of restraint he had not to kill him where he stood, but that man wasn't the person he had a problem with. The issue was with his woman, and that's who he planned to deal with. That man didn't owe him shit, but she did. All this time his suspicions had been dead-on. He recognized Kendall as the nigga he saw her talking to months ago while he was at the bank.

When Nikki's eyes met his, she suddenly felt naked and completely exposed. His eyes roamed her entire body, and as usual, it turned her on. She bit her bottom lip, attempting to hold in the sigh that threatened to escape from seeing his handsome face after months of being apart. Junior looked back and forth between them a few times before deciding it was time for him to move around. Mentally, they were fucking the shit out of each other, and it was too much for him.

"See you inside, boss," he said, shaking his head as he walked away.

"Marcus, I shouldn't have just popped up here today. I just needed to see you, but I realize you need your space right now. I'm sorry," she said sadly before turning to leave.

"Come here, Li'l Bit," he called after her. She paused and turned to face him, terrified of what he might say. Her fear kept her feet planted. "I said come here," he demanded. He pointed his finger, indicating to her where he wanted her to be, which was directly in front of him.

She moved slowly, and once she was where he wanted her, she looked up at him, timidly searching his eyes. Unfortunately, they gave her no indication of what he was feeling, so she was unsure if he still cared or if he was really done with her. His gaze was intense and penetrated her to her soul. Even if he told her right then and there that it was over and she didn't stand a chance with him, she couldn't leave there without telling him how she really felt about him.

"I love you, Marcus, and I'm sorry. I offer no excuses for the things I've done, but I hope that one day you'll be able to forgive me. It's just that—"

"You love me?" he quickly asked. Sometimes he thought she did, but others he wasn't so sure.

"I do. With all my heart, I do," she confessed. The sincere look in her eyes told him she was being honest.

"I love you too." He pulled her into him by the waistband of her shorts, smiling a genuine smile for the first time in a while.

He refused to make her sweat it out any longer after she spoke the three words he'd been waiting to hear for years. He could feel the wetness of her tears saturating his expensive shirt, but he didn't care. All he cared about was the woman he was holding in his arms.

He lifted her head from his chest and kissed her so deeply that she jumped up and wrapped her legs around his waist and her arms around his neck to effectively deepen the kiss. Feeling the heat from her center pressed against his stomach was just too much. He'd been doing okay with the "no sex" shit, but right now at that very moment, he was struggling. To know that she wanted him with this amount of urgency had his dick rising at light speed, so he felt they needed to bring things down a few notches before they did something that they would both end up regretting.

Finally getting a hold of himself, he removed his lips from hers. Stealing a few more pecks, he peeled her body from his before placing her back on solid ground.

"Sorry. I guess I got a little carried away," she said shyly. Carried away was an understatement. She about lost her mind when she felt his dick poking directly at her sex.

"I think we both did," he said as he adjusted his package in his jeans. "Look, we got a lot of shit we need to talk about, and I feel like I've put it off long enough. Our communication with each other fucking sucks, and since we have a hard time expressing ourselves, I think we should have someone help us out with it. Let me run in here, grab my stuff, and let Junior know that I'm gone for the day. I want you to meet me at my crib so we can talk."

"Okay, I'll be there when you get there," she said before pecking him on the lips once more. *God, if this man gives me another chance, please don't let me screw it up,* she prayed as she walked away.

He didn't make a move to go in the building because he was held captive watching her strut in those tiny-ass shorts as she made her way to her car. They would have to set some ground rules before they could go any further, and dress code was going to be at the top of the list. He wouldn't be able to contain his desire for her if she pranced around in anything remotely similar to what she was wearing right now. His feet didn't move until she pulled out of the parking lot and drove down the street. That's how long it took for his dick to go down and his heart rate and breathing to return to normal.

"Couples' counseling?" she asked, surprised.

"Yeah."

They were at his place sitting at the island in his massive kitchen discussing their future. Nikki had since changed into more appropriate clothes. She had some things stored in her drawer in his bedroom. Now she wore a pair of Nike sweats and a plain white tee. It took Marcus a moment to stop picturing her in the outfit she was wearing when he saw her at his shop earlier. That shit was going to be embedded in his memory forever.

"Is that really necessary? I feel like this is something we can work out on our own."

"If that were the case, we wouldn't be sitting here right now after being apart for over two months. It seems like every time I think we're moving in the right direction, something happens that sets us back," he said before taking a deep breath. "Li'l Bit, do you know that I want to fuckin' marry you? That's some shit I never wanted with anybody, but I want that with you," he revealed.

"I want that too, Marcus," she choked out through her tears. She wanted to be his wife more than anything in the world.

"But I'm not doing it if this is the kind of shit I have to look forward to. Most times I don't even know if you really even want to be with me. And you being dishonest and sneaking around with other niggas sho the fuck ain't gon' work. You know firsthand how I give it up. That ain't some shit somebody got to tell you because you done seen it with your own eyes. To have this man in front of me saying what the fuck he been doing with you and the plans y'all was making was like a slap to the face. I could have killed him with my bare hands. I mean what the fuck we been doing all this time, Nichole!" he shouted, getting angry all over again. The question he posed was one he'd been asking himself since all this shit went down. He thought they were building, but Kendall made it sound like her plan was to be with him all along.

She couldn't help but jump as his words echoed throughout the room. Her voice was shaky as she spoke. "I know how it seemed, but you have to believe me when I say that I never made plans like that with Kendall. I was wrong for seeing him, but I never gave him any ideas about us being together like that. I wouldn't do that to you, and you have to believe that," she pleaded.

"I don't have to believe a damn thing you say when your actions show me different," he snapped, causing her to tear up even more.

"You're right," she conceded dismally. She hated that what she'd done caused him to lose faith and trust in her, but what did she expect? "I still want you to know that the most we did was hug a few times. Nothing else happened, babe, I swear."

"He shouldn't have been able to touch you at all, Nichole," he said, shaking his head in annoyance. Just the thought of them having that little bit of contact had murder on his mind. Marcus was pissed that she'd just given him that visual.

"I know, and I swear to you it won't ever happen again," she promised.

"I love you, but I'm gon' be honest with you. That shit hurt me, and I'm having a really hard time moving past it. That's why I thought it would be best to get some outside help. If not, I'm not sure we're going to make it, baby," he finished with his head hung low. He didn't like feeling weak and insecure behind a woman. He normally had a "don't give a fuck" attitude when it came to the females in his life, but she made him fall in love with her, and his love for her was intense and at times all-consuming. So to have her betray him that way was difficult for a man like him to deal with.

Nikki felt like shit, because although she knew what she did pissed Marcus off, she had no clue how badly she'd actually hurt him until now. "Okay, I'll do it. At this point, I'll do anything for us to be able to work this out and be together. I'm in love with you, Marcus. Please don't question that. I've never loved anyone as much as I love you. You might have a hard time believing that because of how bad I messed things up, but it's true. From this day on I'm going to show you better than I could ever tell you. I'm sorry that I hurt you. I'm so sorry," she cried as she stood between his legs and wrapped her arms around his neck.

"I love you too, Li'l Bit," he said after a brief moment of silence. "I'll let you find a therapist for us so we can get our shit together," he said as he wiped her tears away.

"I'll get right on it. One of my coworkers mentioned someone she and her husband went to before they were married, and she's supposed to be really good. I'll give her a call and get the contact information," she said as she stood up. "Oh and I'd also like to apologize for showing up to the shop dressed the way I was earlier. I left home in such a hurry that I didn't think about what I was wearing until everyone was staring at me. That wasn't intentional, and I didn't mean to embarrass you."

"You didn't embarrass me, but please don't do that shit again. I don't want no other nigga seeing you that way. Especially if they were thinking the same things that I was when I first saw you in the parking lot. I swear fo' Gawd I'd have to fuck somebody up," he joked. She laughed, but she also knew that he was serious about what he was saying.

Chapter 19

Another day, another celebration. Tonight the clique gathered together to celebrate Amina's graduation. They had a small get-together for her last day at the shop a few weeks ago, but today's shindig had been a complete surprise to her. Junior had insisted on footing the bill for the party, and Marcus didn't argue with him. He knew his boy had the dough to make it happen, so he wasn't tripping.

Being that they were now good friends, Marcus knew all about the side hustle Junior had with his art. In fact, he'd sold a painting to a big collector out of Seattle a few weeks ago that brought him a nice amount of cash, and it was one of many that he'd recently sold. He was good and was only getting better. Marcus tried encouraging him to come clean with his family, but he still wasn't ready to do it. He wanted to remain low-key for as long as he could.

Junior rented out a small ballroom at a hotel in Arlington. Amina didn't kick it with too many people, so besides her best friend, Cree, and the employees from the shop, there were only a couple of aunts, her mother, and a few cousins. Everyone else in attendance was linked to Marcus or Junior in some way. Just because the guest list wasn't long didn't mean they didn't kick it hard though. The food was plentiful, and the variety of alcoholic beverages left the guests with tons of options.

Amina was happy to be done with school, and with Darius's disappearance she was finally able to enjoy life again. Her baby's father seemed to have vanished into thin air. Honestly, she didn't really give a damn where he was as long as he stayed away from her and her daughter. With him out of the picture she had even been out on a few dates and was getting back into the swing of things. Brielle was growing up beautifully and coming out of the shell she had been locked in for so long. Her baby girl was more outgoing and friendly these days, and she truly believed that Junior was the reason behind that.

Her eyes followed her crush as he directed caterers where to put more food. He had certainly bossed up since she first met him, and now he not only ran the Dallas shop but also traveled to Oklahoma where he managed the shop in the city. Because of his hard work, both shops were bringing in the most money of all five Smoove Ink locations, and she was so proud of him.

His eyes scanned the entire room, and she knew for a fact that he was looking for her. She was able to play it off well, but she had felt his eyes on her all night. When he located her, he smiled and nodded his head in her direction. She returned the gesture before making her way over to him. They had become good friends but still hadn't crossed the line and become involved with each other. He dated other women, and she was doing her thing as well. If she had a say in it, all that was about to change tonight.

"Fuck you smiling for?" he asked once she was standing in front of him. Amina was drop-dead gorgeous tonight. The sleeveless, thigh-length black dress she wore hugged every single one of her curves perfectly. Normally she wore her thick, natural hair in twists that hung down her back, but tonight she had them pulled up in a tight bun that rested on top of her head. She looked amazing, and several times throughout the night he found himself seeking her out from across the room so that he could just stare at her. He loved to see her happy and smiling, and she'd been grinning all night long, so his job was complete. Almost.

"What, I can't smile now?" she teased. *Junior is indeed a good-looking man,* she thought as she bit her bottom lip. Tonight his hair was wild and curly like she liked, and he was definitely dressed to impress. The black printed Roberto Cavalli shirt fit him perfectly as did the slim-fit Cavalli trousers he paired with it. Versace loafers graced his feet, and he opted to forgo the neck bling, wearing only his diamond-studded Versace watch.

"Sure you can. It's just the way yo' ass is smiling. Like you're up to something." He smirked.

"Who, me?" She feigned ignorance with her hand to her chest, making him laugh. "Seriously though, I just wanted to thank you for the party. This is so dope, Junior. I don't have many friends, but you sure made a girl feel loved tonight," she said appreciatively.

"That was the plan," he told her, looking her up and down.

"I did want to ask you something though," she said. This time she licked her ruby red lips. That move drew his attention back to her mouth.

"What's that?" he managed to say while his eyes stayed locked on her full lips. He couldn't wait to kiss her pretty ass. *She gotta know it's going the fuck down tonight,* he thought. The wait was officially over.

"Seeing as how I'm no longer an employee at Smoove Ink, I was wondering if you would like to go out with me," she asked in a sexy timbre while slowly inching closer into his personal space until her erect nipples grazed his chest. Her head was now tilted to the side as she stared boldly into his eyes, awaiting an answer.

Junior didn't bother responding verbally but placed his hand at the back of her neck to bring her closer before crashing his lips into hers. Soon their tongues were dueling, and the shit was so right that Amina damn near forgot who or where she was. His mouth alone was casting a spell on her, and if someone had asked her name right then, she probably wouldn't have been able to tell them what it was. When he finally pulled away, she was dizzy, and her panties were saturated. "I gue . . . I guess that means your answer is yes," she said breathlessly.

"Naw, my answer is fuck yes, baby," he replied before kissing her again.

Junior had planned on asking her out, but she'd beaten him to the punch. At this point, it really didn't matter to him who asked who as long as the shit was happening. He could finally be with her the way he wanted, and he'd have his boo Brielle, too. That little girl was his heart, and he truly loved her as if she were his blood. Even his family had fallen in love with her, with his sisters treating her as their niece and his parents acting as if they had their first granddaughter.

"You mu'fuckas ain't waste no time, huh?" Marcus crept up, catching them off guard.

"Sup, boss man," Junior said, grinning from ear to ear.

"I see your fast ass wasn't bullshittin' when you said you was gon' go for what you know," he said, focused on Amina.

"Bro! I swear I'm not telling you shit else!" She rolled her eyes playfully at Marcus.

"Don't be like that. I ain't gon' tell no more of your secrets," he said, making her laugh. "Come on so you can open up your gifts," he said, leading them to a table on the other side of the room that was overflowing with presents.

"This is just too much," Amina gasped as she opened up another one of her many gifts a short time later. Her friends had gone all out for her special day. She had cash, designer shoes, bags, and even a gift certificate to purchase a whole new wardrobe for work. That one came from Marcus. All of the gifts were nice, amazing even, but it was the final gift that had her in tears and ruining her MAC makeup. Junior presented her with a portrait he'd done of her and Brielle. He had to have taken a picture of them when they weren't paying attention and used that as a reference. She couldn't believe he'd done it off of memory alone. Crazy thing was, that was exactly how it happened. He didn't need a photograph to recreate the image he had of them in his mind. Whatever the case was, she thought he'd done an incredible job, and the detail and accuracy of the picture had her at a loss for words. Brielle's big honey brown eyes, which matched her own, shined brightly, and her chubby legs were just too perfect. She'd seen some of his other paintings and drawings, but in her eyes, this was by far the best.

She really couldn't find the words to express her gratitude to him not only for this special gift but also for all he had done for her and Bri. There were times he would take care of Brielle when she needed to do homework or study, and on occasion when she was dead tired from all she had going on, he would come through to scoop the baby so that she could get some rest. Nicholas Grant Jr. was amazing in every way, and she finally had him exactly where she wanted him. Still unable to speak, she thanked him the only way she could, and that was with a kiss that she probably should have given him behind closed doors.

After she released him, he said the magic word. "Damn!"

It was safe to say he'd gotten the point.

"I let Bri paint this one for you when she was at the house with me a few weeks ago," Junior said, handing her a much smaller painting that held nothing more than splashes of different colors with her daughter's hand- and footprints embedded, but it was beautiful because her baby made it just for her.

Amina had never felt more special than she did tonight, and as she looked around, she realized that all the people in the banquet hall had helped her in some way or another since she met them, but her former bosses Marcus and Junior had both gone above and beyond. She had long ago stopped feeling bad about accepting help from others because she believed that God placed this particular group of people in her life for that very reason, and she was grateful for them.

"Junior, that picture is amazing. You are so awesome, and I love you," Nikki said as she embraced her brother. His parents and older sister, along with her sister's husband, walked over to join them.

"Thanks, Nik Nak. Love you too." He smiled.

"Yes, baby. It's just beautiful," his mother complimented him as she hugged him first then turned to hug Amina. Christine Grant was claiming this beauty as her daughter-in-law already. In her opinion, she was just perfect for Junior, and a mother knows, honey.

His father waited until everyone had sung their praises before he finally approached his only son. "Nicholas, I'm proud of you, son. You really do great work," he said.

"Thanks, Dad. That means a lot to me."

"So, why have you been keeping this to yourself for so long?" he wanted to know.

"Keeping what to myself? You know I've been into painting and drawing since I was a kid," Junior replied, trying to make light of it.

"I do know that, but that's not what I'm talking about. I'm referring to the whole Leo Grant thing," his father said, putting him on blast.

Junior's eyes damn near bugged out of his head when his father mentioned the pseudonym he used for his artwork. He simply dropped his first name and used his middle and last name. As far as his family went, Nichole was the only one he told about his art. She and Brielle were the only ones to ever set foot in the studio he had in his condo. His parents only recently learned of the condo he'd owned for over three years. He hated being so secretive, but he didn't feel like answering questions about why he would come live with them when he had a big place of his own. They were probably already curious about how he managed to drive a luxury car and stay dressed in designer clothes even before coming to work for Marcus. It was no secret that up until then he could hardly keep a job.

"I just didn't want to make a big deal out of it. I enjoy it, but I'm not really trying to be out there like that. Not yet anyway. I'm able to have fun with it and make a little money in the process. Flying under the radar is how I want to play it for now," he informed his father. "How did you find out anyway?"

"One day you kids will learn that you won't be able to keep anything from me. Always want to know how I know what the hell I know," he fussed, making everyone laugh. "Seriously, son, I understand what you're trying to say, and I respect it. I don't ever want you to feel like you can't tell me what's going on in your life. Just like I look forward to celebrating your sisters' accomplishments with them, I want to do the same with you. Be so damn happy, folk would think I was the one who painted that shit," he joked as more laughter ensued. "Just know that you can always come to me, Nicholas," he assured him.

It seemed his son didn't want him to interfere in what he had going on with his art. He probably knew that his father would spread the word, and soon everyone would know about his talented son the artist and he'd be in high demand. With his connections in the entertainment industry as well as here in Dallas, his father would send anyone and everyone his way to make sure his son's pockets stayed plump. After all the exposure that his parents could bring him, the galleries along with everybody and they mama would be after him, and he knew his son well enough to know that he didn't need or want to be in the limelight. He was chill and liked living a low-key life. Nicholas Grant could do nothing but respect his son's wishes.

"Thank, Pops," he replied as his father hugged him. It felt good to have everything out in the open. Now all he had to do was wait for the night to be over so he could tend to his unfinished business with Ms. Amina. Tonight he had to tell her the truth.

"Uhh, Nicholas!" she moaned loudly as her entire body vibrated with pleasure. She'd always imagined that sex with him was going to be good, but this shit here, this shit here was extraordinary.

"What is it, baby?" he asked as he slowly stroked her. "Talk to me," he coaxed. He absolutely loved communicating verbally with his partner during sex, and he wanted to hear every single word Amina had to say tonight.

Her mind was so jumbled from the long overdue beating he was putting on her pussy that his name was all she could get out. "Nicholasss," she whimpered when he hit her spot.

"I love the way you say that shit," he groaned as his warm breath tickled her neck, adding to the extreme pleasure she was experiencing. Her pussy was so damn tight, and the depth of her tunnel had him sprung from the first stroke. He licked and bit her neck some before he spoke again. "Say it again, Amina. My name, love, shiittt say it again," he begged as he continued digging her out. He noticed her voice was raspier when they made love, and traces of the accent she shed years before could be heard, elevating the level of sexy like ten notches for him.

"Junior, baby, wait! Ooh, fuck," she called out. His stroke game was just too much, and he had her feeling all kinds of shit at once.

"Wrong fucking name," he chastised as he began pounding into her relentlessly, causing her to scream out louder. He planned to continue his assault on her pussy until she said what he wanted to hear.

"Nicholas! Nicholasss, please!" she pleaded as she wrapped her juicy legs around his waist, allowing him to dig even deeper. She could feel what was sure to be a powerful orgasm building, and this one was going to be life changing, even better than the first two she had when he blessed her with the best head of her life.

"There you go, baby. That's what I wanted to hear," he praised her as he switched back to his slow grind. He kissed her passionately, bringing her that nut she was desperately searching for, prompting her to howl and cry out in pure ecstasy. She never missed a beat, continuing to milk him and meet him stroke for stroke. It wasn't long before he detonated, spilling his seeds into the condom. "Goddamn, Amina! That shit was so . . . so . . . umm . . ." he stammered. He lost his train of thought while attempting to catch his breath.

"So damn good," she said, finishing the sentence for him in between breaths.

"That's it," he laughed as he rolled over, pulling her thick body next to him so that she could nestle her face in his neck.

Amina ended up screaming his name at least a hundred more times that night. All she knew was she was never calling his ass Junior again, because every time she yelled out his government name he went sicker and sank into her deeper. Nicholas was a fool with the dick, and she enjoyed every second of their lovemaking. Tonight they had a room at the W, and they'd been rumbling in the sheets ever since they made it in from her party. Brielle was with her mother for the weekend, so this room and this bed were where she planned to remain with her man until checkout time come Sunday morning.

Resisting being with Amina all this time had taken a great deal of restraint on Junior's part, and he was glad that the wait was finally over. And boy was it worth it. He fell in love with her body as soon as the last stitch of her clothing had been removed. He didn't know if he expected her to be self-conscious because she was what society deemed overweight, but the fact that she wasn't turned him on. He'd been with more women with low self-esteem and body-image issues than he cared to admit, so maybe he did expect it. Thin women with the bodies of supermodels still seemed to find something wrong with themselves. Or there were the ones who were on the juicier side and were uncomfortable with their weight but did nothing but complain about it. Ask her to hit the gym with you and her ass would look at you like you slapped her mama or some shit. It didn't matter one way or the other to him, but his thing was if you didn't like something about yourself, change it or shut the fuck up. When it all boiled down to it, he was fucking either way. For him, as long as a female looked decent, was confident, and kept up her appearance, he could get with it.

Amina was a beautiful girl, but her confidence was what he had been attracted to from the start, and that it wasn't just a front and she was actually comfortable in her own skin had him loving her even more. When he undressed her with all the lights on, not once did she shy away or cover up. She bared it all and granted him the time he needed to take in her beauty and appreciate every inch of her. And appreciate her he did. In fact, he appreciated her beautiful ass all weekend long.

Before they got to the intimate part of the night, he told her that he had something very important that he wanted to talk to her about. His tone and the seriousness of his expression scared her at first, and she was unsure if she even wanted to know what he had to say. "It's about Darius," he said, not knowing how she would take what he was about to say. All he knew was that he couldn't go there with her or move forward in their relationship until he came clean about everything. Telling her after they fucked seemed like some snake shit. He wanted her to know beforehand just in case she wanted to opt out of being with him. Junior didn't feel bad about what went down because it was literally her and Brielle's lives or that nigga's. Without question, he chose them.

"What about him?"

"He ain't ever coming back," he replied, hoping she could read between the lines. Junior's face showed no emotion or regret. He didn't feel anything when it came to the man, so it was fitting.

"You killed him?" she asked with the same amount of emotion his voice held: none.

"That was the plan, but it didn't exactly work out that way," he said truthfully before going on to explain.

They'd caught Darius slipping as he made his rounds around town, stalking her. Junior, along with Marcus and Big B, wasted no time snatching him up. Finding the kill kit in the trunk along with a suicide note sealed her baby daddy's fate. According to the letter, he planned to take himself out after killing Amina and his own daughter. Since the nigga had plans to end his life anyway, they helped him do it the Joe Clark way: expeditiously. Only thing was that he wouldn't be taking Amina and Bri with him.

Following his confession, Junior looked into her eyes, awaiting her reaction. He had no idea what she was thinking at that moment. He didn't think Amina had feelings for dude, but he was her daughter's father, so she might feel a way about Junior and Marcus being involved in his disappearance and death.

Before Junior's admission, Amina's gut told her Darius was dead. A few times Junior and Marcus slipped up and spoke of her baby's father in the past tense, like they knew he was no longer among the living. Plus, there was no way that he was alive and not coming around to bother her. He once told her that death was the only thing that would separate them, so she figured that he'd somehow met his Maker.

"Thank you," she said before throwing her arms around his neck and slipping her tongue into his mouth. She knew better than anyone that Darius would have never stopped until she was dead, and if she'd had the courage to do it, she would have killed him herself. Because she had a good man who wanted to protect her, she didn't have to worry about getting her hands dirty. For his chivalry, he was rewarded with the best loving he'd ever had in his life.

Chapter 20

"I hope whoever you found is good and knows what the hell they talking about," Marcus fussed as he drove them to their appointment.

"Trust me, I did my research on this one. I couldn't take the chance of the situation that happened last time happening again," Nikki said, rolling her eyes to the sky.

"Let that shit go, Nichole. We've argued about it enough. There was no way I could have known that shit," he told her for the last damn time. If she brought that shit up again, her ass was getting thrown out of the car. She knew not to push further, so she just huffed and folded her arms across her chest like a kid. She didn't dare say another word though.

This afternoon they were on their way to couples counseling. Actually, this was their second attempt since the first was a complete disaster. Going to see the therapist that was suggested by her co-worker turned out to be a mistake. As soon as they walked into her plush downtown office and Dr. Evan's and Marcus made eye contact, Nikki felt the tension mount.

"We gotta go see someone else," Marcus said immediately and started moving backward toward the door.

"But why? They say she's the best there is," Nikki asked, not understanding what was going on. When she turned and caught the look Dr. Evans was giving Marcus, she got the answer to her question. "Shit, you slept with her, didn't you?" she asked, looking back and forth between

*him and the doctor. It never failed. Not even relation-
ship counselors were safe around Smoove. What were
the odds that she'd signed them up to see someone her
man had smashed? Nikki couldn't believe her luck.*

*While reviewing the paperwork of her newest clients
the night before, Dr. Evans came across his name and
hoped that it was really him. They began sleeping
together years ago when she was doing grief counseling,
and she helped him through the tough time he was
having after his family members had been killed. She
ended up helping him in more ways than one. He was
even more handsome now than he was back then, and
she also remembered how great he was in bed. Marcus
Tate wasn't the first client Dr. Katrina Evans had
fucked, and he wouldn't be the last. He was definitely the
most memorable. She just hoped that seeing her today
would spark memories of how good it was when they
got together, and just maybe for old times' sake he'd
want to do it again. Sure, she was supposed to help fix
whatever was going on with him and his little girlfriend,
and being the multitasker she was, she had no problem
doing that too.*

*"Li'l Bit, that shit was years ago, so don't even start,"
he warned her.*

*"Look, Ms. Grant, I'm a professional, and he's right. It
was years ago. I can still help you two if you let me. I can
do my job properly without letting past relationships
get in the way of that," she tried to assure Nikki.*

*Marcus was about to ask her if she was fucking crazy,
but his lady spoke up first. "No offense, Doc, but that's
not about to happen. We'll find someone else," she said,
looking up at Marcus. As usual, Marcus felt like he had
done something wrong. He just shook his head at Nikki
and turned to walk out. It seemed that he couldn't win
for losing with her.*

"It was good seeing you again, Marcus," Dr. Evans called out behind them.

Her seductive tone caused Nikki to stop dead in her tracks. This lady was really trying her today. Dr. Evans's sneaky ass wasn't fooling nobody. First, she looked at her man like she wanted to jump his bones as soon as they walked through the door, and now she was outright flirting with him. Hell no! "Lady, you must want me to slap that silly smirk off your face," Nikki threatened as she began making her way back into the office to give the harlot a piece of her mind and her hands. Before she made it to her, Marcus grabbed around her waist from behind.

"Baby, let's just go." He couldn't have his woman out here acting crazy behind some looney-ass doctor. It took him threatening her license for her to leave him alone last time, and he didn't want anything to do with her ass. He was twenty-two years old when they met, and he was going through a difficult time in his life. One minute he was laid up on the couch in her office, spilling his guts about his life, and the next he looked up to find her butt-ass naked, perched on her desk. Being the player he was at the time, he gave her exactly what she wanted, and he did so each and every time they had a session. It came to a point that he no longer felt she was helping him with his real issues, so he found another doctor. It was safe to say that Dr. Evans had a hard time letting go.

In the car after they left her office that day, he'd told Nikki all about his previous involvement with the doctor. She couldn't believe that someone who was supposed to be helping people through their problems would be so careless. To sleep with someone who was emotionally damaged and dependent on you to assist them with moving through their issues was just plain sick in Nikki's opinion, and she wanted to do something about it. The lady needed to be stripped of her credentials, but Marcus begged her to let it go. It was in the past, and he just wanted to focus on their future. His voice brought her back to the present.

"Stop pouting and kiss me," he ordered after parking in front of the beautiful glass building that housed multiple doctors' offices. She smiled and leaned into him for a quick peck.

"I'm sorry, babe," Nikki apologized. "I just hate that that crazy-ass lady has already had something that I want. Something that I need, Marcus," she whispered seductively against his ear. She had been on her man hard trying to get him to give in and agree to have sex, but he wasn't having it. Being married first was no longer important to her, but for some reason to Marcus, it was.

"Nichole, we already talked about this, and we're going to do this shit the right way," he stressed as he tried not to focus on the stiffening and lengthening of his mans down below. Her sexy voice and breath on his face and neck was wreaking havoc on his willpower.

Lately, Nikki had been on some straight bullshit and was trying her best to make him fold under the pressure. Little did she know, he prayed for the strength to resist her ass damn near ten times per day. First, she started with the clothes. Around the house when they were chilling, she would put on the tiniest shit, which would have him salivating at the mouth like a rabid dog. When they worked out in his home gym, she made it her business to wear the skimpiest workout gear, and he could hardly focus for picturing himself licking every drop of sweat from her body. When her attempts to seduce him with her body didn't work, she came right out and told him that she wanted to fuck. She felt that since they were planning to get married someday, it didn't matter if they had sex now or later, but he didn't agree. He hated that she felt he was only doing this for her. His decision to abstain was just as much for himself as it was for her, but she was too self-absorbed to see it.

They had just left their third session with Dr. Wortham and were both in deep thought as Marcus drove down 75 headed to Allen. It was couples' night, but neither of them seemed to be in the mood to hang with their friends. So far, seeing Dr. Wortham had been an eye-opening experience for the both of them. They'd learned a lot about one another and about themselves in the last three months, and although working through their problems was hard, it also brought them closer together.

Nikki would always end up apologizing to Marcus every time they left counseling because she would realize another mistake she'd made or problem that she had somehow caused in their relationship. It wasn't that Marcus was perfect and didn't make any mistakes, but a majority of their issues stemmed from something she did or said. She spent all that time not giving Marcus a chance because she thought him to be a player who was only out to break her heart, but she was the one who ended up emotionally cheating on him. She pushed him away because she didn't think he would be down to wait until marriage for sex, but now she was constantly pressuring him into it. All this time she thought they weren't having sex because he wanted to be a gentleman and make their first night as husband and wife special. Today she realized that Marcus was doing this for himself as well, and she hated that she hadn't been listening to a thing he'd been trying to tell her.

"Baby, you know we can head back to my place or yours tonight. We don't have to do this couples' thing if you don't want to," he said, grabbing her hand. As usual, she had been quiet since leaving Dr. Wortham's office.

"No, I want to go. I was just sitting here thinking of some of the things we talked about today, and I feel so bad," she pouted.

"There is nothing for you to feel bad about. That's why we're going to counseling in the first place. So that we both can do better," he reassured her.

She had changed a lot over the last few months. He noticed her starting to pay more attention to his feelings and not just her own. On top of that, she was courting the hell out of him. He hated to seem like a sucker, but he really enjoyed that shit. Special gifts, notes, and sweet texts telling him how much she loved and appreciated him made him feel like he was important to her. She was doing for him what he'd always done for her, and it felt nice to no longer question how she felt.

Nikki spent her entire life being pampered and catered to by everyone around her, and she wasn't really used to having to do that for her man. Like many women, she didn't realize that not only did she have to show her man she cared, but she needed to tell him as well. It's important that men, as well as women, be lifted up and told how their partner feels about them. Her doing that for him improved their relationship a great deal.

"I know, but I do want to tell you that I'm sorry for the way I've been behaving with the whole sex issue. I never even bothered to ask you the real reason you wanted to wait. I always assumed that you were only doing it because it was what I wanted in the beginning," she admitted.

"I know, Li'l Bit, and it's cool. When you first came at me about you being a virgin, I had no problem waiting because I wanted to be with you. All the reasons you gave me for wanting to wait became my reasons. Then I started reading some of the books in your library on celibacy, and after educating myself, I made a promise not only to you but to God and myself as well. It became a big deal and something that's important to me. So big that I fucked up and told Jakobi about it. His childish ass had all the homies calling me a born-again virgin and shit." He laughed and so did she. "But seriously, the way you were passionate about it when we first hooked up is what inspired me to see this thing through. I get the same urges as you, and I know how hard it can be, but we can do it," he assured her.

"I know we can, baby," she agreed.

"I won't lie, I didn't think I was gonna make it when yo li'l ass was walking around the house half naked though. You almost broke a nigga down," he admitted.

"I shouldn't have done that to you. I'm such a horrible person," she giggled while hanging her head in faux shame. She was going all out with her plan of seduction, and he turned her down each time. Nikki tried to figure out where along the line she lost herself and began to disregard her morals and the vow she made to God. This exact scenario reversed was what kept her from giving Marcus a chance in the beginning. It had happened many times with men she was dating, and now she was doing the same thing to him.

"It's all good. You're lucky I didn't go through with my plan to get your ass back." He smirked.

"Exactly what were you planning to do, Mr. Tate?" she asked, eyeing him curiously.

"I was gon' walk around the house butt-ball naked all day right in front of your ass," he said and fell out laughing.

She didn't laugh with him because she was too busy imagining his naked body. She had never seen him completely naked, and she couldn't wait until the day that she could. They slept in the same bed together, but both dressed very modestly so as to not tempt the other.

When she was trying to seduce him with the sexy clothes, he stayed away from her place and refused to let her come over to stay the night with him until she promised to stop playing games.

"Girl, get your mind out the fucking gutter," he teased, snapping her back to reality. He could only imagine what she was thinking right now.

"Whew, my bad," she said, fanning herself as they walked up to his brother's front door.

Marcus only shook his head and grinned because he had a feeling that once they were married and he was giving her the dick on the regular, she was going to be a problem. When they kissed, her passion and neediness couldn't be missed. Marcus believed that very same passion would translate in the bedroom, and he couldn't wait to awaken that inner freak he knew lay dormant inside the soon-to-be Nichole Tate.

"Ump, now whose mind is in the gutter?" She laughed and wrapped her arms around his waist as he rang the doorbell.

"Hey, lovebirds," Alana said as she opened up to find her brother-in-law and her friend all hugged up. She never thought these two would actually get it together, but she sure had prayed for it. Tonight was going to be so awesome.

"Hey, sis," Marcus said, hugging her.

"Hey, boo," Nikki said, getting her hug in as well.

"Come on in. The crew is in the den," Alana told them.

"Uncle!" screamed Kiyarah as she ran full speed at Marcus.

"Hey, YaYa," he said as he scooped his baby up in his arms to kiss her forehead. His youngest nephew was coming his way as well. "Kash Money, what's up, my man?"

"Wussup, Unc," he said coolly, making everyone laugh. It seemed he'd been spending a lot of time with his big brother, Gavin. Kash had to be the coolest three-year-old he knew, and he was no longer considered a tittie baby. Jakobi had effectively broken him from that crybaby shit, and he was enjoying being called a big boy by everyone.

"Unc, what's good," Gavin spoke as he exited the kitchen, wearing baller shorts and a beater while smashing a big-ass bowl of cereal.

"Damn, G, you gotta slow down! Yo' ass done grew a few inches since last week. I can't have you getting taller than me, nephew." Marcus smiled as he did the guy handshake and shoulder bump thing with his nephew. This right here was what he lived for: family. Alana coming back into his brother's life was the best thing that ever happened to him. Not only did she make his brother the happiest man on the planet, but she blessed them with these three awesome children, and because of her, he met his best friend and soul mate. Nikki was the love of his life, and he couldn't wait to officially make her his.

"Okay, li'l ones, come on up to my room with me," Gavin spoke to his younger siblings. Of course, Kiyarah wasn't feeling going upstairs and wanted to stay by her Uncle Marcus. "Come on, YaYa. I'll let you play some games on my computer," he told his baby sister. That was all it took to convince her to go upstairs with him. He was getting paid a hundred bucks to keep the twins occupied while his parents hosted couples' night, and he wasn't trying to have his pay docked because they didn't want to act right. Kelsey's children would normally be in the mix as well, which would have doubled his pay, but they were on vacation with their grandparents until next week.

Nikki sat curled up in Marcus's lap, cracking up laughing. They were in the family room playing a card game called Black Card Revoked, and of course, the clown of the group had everyone dying laughing. His goofy, ghetto behind had answered every question correctly while adding his hilarious commentary and effectively securing a win for the men. Marcus had always been able to make her laugh until she was snorting and her sides ached something terrible. She didn't even know humor was something she needed in a man until she met him.

"Don't ever question my blackness," he said, making them laugh some more. "Y'all laughing and I'm dead ass," he added before kissing his woman sweetly on the cheek. Taking it a step further, Nikki offered up her lips to him, and when they finally came together for a kiss, it seemed as if no one else existed, and that was fine by them. At this particular moment in time, everything was all right in their world.

"Marry me, baby," she whispered against his lips. This was nothing new. Everyone in the room had heard her ask him that question plenty of times, but she didn't care. She kept right on asking and planned to keep on until he said yes. She wasn't embarrassed at all. This was the man she loved, and she wanted to be his wife. It was as simple as that to her.

"A'ight," he answered with a nonchalant shrug.

"For real?" She pulled back and looked into his eyes excitedly.

"Naw, girl," he answered jokingly. He hated to shoot her down again, but there was no way he was going to let his baby propose to him.

"You make me sick, dude," she pouted as she lightly pushed against his chest. "I'm going to break you down, Marcus Tate. Mark my words," she said, standing.

"Where you going, bae?" He looked up to her, still holding on to her hand.

"To the restroom. I'll be right back," she said before leaning down to kiss his lips once more.

"Fuck, I almost said yes for real that time," he said once she was out of the room. The crew cracked up laughing at that.

Nikki was only gone for about five minutes, but when she returned, the room had been cleared, with Marcus the only one remaining. He sat on the edge of the chaise waiting for her, and he seemed to be in deep thought. "Where did everyone go?" she asked.

"I think they went out back." He shrugged.

"Out back? What for?"

"Hell, I don't know, Li'l Bit. I'm just sitting here waiting on yo' ass," he replied, fake annoyed.

"Come on, rudeness," she snapped back while reaching for his hand so that they could join their friends outside. Marcus released her hand just as she stepped onto the veranda. It was pitch-dark out, and her friends were nowhere in sight. "Babe, no one is even out here," she said, turning to face him.

On cue, the backyard lit up due to the many rows of decorative hanging string lights. Nikki looked around and found herself surrounded by countless vases of pink roses, which were her favorite. They were literally everywhere. Marcus was on bended knee as Hi-Five's "Unconditional Love" played in the background.

I will climb the highest peak
Swim the deepest sea
I will cross the desert land
I would do anything for your love, yeah

By the time it sank into her mind what was happening, Nikki could barely see Marcus for the tears clouding her eyes, but she did feel him take hold of her hand.

"Li'l Bit, from the moment I met you, I knew there was something special about you, and it didn't take me long to realize that you were the woman I needed in my life. Of course, you thought otherwise and refused to give in to me." He laughed and so did she. "So instead of becoming my woman like I wanted, you became my best friend and someone I knew I couldn't live without. You made me work hard to gain your trust and capture your heart, and I'm so glad that you did, because it makes me appreciate what we have that much more. Over the last few years, we've been through a lot with our friendship as well as our relationship. We've tackled some rough stuff, but we made it through, and that's why I'm confident that we can make it through anything else that may come our way. So I'm asking you to continue this journey with me as my wife. Make my dream a reality by becoming my wife. Marry me, baby," he proposed, opening the pink ring box.

Nikki kept her eyes glued to his and didn't even bother looking at the ring. She didn't really give a damn what it looked like or how many carats it held. All she cared about was giving him his answer. "Of course I'll marry you, Marcus Tate. I love you," she said, smiling brighter than she had ever smiled before with her deep dimples on full display. With her hands touching the sides of his face, she bent down and planted a kiss on him that damn near knocked him on his ass. "I told you I would break your ass down," she said against his lips, making him laugh.

"You remember when I put my number in your phone that night at my brother's house?" he reminded her as he stood.

"I do."

"You remember what name I saved my number under in your phone?"

"Yes, and to this day I've never changed it," she admitted as tears flowed from her eyes.

"So, it's safe to say that I'm the one who broke you down. I didn't know how the fuck I was going to pull it off, but I was determined to make you my wife. Thank you for making me the happiest nigga on the planet, Li'l Bit," he said before kissing her again as more tears spilled from her eyes.

Their tender moment was broken up by applause, and she looked up to see everyone who was important to her standing around with tears in their eyes. Her immediate family was there along with her close friends. Even Eric had shown up with his new boo, Denny, to share in their special moment. He'd done well in rehab over the last few months but was still dealing with the emotional damage left behind due to his mother's and Rae's actions. Nikki was glad that her friend had someone who cared for him by his side to help him through it.

"Congratulations, baby girl," her father said as he wrapped her up in a tight hug.

"Thank you, Daddy," she gushed.

"Marcus, job well done, son," he said, shaking his hand. This was going to be a hard one for Nicholas Grant. Turning the love and care of his darling Nikki over to another man was difficult to digest, but he had no doubt that his daughter was in good hands. Plus, he'd had plenty of time to prepare, since Marcus had asked for her hand back when they hooked up the first time.

"Thank you, sir," Marcus said, blowing out a breath of relief.

After giving her family a chance to congratulate them, her best friends rushed her for a group hug and a celebration of their own.

"Boo, I'm so damn happy for y'all," Kelsey said, wiping tears from her eyes.

"Thank you for making my brother happy," Alana said as she embraced her.

"Thank you both for being great friends to me. I know I was stubborn and made so many mistakes where Marcus is concerned, but you two stayed down with me through it all. I swear this man is the best thing that ever happened to me," she told them as she made eye contact with Marcus, who was being congratulated by his boys. He mouthed to her that he loved her, and she repeated the same to him.

Chapter 21

"I don't want to wait too much longer to get married, Marcus. It's like everything I thought I wanted has drastically changed. Certain things that I thought were nonnegotiable for my wedding day have suddenly become insignificant. It's about you and me, nothing else. I'd honestly be content going down to the courthouse and doing it that way," Nikki said to her fiancé.

"Your moms would have a heart attack if we did that shit, Nichole. Hell, I believe your daddy would too," Marcus joked. "Did you see how happy they were when I proposed the other night?"

"Yes, babe, I recall," she pouted as she browsed through a table lined with colorful skinny jeans in Macy's. She and Marcus were partaking in their favorite pastime: shopping. "Maybe we can do something small then. That way, everyone is happy in the end. Mama will get to do her planning, Daddy will get to walk me down the aisle, and I'll become Mrs. Tate, which is all I want out of this whole thing," she said seriously. "Is that okay with you or did you want to do something big? Because if that's what you want, I'll do that for you. I understand that this is your day too, and it's not just about what I want." Nikki didn't want to assume that he was cool with what she had in mind.

"Look at you," he teased. He loved that she was taking into consideration what he wanted. She could be all about herself at times, but she was getting better. "I think

I can get with the small thing, but only if you let me plan it. I'll get ya moms to help so that she won't feel left out."

"Are you serious? You want to plan our wedding?" she asked in disbelief.

"I do. Since I met you I've had this recurring dream of the day we got married, and I want to use the images in my head to plan our big day," he told her. She was already cheesing hard, so he knew his confession pleased her.

"Okay, you can do it, but I'm giving you three months to put it together, or we're going to the justice of the peace. I refuse to wait any longer than that, Marcus," she said straight up. Just that quick she was back to being spoiled and getting her way.

"You think you're slick, Li'l Bit. You just trying to hurry up and get married so you can get this dick!" he said while gripping himself, causing her to fall out laughing. Back when they first met, she would have gotten on his case for saying something like that, but she was used to his filthy mouth and playfulness now.

"Oh, I'm most definitely looking forward to getting that dick," she countered, triggering wide-eyed laughter from him. She knew saying that in her proper voice was going to tickle him. "Seriously though, babe. It's just that I love you so much and I can't wait to be your wife. You are who I've waited for all my life, and you are who I want more than anything or anybody. More than an extravagant wedding. More than some luxurious honeymoon in some exotic location. I only want you, Marcus," she expressed to him, her words heartfelt and honest. Her declaration of love moved him, and it showed all over his face.

"I can do it in a month," he said quickly. "Find your dress, and we'll be married thirty days from today. I just want you too, baby," he whispered in her ear with his arms wrapped tightly around her. To know that she felt the same for him as he did for her made him the happiest man alive, and whatever she wanted was what he would do. His sole purpose in life had become to make her smile and keep her happy. If all she wanted was to be his wife, he'd make that happen for her.

She suddenly broke away from him and started acting a fool. "Whoop! Thirty more days until I get that dick," she cheered while humping the air in the middle of the crowded department store. Folks were looking at her like she had lost her mind, but she didn't give a damn. By the time Marcus was able to stop laughing at the way she was carrying on, his face was wet with tears. He had clearly rubbed off on her, because she was becoming too damn silly. She walked back over to him and used her palms to dry his face. "I love you so much, Smoove."

"I love you more, Li'l Bit." After a quick kiss, they continued with their shopping.

"Nichole?" a male voice called from behind them as they made their way through the cookware section. She and Marcus turned at the same time to find Kendall standing there with a confused look on his face.

"Uhh, hey. What's up," she answered, instinctively grabbing Marcus's hand. She hadn't talked to him since she blocked him from calling her phone a while back.

"Not too much," he replied before turning to her friend. "How you doing, man? I'm Kendall, and you are?" he asked the man standing with Nichole like he had every right to know. He recognized dude from the bar the night he ran into Junior and was being petty by pretending he'd never seen him before.

Marcus knew that this square-ass nigga knew exactly who he was, and he wasn't about to stand there playing games with him. He simply looked down at the man's extended hand and back up to his face with a serious mean mug. Kendall arrogantly shrugged it off.

Sensing her man was about to knock Kendall out, she moved to stand in front of him, with her back to him. Naturally, he wrapped his arms around her waist. "Kendall, this is Marcus, my fiancé," she said happily.

"Fiancé?" Kendall asked, shocked.

"Yes, we're getting married next month." She beamed as she watched his face contort in anger. Her goal wasn't to make him jealous. She was just happy was all. In one month she would be Mrs. Nichole Elise Tate.

"Married?" he scoffed.

"Yeah, nigga, married," Marcus finally spoke up. This clown was really starting to piss him off, repeating her words like her marrying him was that unbelievable.

"Well, I'm just trying to figure out how your fiancée went from kicking it with me to getting married to you next month," he challenged.

"Kicking it? Kendall, we went out to eat a few times, and that was months ago. Marcus already knows about it, so what do you call yourself trying to do?" she asked heatedly. Was he really standing here trying to tattle on her? Ol' lying, corny, wack ass. He was behaving like a bitter side bitch, and if she weren't so mad, she would have thought it was funny.

"I'm just trying to understand what kind of game you're playing, Nichole. You had me thinking we were working things out, and then you just dropped off the face of the earth," he complained. He had no idea what had occurred that caused her to stop communicating with him, but seeing her here with this man gave him an idea. She told him upfront that she was involved with someone, but he thought maybe things had ended seeing as how she was spending time with him. Now Kendall understood why dude stormed out of the bar that night wearing a murderous scowl. By sharing the news of his reunion with Nikki, he had inadvertently outed her as a cheater to her man, but it seemed he had since gotten over it.

Marcus had officially heard enough. "Man, look here, there ain't shit you can tell me about my woman that I don't already fucking know. I don't give a fuck about no ho-ass lunch dates or whatever the fuck you thought was gon' happen with y'all. What I do know is that this one right here is all me, all fucking day, until the day I gotdamn die! Fuck what you heard," he said, possessively tightening his hold on her. "After today, ain't no need for you to call her, text her, or even speak to her when you see her out and about. If you can't get with that, then you gon' have to see me, and believe me, you do not want that. May as well kill yo'self right now," Marcus spat angrily. He never planned to come for this nigga, but since he wanted to flex, it was on. All he needed was an excuse. If he contacted Nikki one time after today, it would be a wrap for his wack ass.

"Come on, babe, let's go," Nikki said, pulling him away from Kendall before things got out of control. She didn't even bother saying good-bye. There was no need to, and she prayed that he took heed of Marcus's warning.

"You good?" she asked once they were alone. For a minute he didn't speak, and she thought maybe he was upset with her.

"I'm cool, baby. Gimme a kiss," he said as they exited the store and entered the actual mall. She gladly offered up her lips to him, unaware that Kendall watched from the upper level with pure jealousy.

Kendall knew that he screwed things up with her before, but he actually believed that this was his second chance to do right by her. Even after not hearing from her for a while, he still held on to hope that they would eventually be together. The way things just went down with her man made him realize that it would never happen for them. How she ended up with a thug like that was beyond him. Although he wanted to get her alone to see if he could possibly talk some sense into her, something told him to leave the situation alone. Dude didn't look like one to make idle threats, so Nichole Grant was officially the one who got away.

Chapter 22

"Good morning, husband," Nikki purred into Marcus's ear, waking him from the good sleep he was getting. She hated to interrupt his rest, but she needed him right now, and he was taking too long to open his eyes. They'd been home from their honeymoon for a few weeks, and she still couldn't keep her hands off of him. Marcus broke her in on their wedding night, and they had been going at it all day every day since then.

"Morning, baby," he murmured. He was still half asleep, but his natural instinct was to pull her closer to him where he felt she belonged.

Nikki lay there for a while taking in his scent and admiring the beautiful ring that he'd placed on her finger weeks before. Her husband had truly exceeded her expectations, not only with the ring but with the wedding as well. She never dreamed that she wouldn't want to be more involved in the planning of what was supposed to be the biggest, most special day of her life. When she told Marcus that all she wanted was him, she meant just that. She'd tossed her wedding scrapbook the night he proposed and hadn't looked back.

Although it was a small affair, Marcus still managed to make it one of the most memorable and amazing days of her life. He made the dream he'd been having of their wedding day a reality. It was basically everything she'd ever imagined on a smaller scale. It was absolutely perfect. Her man did the damn thing all the way down to the pink and platinum color scheme. Jakobi served as his best man while O'Shea, Junior, and Big B were the groomsmen. Brandy was her matron of honor and Alana, Kelsey, and Amina were her bridesmaids.

Under Marcus's orders, all she had to do was find a dress and write her vows. The dress was already covered because she'd had it for some time. Ironically, around the time she first met Marcus she was helping her mother sort through some clothes that she wanted to donate to a local women's shelter, and they came across the wedding dress her mother wore when she married her father. Instead of letting her mother donate it, Nikki asked if she could have it.

The dress was nothing like the one she had glued down in her scrapbook, but for some reason she was drawn to it, and she had to have it. Brandy hadn't wanted to get married wearing it, so Christine didn't bother offering it to her youngest daughter, who was extremely picky. After some updates and modifications, she had the perfect wedding gown.

It was clearly a hit with the groom, because when the double doors of her childhood church opened and she came into view, Marcus was overcome with emotion. Seeing him that way touched her heart, evoking those very same emotions within her. It took his brother's hand on his shoulder and the whisper of a few words in his ear for him to get it together. Her father's arm looped tightly through hers kept her from falling apart or doing what her mind was telling her to do, which was chuck her father the peace sign, then sprint down the aisle toward her man and her future. She was sure her father could feel her pulling him along. It couldn't be helped, because it was imperative that she get to Marcus quickly.

As they recited their vows, sniffles and the clearing of throats could be heard throughout the building. The sincerity, truth, and raw emotion of the words they spoke to one another was enough to bring the hardest man to tears, or at the very least, make him believe in love. Jakobi was shocked when he caught sight of Big B flicking his nose and dabbing at his eyes. He understood though because the ceremony was just that moving and special.

And because nobody partied harder than the crew, the reception was fucking lit. The vibe throughout the whole day was everything. The music, food, laughter, and most importantly the love that surrounded them was something unexplainable. For their first dance as husband and wife, Kelsey's cousin-in-law, Chelle, who was married to Nate, sang Tamia's "You Put a Move on My Heart" and brought the entire house down. It was one of Nikki's favorite songs, and Chelle could truly blow. She sang from her soul, touching every heart in the building. Nikki loved that her man paid attention to her, because she had never even come out and told him how much she loved the song. She did, however, play it and sing along to it often enough for him to have figured it out.

They kicked it until the wee hours of the morning since they weren't scheduled to leave for their honeymoon until late afternoon the following day. She'd moved into his place a few weeks before, so that's where they went after the reception. He wanted their first time to be in their home and in their bed, which was his reason for planning the late departure. Their coming together as one had been the sweetest thing, and every time the memory came to mind, she wanted to do it again and again.

"So, I take it you like the ring," Marcus spoke low while nibbling on her neck and ear, interrupting her trip down memory lane.

"I love it, baby. I love you more though," she said, tilting her head back to kiss him. She then wrapped her arms around his neck to deepen the kiss, and the next thing she knew she was straddling him.

It seemed that her body operated by its own accord when Marcus was around. They could be having an innocent conversation, and before she knew it, she would be reaching in his pants for her new best friend. She was addicted and wasn't ashamed to admit it. Since that first time they made love, she'd practically become a fiend for her husband's loving. She craved him every minute of the day, and she doubted that her thirst for him would ever be quenched. She was still adjusting to his size, and some positions were painful, but the pleasure he gave her canceled out the discomfort. "No pain, no gain" was her motto these days.

"Damn, Li'l Bit," he groaned when she leaned forward, allowing him to gain entry to her juicy tunnel. Her shit was piping hot and leaking like crazy. No pussy he'd ever had felt as good as hers. Just as Marcus predicted, Nikki's passion for him was out of this world, crazy, and intense. The good thing about it was that it was equivalent to the passion and love he had for her.

The first couple of times they made love, he took his time and was as gentle with her as he could be. He knew what he was working with so he had to be delicate in the way he handled her, at least until she became acclimated to his size. She was cool with it at first, but two days into their honeymoon in the Maldives in South Asia, she was done playing games and begged him to give it to her nasty and rough. Since he didn't make it a habit of telling her no, he gave her exactly what she asked for.

She came completely out of her shell that night and hadn't gone back in since. He doubted she ever would. Marcus had created a monster, and she'd been putting

the pussy on him so good that she had him confused.
He didn't understand how she could do all the shit she
was doing to him and do it so well when she'd never
done it before. He wasn't questioning if she was really a
virgin bride because that much was evident when he first
entered her. That incredible feeling was indescribable
and unmistakable. Although her word was good enough
for him, the feeling of that cherry popping and the blood
on the sheets of their marriage bed confirmed to him
what was real. He still couldn't resist asking her how the
hell her little ass got to be so freaky, seeing as how she
had never fucked before.

"Baby, it's your fault," she'd told him. "I have years
of pent-up sexual tension and energy to burn off. Even
though I fought it in the beginning, I wanted you so bad.
And just think of all the how-to and 'what not to do' sex
guides I've read over the years. Then you also have to
take into account that my two besties are sex experts who
don't mind sharing their extensive knowledge in the area,
so this is the end result." She shrugged. "I've had nothing
but time to prepare for being with you."

Thing was, she said all this right before slipping his
dick into her warm, wet mouth. Prepared? His wife was
prepared like a muthafucka. Baby blew him the fuck
down and in the process blew his mind by giving him the
best head he'd ever received, right there in the cabana
they were relaxing in, above the clearest, bluest water
either of them had ever seen.

What she didn't tell him was that Kelsey and Alana
actually gave her several tutorials on blowjobs, props
included, so she was pretty confident when it came to
this aspect of lovemaking. And it would only get better as
she became more familiar with her husband's body. With
Marcus, she felt free and able to relax and be herself, so
jitters or anxiousness didn't exist in their bedroom. Her

husband was a master of sex, and she was glad that she was able to bring him as much pleasure as he brought her.

"Fu . . . fuckkkkk!" he moaned, focusing back on the present. He watched in awe as her tiny ass bounced up and down on his shit like he wasn't packing damn near eleven inches of hard dick. She was damn near going all the way down on his shit, and that pussy had him stuttering. He guessed the saying about smaller girls being able to take the dick better than big girls was true. The grip her pussy had on him had him writhing and bucking up off the bed. She took every thrust like a trooper, and when her nut hit, shaking her entire existence, she cried real tears as her walls convulsed and creamed all over him. A few more pumps were all it took for him to explode, shooting a copious load of hot semen inside of her. Nikki fell against his chest and was asleep within seconds.

"I love you," he panted as his eyelids became heavy. Moments later, after his breathing returned to normal, heart rate slowing as he teetered between sleep and alertness, he heard her sweet voice.

"I love you too, husband. More than anything or anybody." Busting that nut had her temporarily sedated, but like always, she never failed to tell him how she felt about him. Her voice was low, barely above a whisper, but the intent and truth of the words she spoke touched him in the same way it always had and would forever. His wife was letting him know that, right under God, he was king in her world, and most importantly he was worthy of her love.

Epilogue

"Husband, I need to feed her," Nikki said for the third time. She had been trying for the last ten minutes to get Marcus to hand over their newborn baby girl so that she could nurse her, but he wasn't having it. Nikki needed to feed the baby then clean her up and dress her before their company arrived.

"Fine," he conceded before reluctantly passing the five-week-old to his wife, but not before kissing each of her chubby cheeks several times. Nikki giggled and blushed when he turned his affections on her, planting soft kisses to her face and neck as the baby latched on to her left breast. "Damn, babe, you're so fucking beautiful, and so is my baby girl," he said, shaking his head in disbelief.

He didn't know what he had done in this life that was so good that God felt he deserved to have Nikki as his wife. Maybe he felt sorry for him for all the pain he had endured early on, but whatever it was he was grateful to have her. She was an excellent wife and took good care of him, their children, and their home. They had come so far from when they first met, but somehow he knew the first time he saw her that she would one day belong to him. It took a lot of work for them to get here, but it was worth it. He finally had a family of his own, and he thanked God every day for them.

Miles was knocked out in the bed next to his mother. His son had turned a year old just two weeks ago, and they already had a five-week-old. So for a few weeks, their children would both be the same age come this time next year. They had definitely been getting it in.

"You're so sweet," Nikki replied, gazing at her handsome husband. She couldn't wait for the six weeks to be up so she could make love to him. Three years later and she still couldn't get enough of Marcus. "You hear that, Sky? Daddy said we're beautiful," she informed her daughter, who was oblivious to what was going on around her, just sucking away with her eyes closed.

The couple went with a home water birth just as they'd done with Miles. The experience was just as grueling, rewarding, and amazing as it had been the first time. Their family and friends hung out in the family room, quietly awaiting the arrival of Miss Skylar Cryslynn Tate, her name a combination of Marcus and Jakobi's late twin sisters, Skylar and Cryslynn. Miles was named after his father.

Just like the first time, her husband was supportive, encouraging, and loving throughout the whole process. And like before, he bragged to anyone who would listen about being the one to catch his babies when she delivered them. Marcus was amazed by his wife's strength. She took the pain of having her children naturally, like a straight-up G. Being there to witness and assist in bringing his children into the world was a truly humbling experience and something he would never forget.

Once his son woke up, the family went about the business of getting themselves together for the day. Marcus showered and afterward came to retrieve his son so that he could bathe and dress him, while Nikki tended to Skylar. As soon as the baby was ready, Marcus came and took her so that his wife could shower and jump fly.

Later that afternoon, as Marcus sat on the steps of the deck out back with his sleeping daughter cradled in one arm and his gorgeous niece Kiyarah snuggled up next to him, he took a moment to look over each member of his family. Junior, who was more like a blood brother to him now, was pushing a very pregnant Amina on the swing as they laughed and talked. It was good to see them back together following a brief separation.

After being together for nearly two years, Junior asked her to marry him. To everyone's surprise, she turned him down. Junior wasn't as shocked as everyone else had been, because anytime he brought up the subject of marriage she would shut down. He felt he set himself up for that one. There was no doubt in his mind that Amina loved him, but for some reason the thought of forever frightened her. The fear of him changing and becoming like her ex was one of her biggest worries. She didn't feel they needed a piece of paper to prove their love and dedication to one another. Marriage changed people and not always for the better. For that reason, her mindset was, "If it ain't broke, don't fix it."

Junior, on the other hand, wanted her and Brielle to have his last name, so after being rejected, he broke things off with her. He didn't see the point in continuing if marriage wasn't the end goal. He still spent a great deal of time with Bri, but he made it clear to Amina that they were over. It didn't take long for her to come to her senses and realize how stupid she had been to let him walk away, so she begged him to come home. Junior didn't give in right away though. He asked her to take some time to make sure that marrying him was what she really wanted because there would be no turning back after they said I do. They reconciled a few months later and were married at the courthouse two weeks after that.

Since her birth father had been found dead, Junior adopted Brielle, and they had another baby girl coming next month. Junior still managed the Dallas shop, but someone else had taken over the duties in Oklahoma City.

He was also making a name for himself in the art world, and for the first time he was comfortable with his name being out there.

Marcus chuckled watching his in-laws looking like two big-ass kids as they played with their grandchildren, Alex, Bri, and Miles, in the treehouse. Despite how mushy and silly they acted with the kids, Mrs. Grant was as regal and fancy as she'd always been, and Mr. Grant was still the epitome of a boss. The crew often speculated and joked about Nicholas Sr.'s past. Kobi said the man had to be a former hitman, while Big B said the nigga was probably down with Dallas's infamous Gorilla Mobb. Marcus guessed him to be a former dope boy who turned his life around after meeting the love of his life. He could definitely relate.

Brandy and her husband were not present today because they were on a weeklong baecation. They were remarried and happy as ever. Counseling, compromise, and communication helped them get back to that happy place in their relationship.

As for Eric, who was also absent, he married his partner of the last three years in a small ceremony last year, and they were now the proud parents of a beautiful baby girl they adopted from Gabon. Surprisingly, his mother had been trying for years to contact him to reconcile, but he wanted nothing to do with her, which was understandable. He was truly happy and in love, and in his opinion, she didn't deserve to be a part of that.

Kelsey and O'Shea had their grown asses out there racing while their children judged. They were a competitive bunch, even with one another, but they would team up to put the smack down on anyone who challenged them as a unit. With children ranging from ages nine months to eight years old, the couple said they were officially done making babies. O'Mega, Kelis, Kinsley, and O'Shea Jr. kept them pretty busy.

O'Shea was retired from the league and now spent all of his time with his family. The years on the road playing ball and being away from his family were hard on him. Kelsey had spent nearly nine years working and taking on most of the responsibility with the children, and Shea felt it was his turn now. While his wife continued to work, he was now the one driving the kids to and from basketball practice, piano lessons, and karate class all while heading their non-profit organization for adopted children. His boys constantly clowned him, calling him Mr. Mom, but he didn't give a damn because he cherished the time spent with his children. It only made him realize how hard Kelsey had been working to hold them down all these years, which made him love and appreciate her that much more.

"I love you, Cocoa Baby, but I dusted your ass!" he bragged, and everyone fell out laughing. Of course, his wife called him a cheater and added a few choice words, making them laugh even harder. That girl still had a mouth on her, and the shit was hilarious.

Jakobi and Alana were cuddled up on the swinging hammock, kissing and whispering to one another as usual. Alana had completed NP school and had joined Kelsey to open a practice in South Dallas. His brother was still running multiple businesses and spending all his free time with his beautiful family. Kobi recently confided in Marcus that he was trying to convince his wife to give him another baby, but she was reluctant due to the recent opening of her clinic. It wasn't that she didn't want more children, she just wanted to wait awhile. The Tates were happy as a unit, but Kobi longed to expand their family. If it were up to him, Alana would stay barefoot and pregnant. He wanted a house full, but he needed to get his wife on board. He had no clue that Alana was already with child, and she planned to share the news

with him later that night. Looked like God had plans that
didn't line up with what Alana had in mind, and after
finding out that she was pregnant, she was perfectly fine
with that.

Gavin would soon be leaving to attend college at
the University of Oklahoma, and they were all excited
about that. Alana wasn't exactly thrilled that his girlfriend would be attending the same school, but there
was nothing they could do about it. They all just prayed
that he didn't come home with no babies. YaYa was still
Marcus's boo, and Kash was still as cool as the other
side of the pillow. It was a trip to watch the interaction between him and Kelsey's daughter Kinsley. They
were thick as thieves and very protective of one another.
O'Shea often said that their bond reminded him of the
one he and Kelsey had coming up. Only time would tell
how that all turned out.

As for Mr. Marcus Tate, the guy who thought he'd be
a bachelor for the remainder of his days? The smooth-
talking player who didn't think love was something he
wanted or needed to be happy? Life was good for that
dude. Actually, it was better than good. It was fantastic. He felt complete now, and he owed it all to his wife.
Before meeting Nikki, it always baffled him how Jakobi
and O'Shea could be so damn crazy in love with one
woman. Caring for someone that much had been a foreign concept to him until he met the woman who would
become his wife. Loving someone so deep that you
would literally lay down your life and die for them was
like the dumbest shit he'd ever heard until he found her.
Knowing he had someone in his life who would do the
same for him was what he needed. Marcus was a better
man because of his wife and children, and for them, he
would do anything.

His eyes searched for and landed on his wife, who had
been watching him the entire time from her spot on the

cushioned wicker sectional situated on the upper deck. Her tiny body gave away no indication that she'd given birth one month prior. Her hips spread a little after having the babies, but she was still his Li'l Bit. He locked eyes with his queen, and they silently began communicating with each other. It was clear that they wouldn't be able to last the full six weeks. One more week was just too long. Reading his mind, she smiled bashfully and discreetly nodded her head in agreement.

Later that night after everyone was gone, Marcus made his way upstairs to lay Skylar down. Nikki's parents insisted on taking Miles with them for the night, and they received no objections from his parents. Marcus didn't have to look back to know that his wife was coming to him. They were so in tune that he could feel her energy. She wasn't on any type of birth control yet, and he wanted to give her body a break and not get her knocked up so soon after giving birth, but he wouldn't deny her. Telling her ass no and that they should wait was not an option. He lied and told himself that he would just have to pull out. Once he was up in that gushy shit, the likelihood of that happening was slim to none, and using a condom with his wife was preposterous.

By the time he emerged from taking his shower, Nikki sat on the bed freshly bathed in her birthday suit with her legs folded Indian style. After washing Skylar up and feeding her, she took a quick shower in the guest room next to the nursery. "Baby," she called out to him desperately. She rose up to her knees and beckoned him with her index finger curled. Nikki planned to get in a few rounds with him before Skylar woke up for another feeding.

Marcus's eyes zeroed in on his name tatted on her right hip above her pretty pussy. That shit was so damn sexy to him. Of all the tattoos he'd done on her, that one was by far his favorite. She was his, and he didn't want her to ever forget it. "What is it, mama?" he asked as he traced his name with his index finger, causing her to shiver.

"Smooveee," she whined. She wanted her husband in the worst way, and he was teasing her. When he laid her down and pulled her to the edge of the bed, her breathing became labored. Seeing him drop to his knees had her lifting her ass up off the bed, offering herself to him on a silver platter. His head game was out of this world, and her box was already leaking its fluids in anticipation of feeling his mouth on her. Marcus Tate was the only man who would ever know her this way, and he handled her body so well that she had no issues with that. She was convinced that no one could do it better.

"I got you, Li'l Bit," he promised before he proceeded to make sweet love to his best friend, his rib, and his soul mate like it was the very first time.

The End